PROLOGUE

The glowing lights of the Hearst castle high on the distant hill soon disappeared in the rage of the Pacific storm. The off shore winds increased, hurling their powers into a cyclonic monster, howling in anguished ferocity and without mercy. The temperature had dropped like a rock from on high, followed by giant sneaker waves without warning, swamping the freighter and her crew at their midnight work. Thus arrived the storm of the century. Under tremendous flashes of lightening, in the escalating winds, the Hearst coastal freighter, the once proud San Bella, now struggled like a wounded sparrow seeking to escape from its hidden nest in the coastal cove.

Captain Escalante gave orders to stop unloading their precious cargo and reverse engines as he frantically began to nudge the San Bella's bow out of the dangerous shallows. Lifting her anchors, the ship began to power up, trying to prowl her way back into safe waters.

This storm had come rushing over the black western horizon like a roaring lion, pouncing upon the San Simeon coastline, catching the small freighter in its crushing teeth. Immense waves rolled over her bow as the crew fought to bring her about and head out to deeper waters. Suddenly word came up from the engine room that their shovelers had been crushed in the shifting tonnage when the coal bunkers had caved in. With her engine power going down, the lights of the san Bella started flickering, and went dark.

Captain Escalante yelled to lock down the hatches as he tried to turn his ship seaward. But as the power went dead, a great wave rolled over the port beam, smashing its way across the decks–creating a battering wall of thrashing metal debris. The freighter dangerously rolled with each smashing wave. The ship's bell was clanging its last hope of pure madness when suddenly it went silent as the bell was flung into the howling night.

Escalante's first mate had not responded to his call for assistance. Then one of the deck hands screamed up to the bridge that first mate, Turlock, had been washed overboard! Captain Escalante had been in trouble before, but this time, survival seemed impossible unless there was a chance for recovery of the ship. With her cargo mostly gone the San Bella had become a cork on the convulsing sea. Monster waves towered, rolling into the cove, fuming in their fury, reaching up the sheer jagged cliffs. The only chance they had was to turn out to sea or they would be bashed to death upon the cliffs waiting behind them. The night was painted black as velvet, overlaid with the screaming storm of death reaching for this tossing piece of steel. The sea had become a war zone of on-rushing waves, continuously pelting them with blasts of hail, while relentless bomb-like blows thundered against the struggling ship which was seeking out a desperate white flag retreat. Every instrument was dead, the only light now coming with explosions of lightening. Captain Escalante 's hope of survival turned on the thought that, overboard, the waves might carry himself and his crew to shore.

Every ear could hear the steel girders groaning as the small freighter twisted itself over and through the massive mountains of rushing ocean. Lightening and thunder shook the decks as the cargo cranes were torn to pieces and hurled like deadly spears into the sea. Each wave punched out rusted rivets; stripped away scarred steel planking, until nothing but a skeleton frame, bound by wires with flapping iron skin remained. Water washed over and through her guts, with tons of icy water gushing, reaching the upper deck and flowing into the wheel house. As the ship's wheel began spinning freely, the Captain knew it was all over–his ship had become a broken iron corpse waiting for its watery grave.

Barnardo Escalante, the old Greek captain, spit out his shredded cigar as he pounded his gnarled fist against the gyrating compass. Turning his frightened eyes to the distant shore where a brilliant sheet of lightening flashed across the hills, he saw the Hearst Castle rising out of the storm. In anger, he cursed the night, the sea and the Hearst family. In a tirade of godless screaming he spewed out his last words, "For what–my ship, and our lives lost? So some Tsar blooded family might hoard up more treasures in secret under the cover of the night?"

Escalante realizing this was the worst storm of his life, grabbed hold of the chain and the cross around his neck, finished his curses and cried out his earnest prayers, but way too late! Disaster was upon them, the San Bella , with the loss of her power did not stand a chance. The cry to abandon ship had gone out but who it might have reached was unknown. Nothing but the fury of the wind and the spew of the roaring Pacific could be felt. In one horrific groan, the San Bella lifted and rolled, but this time she did not regain her float but went over and was sucked down, disappearing into the deep dark waters. Forever gone silent.

That was it, the San Bella was lost in the night. Only bits of twisted wreckage would now and then be found buried in the sand and rocks along the lonely shore. Some pieces would even be found embedded high up in the cliff sides, but the San Bella was never seen again. Stories of her treasures and her phantom disappearance were told, but no one knew where she had vanished to, with much of her secret treasure still aboard.

incomprehensible, shake up.

A new chapter of experience was suddenly opened unto us. A mystery beckoned: drawing us out of a simple introduction, pulling us into a full fledged adventure novel, with so many twists and plots that it would take years to fully understand. Without knowing it our lives would be rearranged, changed and enlightened; with all that was to happen, they would never be the same again. Then the earthquake was over. Dylan 's craggy voice stopped skipping and went on with the changing times.

My traveling companions barely stirred out of their sleep while I was fearfully expressing my wild eyed "whoops." Staying real cool like, I let them know that they had missed the fun. They could care less, tired and anxious to get home, they were still locked into their California dreams.

The day was beautiful until that rolling shaker showed up on the scene. I had been through some big ones before and this seemed to be nothing less than a little wrestling match deep in the earth; some thumps and adjustment in deep hidden places, I thought, except for those snapping lines and swaying poles.

My journalistic thoughts, ever open to making connections, were never still. Especially with these unexpected events, my mind began wondering if this might mean something more than just a physical shaking of the land. These types of strange occurrences had happened to me in the past. From experience, I was wary. One most significant lesson, which had pretty well laid the pattern for my suspicions, had scratched itself deep into my curious mind.

A falling star had passed directly over my home back in Canada. Then, within the week, my grandparents, my

Chapter One

The Home Stretch

We were worn and ragged, finally on the home stretch, rolling south coming out of the rugged coastal mountains of Big Sur. Irritating enough, the 'oldie but goody' CD began skipping on Bob Dylan's "The Times They Are A Changing." Just as my palm came down on the dashboard to stop its repeat clicking, I realized that our entire van was skipping. Was it a flat tire I wondered? Then, in the midst of my preoccupations with our journey home I noticed the telephone line stretching tight as guitar strings, nearly snapping while the poles swayed like palm trees in a tropical storm, and I knew for sure things were a-changing. The road ahead was shimmering while our travel van danced across Highway 1, to one of those famous California earthquakes.

It was a frightening moment—having to deal with the on-coming traffic and the unknown. First, the atmosphere began to shimmer and vibrate. Then the road ahead began rolling towards me as if small beach waves were swirling up to my ankles. Slowing down, I had no choice but to drive over each on-coming swell as I whooped out some corny, "Ride-em, cowboy" phrase!

Fortunately, we had just come out of the mountains and were driving along the flat stretch alongside the Pacific Ocean, on the San Simeon coastline. This left us free of any falling mountains and tumbling boulders; however, our three week research jaunt suddenly managed to take on a life of its own. Without a chance to acknowledge or grant our approval to such forces, our journey would now transform itself, from a peaceful business venture into an unexpected, nearly adopted caretakers, were both killed in an unfortunate airplane crash, pretty close to where that flashing star had seemed to hit. Some three years back, this tragedy had shocked my life and left me without family and almost no friends. Everything had changed for me during that time. Suddenly left alone I was forced to deal with events which could only be considered experiences on a grand scale.

As a young struggling student of life I was suddenly awakened to the real world. Not only did I lose the grandparents who were my guardians and best friends while I grew up, who had adopted me from a child after my parents were lost at sea, but my inheritance was caught up in overwhelming law suits, endless court and lawyer battles, as I was being forced away and out.

I was left nearly destitute and only a few distant friends from my college days came to my rescue. Through these events some kind of alert code had been programmed in my thought processes so that any type of odd event would awaken my thoughts to what it might mean for me. And so it was with this earthquake.

For now, I saw that in the south the sky was blue, but that perfect off-shore breeze from the north was already chasing us with a hazy bank of fog. I thought we could beat it and make it up to Highway 101, but something more was about to happen. With the sudden quake and the on-rushing fog, I felt an uncertain change ready to pounce on my bones and tear into my life—and so it happened.

Chapter Two

The Breakdown

We were heading home from a long tiring business trip and we really didn't need any troubles. But, with just our luck—there's that 'but' word again, trouble seems to find its way into our adventures, just when things seem to be moving along fine. Sure enough, the 'but' dilemma show up: my old traveling van decided to bring forth formal objections to its ongoing abuse. I wondered if this was the quake taking on its real purpose of alerting me to something greater yet to come, but I laughed that thought away.

Things took a strange turn downhill for us at this time and we were left behind as the fog began whispering "change" around us. Sure enough, we were stranded—as my camper van began sputtering until it finally broke down just north of the famous Hearst Castle along the lonely California coast.

We had just spent several long weeks on the road, researching and drumming up business. There was that first week in Half Moon Bay at the annual Surf Show, then a good week of visiting beaches on our way to Monterey. Then we spent time in Carmel, the lovely city by the sea. There, we spent a good week of visiting surf shops and reestablishing old friendships. Then we headed home, venturing south through the rugged coastal mountain range of Big Sur.

It was late afternoon when my well-worn camping van decided to bring forth fits until it jerked to a stop alongside the vast stretch of grassy fields running between the highway and the beach. Old Betsy seemed to be in obedience to the whispering fog touching and swirling around us. Or, I laughed, she had been scared silly by the earthquake. She began to limp and then spluttered for a time, giving a few last breaths, before she died all the way. Of course I was pumping the pedal and yelling obscenities, urging another 100 feet out of her, trying to reach a good place to stop alongside the barbed-wire fence to clear the way for passing traffic. Then and there, the weather changed. The storm of our life broke and poured forth upon us all its hidden twists and strange winds.

Theo, or I should say, Theodore Vontempski, my long-time traveling companion, an up and coming photographer, inventor and entrepreneur, was stirring awake in the reclining passenger seat. We often traveled together on my research ventures, investigating and searching for new articles. He did his photography thing while I did my research. I had been a freelance writer and endeavoring journalist for the last five years, constantly searching out uncommon topics and specialty subjects.

We were on our last stretch of the trip home from the International Surf And Sports Show, which always offered up great new inventions and insights to my article writing. The big northern California surf show always presented new technology in water sports equipment and great insights into the new and upcoming water sport arena. We were more than interested in the new high tech surfing boats and boards, because one of those high tech boards had been designed by Theo. Not only was it one of the fastest boards on the water, but it had a built-in super-sonic sound box designed to pulse out an underwater sonic wave to drive away prowling sharks. It was being tested and had won some approval, especially with the Australian surfers and was now going world wide.

I was trying to tell Theo about the quake they had slept through but nothing more than passive nods came forth in response as if he didn't believe me. To prove it to him I turned on the radio to hear some news. Bad reception mixed with garbled reports of the earthquake, registered at point six, with no real reports of damages as of yet. Theo was tousled, looking like he had just escaped out of some Turkish prison. He rubbed his eyes, trying to release himself from whatever dream he had been languishing in.

We had brought along the nephew of my good friend Dustin, who was also my lawyer and my publishing agent and editor. Jason Jenson, his nephew, better known as JJ, was one of the top young west-coast surfers who would offer his irritating punk kid attitude along with his expertise on some of the new equipment. We had been on the road for several weeks now, somewhat tired and in a hurry to get home, and things were going along fine—until the shaker, and until my traveling van began its woeful protest. I knew it was the fuel pump, but had neglected to have the work done, hoping to make it home first. But I still wanted to pass blame onto the earthquake. Dustin, my friend, editor and lawyer, had always said that I was too bold, maybe too confident, and for sure—I had stretched my luck out on this one, and it snapped!

The trip up the California coast had been planned for several months now. It had served a few different purposes. I could do my background work for several upcoming articles and it would allow Theo to continue promoting his new sonic board and his Water Play Shop in Newport Beach, near Balboa Bay along the southern California coast. At the same time, we were trying to hustle up funding or gain backers for a surf movie we wanted to produce. We were on our way home from the annual International Surf and Water Sports Show up in Half Moon Bay, just below San Francisco and all was going so well. For once, I thought we were finally getting it all together when the hand of fate sent an unexpected sneaker wave of troubles across the last part of our trip.

Theo managed to sit up, and of course, decided to mutter forth his misgivings, "Holy gum drops and Hungarian camel turds." Good old traveling companion, Theo, then announced with his abnormal exclamations, "Hey Luke, now what the crap we gonna do?"

"Kripe, right now I am so pissed at this turd of a van, that I can set it afire and walk away," exclaiming in anger as I was hitting the wheel, as if to punish this bucket of on-going trouble. I pushed my hair back and grabbed hold of the chain and flash drive around my neck. I really did not need this right now; my life was filled with more than enough concerns, most of them built around money or—better said—the lack thereof. This little expedition, with its expectation of collecting insights for new upcoming articles, had cost me dearly. We were also hoping for some good sales with Theo's new board design and maybe a shot in the arm for his shop. Then there was my agenda with lawyer meetings for the month, full up.

Dustin Arrow, my friend and lawyer was scheduled to meet with several Canadian lawyers who were pressuring me to give into their demands regarding my inheritance. A hundred law suits had been filed against my grandparent's trusts and will, all trying to push me out. It was already dragging out to a three year battle with the end nowhere in sight. It had been an on-going heartache and a costly hardship for Dustin and myself; it seemed we were on the butt end of the legal gavel. This breakdown of the van was not on my agenda, but troubles were nothing new to me. Still, why now?

Then hot-shot Jason's head popped up from the back bunk.

Still half asleep, he mumbled, "What's up guys? All that bellowing woke me up from a really good dream named Lulu."

"Ahh, go back to sleep. It's this stupid junk tin-covered wagon again. I think it's the fuel pump finally gone down," I fired back to his complaining, while considering what the problem was.

Theo agreed as he raised his nose as if sniffing gas fumes, "Yeah, I think so too. That is either JJ or some strange gas." The question now in all our minds was: what are we going to do? We were all aware of the present dilemma.

"Easy enough friends. If it is the fuel pump, someone is going to have to hitch-hike into San Luis Obispo and bring one back." I announced the dirty burden into the van's interior, adding this to the declaration, "Remember, I dealt with the first two breakdowns up north. I think it is someone else's turn to get some needed exercise and take a walk."

It was quiet for a while, then one of those monster trucks came roaring up out of the fog and went flying by, no more than a foot away. We saw that it was a huge tow truck and it came so close that its right-hand extended mirror caught my side mirror, tearing it off as if it were a dandelion flying in the wind.

I could not believe it, one moment the mirror was there and then it was gone. Our whole van was shaking in the aftermath of the gust of foggy wind, stirring up a dust cloud and leaving us with thoughts about being smashed to bits. That driver either was drunk or the fog had blurred his view, but it was a close call.

"Oh sheet! Did you see that?" JJ nearly screamed, pointing into the swirling fog as the truck vanished.

I was sitting there rather freaked out myself. What if I had opened the door or had my arm out? I was thankful that the mirror had been sacrificed instead of my arm or my life. I felt the alarms within me go off.

After a few minutes getting over our shock, Theo spoke up, "Hey, that is going to cost some bucks to get fixed. We better start doing something to get off the road and figure out what to do." In the same breath he added, "I did the dirty work last time with the tire thing, in Big Sur, remember. I think it's JJ's turn to do some humping."

Theo Vontempski (the Third, if you wanted to get technical) was a half genius in computers and part-time tech in electronics and photography. However, his true passion was in marine biology and he was forever enjoying the activity of the world's oceans as a photographer. His abilities were not lost, for he had slowly carved out a reputation in the surfing world and was a known name in its on-going activities. Even though his inventive and technical genius provided a modest income for him, it was his fledgling Water Play Shop in Newport Beach and strange inventions that gave him the most pleasure in life and kept us afloat. I had invited him along on this trip, for his expertise was forever helpful in my personal endeavors. His compassion for adventure had teamed us up on more than one occasion; I felt I could trust him with my life. It was obvious that at this moment, he had JJ in his sights to take on some responsibility.

From out of the back Jason's voice bemoaned, "Come on you guys, I don't know anything about engines, much less fuel pumps. You know the odds are against me this time."

JJ's references to gambling seemed to be firmly attached to his personality and this was something we were dealing with. There I go, he's even got me talking gambling.

"No big deal. You just go to a parts house and give them the make and model which I'll write down for you, then they'll get one for you and you hitch back and we put it on—voila! that is it." I lined the whole thing out in one sentence.

"Oh yupski, sure sounds easy. Where am I going to get the bucks? And what is a parts house?" Jason whined.

Theo and I both laughed at his ridiculous question—but then I thought that this kid might not really know what a parts house is. He might think it's something to do with tanning or bodies, or whatever. None the less, I immediately dug through the emergency box under the front seat and counted out $150 and handed it over to Jason, "This is the last of the kitty. A pump for this shouldn't be more than fifty bucks, but just in case, there's a few extra bucks. Don't lose it in one of your card games or spend it on junk or bunny parts if you know what I mean. That is the last of our cash. We'll probably need every extra penny for gas to get home, we're running real low."

Even though JJ had contributed to our welfare fund through one of his poker games, he knew that we had broken down several times and spent most of our funds on van repairs.

Young Jason was my lawyers nephew. Dustin, my life-time friend, had taken Jason under his wing when Jason's father, a well known gambler, had run onto hard times. His parents lost their home and were on the edge of divorce. Jason became a part of our team on request from Dustin, who asked me to take Jason along and apply some needed discipline and some reasonable common sense to his spoiled and lazy life. Thus, JJ had been with us for several weeks now.

He was not a bad kid, a near genius in the card playing trade, sharp and witty; somewhat intelligent in general matters, but careless in many ways, JJ was definitely in need of some maturity. We wanted him to know that life was more than fun and games. It seemed to be working: we could see a change taking place in this young man's life, and positively enough—he knew it too. This shaggy haired human, a tall, freckled-face lanky kid, was a man in the works. We had more or less adopted him into our traveling team possibly to guide him into constructive ideals and pull him out of his careless gambling and surf mentality—surf is everything and cards are next in line! He was a good looker, forever attracting surf bunnies and always hanging ten on the edge of troubles.

Nevertheless, JJ was still the sophomaniac—one of those new generation kids full of delusions, thinking they are somehow incredibly intelligent—NOT!

He was enjoying this adventurous life and we were slowly handing over bits and pieces of responsibility to him and this seemed the perfect time to give him a good chunk of it. Handing over the cash and in perfect harmony, Theo and I both yelled, "Amen, that is it." Thus was Jason elected.

"So happy people, what are we going to do in the meantime? We can't sit here all night next to the road," Theo said as he was looking over the fence and off through the drifting fog towards the beach area.

"The first thing is to bale out and push this barge down the road to a wider clearing, get a ways off the road, and escape death by big booming crash!" I pointed towards the grassy fields running alongside the private beach. "Then looks like we're going to spend the night under the stars, or should I say the fog, and wait for Jason to return."

Theo was looking out across the wavering grass towards the ocean, watching the wispy tails of fog move across the field, "Wow, that beach looks awfully isolated, has that lost and lonely feeling to it, like you see in old black and white movies."

"Just the right place for us to hide out. Maybe we'll have a night of foggy mystery, or at least a mysterious night."

"Ok, so I'll go. But don't expect me to make it back tonight," Jason spoke out indignantly, already making plans for some good times.

"Why not come out on the beach tonight and make camp with us, then leave early in the morning?" Theo suggested.

"That sounds better," I agreed, knowing that JJ would have to spend the night somewhere in town and that meant extra bucks and maybe some hassles; more worries for us than for him. We might be giving Jason a bit too much opportunity to escape our discipline, and that would undo any progress made, a worrisome outcome.

So we piled out and pushed the old van down the road a distance, until we came to a turnout where we stopped alongside a three foot square sign announcing in huge letters 'No Trespassing.' That was strange I thought, I had seen many a no trespassing sign before, but why so big and so official looking? Down in the lower right corner of the sign were the initials HC Security. Must represent the Hearst Castle security company I surmised. Without knowing it, I was just introduced to an organization that would begin playing an incredible role in my already over-complicated life.

We gathered up some grub: stale bread, chips, peanut butter and three apples, along with a few necessities for a night on the beach, stuffing everything into our backpacks. We put our surf boards on the upper inside racks of the van, slid my laptop under one bunk and tossed things around, for a mess always discouraged break-ins. I unplugged my cell phone and made sure Theo and JJ had theirs charged and then waited until the road was clear. I had written an all important note and stuck it under the windshield for the cops to read if they were to investigate our van. This was a long stretch of Hearst beach property with the large no trespassing signs posted every 50 feet, no one but cattle and the beach patrols allowed on the beach, but the sign made an excellent place to climb the fence.

My note in the simplest terms said, "Please do not tow this vehicle away. Our fuel pump went out and we have a service man coming out to fix it today. We will return this afternoon. Thank You."

We waited for all cars to pass, looked around, then climbed

through the barbwire fencing. We ran across the field leaping and dodging around wind blown shrubs as the pasture slowly slanted down towards some good sized sand dunes running between the white sand beach and the pasture disappearing behind us. The van had been swallowed up in the whispering fog and could no longer be seen from where we were, which meant no one from the road could see us. Our little trio made its way against the off shore wind, working among piles of beach debris and old driftwood logs jutting out of the rising dunes. The scene took on a mystical look with the whiffs of fog darting around us and settling into the lower areas.

We walked along searching for a bit of shelter until eventually we came to an over-grown pile of logs, a perfect tucked-away hiding place, and was surprised to find what seemed to be a driftwood hut hidden into a sand cliff. It seemed as though it was waiting there for us, apparently not used for a long time. There was a fire pit and some driftwood shelves towards the back and mounds of nice clean sand, just perfect for our sleeping bags. We were soon getting comfortable and had collected a good amount of firewood, getting ready for the night, but ready for what?

JJ called our attention to an approaching sound to the south. We stood there looking at a pin-point object in the sky until we heard the distant sound of a helicopter drawing closer. Immediately we scrambled into the beach hut, just in time. The chopper came flying right down the beach. It suddenly changed its pitch and we saw it make a turn towards the road, headed directly for the van. It began swooping back and forth, possibly looking for the van's owners. We hoped that our scrambled run across the field and into the dunes had been erased by the afternoon winds. The chopper blew over a few times but soon moved on, heading north. We watched its retreat from inside the cave hut until it was out of sight.

We were just congratulating ourselves when suddenly Jason let out a scream, scaring me and Theo nearly to death! The first thing I thought was that Jason had been bitten by something; but no, he was crawling backwards out of the hut, pointing to the back shelf.

We looked to see what had freaked him out, and, "Omygosh, holy bonkers," there sat a skull in a recessed area, right above the shelf! I shined my flashlight onto the shelf area and sure enough, it was a human skull. At first I thought this must be a joke, just one of those plastic things you buy at the magic store. But Theo, being the curious one, crawled over to it and tapped it with a stick. It did not sound like plastic. Then he reached up and took it down, saying, "Oh wow, what on earth is this doing here? This is real."

"Real? You mean really real?!" my voice crackled out. "I don't have any idea, but put that thing down. It might be one of those curse things, like the Hawaiians have in the islands. It looks like someone is trying to scare us out of this place," I said standing behind him. Just then the wind blew a whiff of soft fog over us and it grew darker.

"Maybe this hut is some kind of burial mound or a ceremonial Indian hut, they had places like that along this coast," Theo suggested.

"Woe-me-down. Say what you want, but no way in hell am I going to stay in this beach hut with someone's skull sitting around. The rest of him and his buddies might be right under us," Jason mumbling, had crawled back into the hut, but stood off as he got himself under control.

As we squatted there on our knees in the sand, a picture flashed through my mind: an iron-hulled ship was swamped by a massive rolling wave. The ship rolled over and went down. Men called out for help while struggling in the water.

This had to be strange for me. I never had anything as intense as this happen before, but I excused it to my over-worked imagination. After this odd moment passed, Theo had finished examining the skull, seeing that it was real, without any obvious damage. Theo our intellectual scientist put it back and said, "Without much cogitation, I am specu-lating that JJ is right. We genuinely don't want to spend the night in this place. I also have an uncanny feeling about this. Let's go yonder and look for something else my friends."

JJ burst out, "See, even the professor agrees with me and has dealt us some honest cards."

It was still early, the sun had not yet settled on the horizon; we decided to further explore the beach. Looking north, up towards the Big Sur Mountains, the beach seemed to stretch wide open forever but with broken clouds of fresh offshore fog tumbling along. This direction would leave us in the open in case the chopper patrol came back. We turned south, towards a prominent rock point that we could see off in the distance. Maybe there was a good rocky hiding place or a sheltered place for us—who knew, maybe even a spot for some good waves. As we made our way, we could see a few nice breaking waves rolling in towards the out-crop of jutting cliffs. This was an uninhabited beach, no prints and no trash or signs of anyone being on it. I had to sum it up as—lonely, really lonely. We weaved our way among the hilly dunes in case anyone from a distance might be patrolling, but we saw no one.

The afternoon breeze was still blowing wisps of fog along the beach, kissing and rippling the dry sands, erasing our prints as we walked south. Within a half hour we came to the rocky point and made our way around it until we came into what we saw as an inviting little cove. The cove itself was notched back off the water a hundred yards deep and about one football field from one point to the far side, with the rocky points jutting out into the waves. The surf had a perfect cove to capture its roar as the tide changed. It was almost as if we had found a secret place, all of our own. Above the cliffs were coastal pines and eucalyptus trees growing thick, sealing the area off and a perfect source for firewood. Ocean shrubbery grew spotted on the cliff with flowers and grasses sprouting wherever there might be enough dirt for them to grow. This was a lovely touch to a bad break down.

Chapter Four

Smugglers Cove

Once in a great while there arrives into one's life, special unexpected discoveries. These are called serendipitous moments. For us, this was one of those rare finds, pleasant to our eyes, and pleasing to our souls.

Theo was the first to express this moment. "Extraordinary! Most astounding. This is incredible. Look at this place, what a fantastic hideaway!" Theo waved his arm while speaking out across the span of the cove, "Who knew?"

I was exploring and talking while clambering around boulders and old driftwood logs near the cliffs that rose about 50 feet above us. "It's like a pirate's cove down here, tucked away from everything. Up on the highway I bet ten thousand people a day drive by and never dream that anything like this could exist, right here."

We came to a small flow of water coming from the side of the cliff and running across the sand, making its way down to the shore. I took a handful of water trickling over the rocks and tasted it. It was fresh water. We followed the trickle to see its source, believing this entire experience was getting even better; for in the cliff, tucked away in the rocks about five feet off the sand, a tiny waterfall fell. As we looked into the boulder-strewn cliff there was a narrow opening, nearly hidden from view. Climbing up we discovered this was a cave that went back about 20 feet into the cliff, allowing us to easily stand upright inside. The trickle of water was falling down the back side of the cave splattering into a tiny pool, flowing along a worn groove on the far side and eventually falling down the cliff onto the sand. This was incredible. We could see a fire pit had been laid with beach rocks and sand that filled most of the bottom of the cave. Someone had been here before, as if leaving it set up for us.

JJ made us check out the cave to make sure there were no skulls or bones lying around. He effectively stood back and stated, "I ain't taking no chances." Theo and I had to laugh at his gambling reference and so we checked it out; the only thing was a few slots where old half burned candles sat.

I was thinking that this could have been a smugglers' cove. During the 1920s, in the era of prohibition, boats from Canada moved down the coast and made secret whisky deliveries in just these types of hidden-away places. "Are you thinking what I'm thinking?" I broke the silence.

"What is that?" JJ said.

"This is a near perfect hiding place for us. We got water, we got shelter, and no one can possibly find us here," I clam- mored on.

"Let's do it." Theo agreed but Jason remained quiet.

"Hey, what about the van—way back there?" asked Jason.

"No problem, when you get back with the pump, just cut across through the grove of eucalyptus trees and climb down here, and we'll head back to the van for repairs."

JJ immediately looked at us with his large expression-filled eyes saying, "You guys ain't really going to send me to town are you?"

"We sure are. Looks like you got the good deal this time," Theo laughed and patted our young friend on the shoulder.

The fingers of fog were reaching over the top of the north point as the sun was going down. We stowed our gear, col- lected some driftwood and settled in for the night.

This had to be one of the best finds we had come to know: our own little hidden cove, right outside the famous Hearst Castle, or at least up the beach from it.

Night had come; the tide rolled in, bringing with it the roar of breaking waves and the coolness of the sea. We were already tucked into our new cave, with a nice hot fire keeping us warm, the interior well lit and the fog held at bay. The candle light flickered off the moss covered walls and sparkled against the trickling spring which filled the worn rock basin at the back of the cave. The water seemed fresh but Theo insisted we boil it anyway. We could not have landed in a nicer and more exciting place as the surf broke outside our shelter in Smugglers Cove, as we so named it, and the coals of the fire glowed red through the night.

Somewhere inside a distant echo, I heard Theo's voice calling out, "What the heck!" Morning light was shining blue into the cave and Theo was standing outside exclaiming something. I went out in my cut-offs and stood next to him wondering what he was jabbering about. He pointed down along the surf line on the beach. I had to laugh; there appeared to be a family of seals, pups and all, playing in the surf and flapping along, half in the water and half on the sand.

It was a beautiful day, fit for adventure. I woke up Jason and stirred the fire, put on some coffee, darkened some toast, added peanut butter and jam, then sent JJ on his way with more instructions than a NASA space launch manual.

Before he left, I made sure he had his cell phone with him and that he was to stay in touch. "Maybe just shoot us a text message now and then. We do not have any means to charge our phones out here, so keep it to a minimum." I cautioned him one more time, not to get arrested, nor beat up or mugged, for we were near broke and could never bail him out. Then to be careful coming back to us across the field, "You might get caught for trespassing. And no lotto tickets or card games with this money!"

After Jason had rolled his eyes up and around, exaggerating every roll at our seemingly endless instructions, rules and warnings, he was happy to disappear over the top of the cliff and fade into the trees.

Thus began our concerns for him. Jason might have been a

punk surf kid with a bag of troubles tied to his back and we were harnessed to taking care of him, but he had some interesting talents. One of the problems in his family was that his father was a professional gambler—one of the most famous card players around. One of those TV competing characters either flying high with cash or crawling low with debt. This had been the downfall to Jason's family and the main reason that my friend Dustin wanted us to help him out. Well, we soon discovered that JJ was one of the most incredible poker players we had ever seen. As young as he was, there were few who could take advantage of him unless he allowed it.

He told us the story of his father, how from the age of 5 he'd taught Jason the tricks and the trade of card skills and playing. No kidding, this kid could have you hold a deck of cards under the table while you pick out any number of cards from the deck and keep it a secret. Then hand him the deck and he would tell you how many cards you had taken. He would tell us to watch him deal and try to catch him. He could deal cards to not allow anyone to know if he were dealing off the bottom. He could hide cards, and could deal himself or anyone at the table a winning hand. It was really something to see or should I say—not to see.

We often sat and had him teach us some of the tricks. It took years of training, and in order to stay sharp with the game he had to handle cards for a good two hours a day. He could tell who was cheating in the game or if there were any marked cards. He could so arrange shuffles and deals to anyone, leading that person on and then take him for nearly everything. We had witnessed his skills and extreme abilities, up at the big surf show one night at the hotel we stayed in. It was amazing to watch. He would be as if transformed into another person. His entire countenance and facial features would go into a meditative trance: he would become Cool

Hand Jason! This kid gained some respect with us, for he had provided us with just enough cash at the right time to keep us going and on the road.

There was one night he sat with many of the older vendors from the surf show, one of those memorable nights to witness. There he was, a shabby surf bum kid sitting with six other men, well older and far more advantaged than this punk kid. We watched him perform his magic; just as he told us he could.

He explained that he had to work slow and easy, not creating any suspicion of knowing he was very capable of taking everyone there for all their nickels and dimes. He could easily be accused of cheating or playing dirty, so he would just win enough to keep ahead of the game, playing dumb but wise. The night finished up with two of the big-shot high-rolling executive vendors from our main competition losing big time. But JJ had so arranged the game to make sure a few of the smaller less arrogant players also got a share of the gamblers pie.

We heard all about this the next day when we found out that a few of the west coast surfers had laughed at the big time Vegas gamblers and told them that this punk shabby-looking kid was one of the best poker players on the west coast. In fact, no one that knew him would play for more than pennies with him. We were glad that the show had come to an end and we were out of there, the same Vegas bigshots were asking around about us and JJ, pissed to say the least, they had wanted our hides or a rematch.

We were not sure how to deal with this acquired skill. Should we break him of it or help him control his involvement in gaming? Dustin wanted us to break him, but he had too many fantastic skills to just crush them out. Besides, he could teach us plenty. On the other hand, his family lay devastated because of gambling and we did not want him to go down this road. The avenue we took might have been selfish, but we decided on a slow alternative—by keeping him busy and involving him in other pursuits. And at the same time having him transfer a tiny portion of his learned abilities onto us, of course, only for the good of a better future for us all.

For myself, while on assignment I would often sit in poker games with others, waiting around for events to happen. But now, JJ had begun to share many of his secrets with us and the one I loved the most was about controlling your eyes and your body language. After he taught us how to observe such things, it was amazing how players would literally give away their game with a twitch or a shake or the raising of an eyebrow. This simple but most insightful understanding would come in handy for me in personal investigations.

As we sent Jason off in one direction, Theo and I strolled down the beach towards the playing seals, to see what they might do. Apparently, they were familiar with people watching them, but still kept their distance. We walked down to the far end of the cove to see what might be among the pools and rocks. After climbing around I found a good knot of fishing line tangled in a ball. There were several hooks and a few lead weights still attached. I sat down, enjoying the morning sun, to slowly untangle the line. It was useable so I thought I might do some fishing. Poking around the tide pools, I dug up a couple of crabs. Soon the line was flying out into the deeper pools off the far south cliff.

It was not too long before I could feel a nibble and then something took my line. I had tied the line onto a stick and I slowly began to wind in the line. Within a few minutes of working my catch around the rocks, I came up with a fairly nice perch. "Hey Theo, take a look at this," and I held up my first catch of the day for him to see.

Theo had gone walking along the cliff, back towards the cave, collecting pieces of driftwood for our fire. He made his way back when I called and was amazed at our good fortune. He said, "Ah, a cold-blooded aquatic vertebrate. Man, perch is good eating. Hope there is more out there. We're gonna eat like kings."

I thought for sure I was going to have to endure one of his ten minute orations on the species of perch, but he saw me casting my line out again and left the subject alone. Sure enough, within a few minutes I had another one. Theo jogged up to the cave to get his knife, returned and began cleaning them. By noon we had about seven perch, nothing to brag about but enough to have a nice meal with. We took the fish back to the cave and rolled them in sea weed and laid them into the bed of coals, making a feast for us. We then sat back at the mouth of the cave dangling our feet and sipping on our fresh brewed coffee.

The sun was above us now, the day had warmed up well and we thought that we might do some exploring. The rising wall of the cove was naturally cut with wide open slots and crevices splitting the face of the cliff, enticing our investigations. Some of them were wide enough that dirt and rocks had long since washed through from above and created mounds of mixed rocks and roots with puffs of grass growing on them. "Maybe we might find some edible berries in those shrubs on top," I suggested.

"At least we might collect a bunch of eucalyptus leaves and bring them into our cave to burn for the aromatic scent," Theo suggested.

Good idea I thought, and leave it to Theo, he was always coming up with these herbal things. We walked towards the north end of the cove where we could see the largest cut or crevice in the cliff. Certainly large enough for someone to have driven through and come down onto the sand; maybe in the past it was a main entrance to the cove. I climbed up the cliff to take a better look around and see how far the cut canyon ran. I followed it back some 100 feet and wondered if this might have been a cave years ago and had collapsed, becoming a canyon filled with debris. The gully soon ended among the trees, over-grown with brush and eucalyptus trees scattered over it.

While looking around and guessing at the geological phenomena I noticed some iron debris sticking out of the dirt below in the slanted canyon. Slowly I stepped down into one deeper impression and tugged at the iron piece. It was buried a little in sand and stuck in dirt. I finally yanked it out. At first I could not figure out what it was but as I broke away the hardened mud I saw that it was a very old sewing machine frame. It had to be old, for it was made out of pure iron and it was heavy. I looked around trying to figure out what on earth would an antique sewing machine be doing stuck in this rocky crevice in no man's land.

Setting it aside I began digging around with my hand, pulling away some of the leaves and debris and soon began to find all sorts of strange things: old odd shaped bits of iron, along with glass and porcelain pieces and some old rusted hinges mixed with parts of tools and things I could not identify. Hey, this is weird I thought. The more I dug down the more things I found. I finally came to what appeared to be large plate tiles, colored blue with some flakes that seemed to be gold. They were in nearly perfect condition after I rubbed off the sand. For sure, this was getting interesting. I thought

I might get Theo and see what he thought. This had to be a treasure trove. He knew a lot about antiques and old things, his parents owned a well known antique store on Balboa Island across the bay from his Surf Shop in Newport. Theo had grown up and spent many hours working in their shop refurbishing and selling, familiar with these things.

I made my way back along the slope of the crevices leading down to the cove. Looking around, I saw Theo out in the shore breaks, trying to do some body surfing. I caught his attention and waved him in. Soon he stood there shaking off the ocean and asked what I had found. I handed him the square blue tiles and one of the old hinges.

"Wow, where in the heck did you get this?" he looked at me curiously.

I pointed to the far corner of the cove where I had gone up the gully, now filled with debris, and said, "I followed that gap up to see how far it went and began to find things buried in it."

"That is strange, let's go take a look. This might be interesting."

We walked to a mound at the base of the cliff, and right away Theo saw something stuck in the sand. He was soon clearing away the wet sand from off a glob of rust that seemed to be junk. It appeared to be things made of iron, somehow washed onto the beach and slowly rusted together. At first we thought we might have discovered an ancient shipwreck piled against the cliff in a storm, but the more we dug the more we realized that much of this debris was from some type of old structure, or maybe out of a shop. Theo finally extricated the large cluster of iron, looking like a strange sculpture, all fused together by years of being in the sand and ocean. He placed it on a rock so we could better examine it.

Taking a sharp stick Theo began digging out the sand and dirt and rocks until slowly there began to emerge objects we could recognize. The first thing he pointed to was a cluster of large old keys. I mean big keys, like you would see in an old monastery prison movie. He broke one off and rubbed it clean. The rust was still thick but it was a huge skeleton key. Holding it up for me to see, he said, "That baby is worth some money."

All I could say was, "Wow, are you sure?"

"Yep, I know a little about old keys and this has got to be something special," and he handed it to me and went back to work breaking off more things from the chunk of conglomerated rust.

As he was working on his piece, I began digging through the mound. Just below the wild beach grass the entire mound was one giant pile of things. I mean things of every sort. One of the most exciting finds was an ornate picture frame about one foot square. I held my breath as Theo scratched off the hardened mud, scratched into the frame, he said, "Great Gobs of Glory! This is silver!"

"You're kidding me. And what the hell is Gobs of Glory?" I nearly shouted.

Theo, one of my oldest friends, was part genius, part inventor, part surfer and had been permeated with his family's intellect. He was a classic collage in character and wit; hard to see him for what he was. He had rebelled against his parents' life blueprint for him by turning down scholarships to several of the most prestigious institutions in the nation, instead joining the west coast surfer groups, eventually opening his own water sports shop. But that could not prevent his genius from working. Inventions and odd ideas constantly came from him, and I will admit some were brilliant beyond common sense and ordinary implementation. His blend of character and personality was different, to say the least, sometimes most entertaining and often too practical to argue with.

He said, "Hey, keep it down. We might have found something that could get us into trouble and it looks like no one has ever touched this junk pile before. And that corny Gobs of Glory expression is one of my father's favorite idioms when he discovers something that glitters below the surface."

When he said this, I looked up at the debris-filled gully and a thought came to me. "You think this crevice might be filled with all kinds of odd things? Could it have been a dumping site for the Hearst Castle when they were building it?"

He looked up at the cliffs, as if seeing things that weren't there, and said matter-of-factly, "You know, you might be right, because old man Hearst was a fanatic about everything. If he didn't like it, he would have it torn out and replaced."

I interjected, "This could have been the place where they dumped all the so-called junk, and because the beach is off-limits, no one would have found it. And as the years went by, the dump area was filled in with dirt and over grown with shrubs and weeds."

"That could be it." Theo pointed to the crevice saying, "It is possible that over the years heavy rains washed a lot of that stuff out of the cut onto the beach and this mound is the result of those wash-outs."

"I bet that is it, I waved the key over the mound and added, "Man, I wonder what else we're gonna find in this mess."

Practical Theo suggested, "I don't know. Let's go get some

shoes and pants on and get started digging through the Hearst Castle junk yard."

Chapter Six

A Taste Of Treasure

We returned to the north cliff, deciding to dig into the larger mound first. If anyone showed up, we would be somewhat hidden in the shadows and could cover the area with sand and play dumb. However, as we began to find and dig out some interesting old items, we chose to take them back to the cave, keeping them out of sight. It was amazing, for every few minutes of digging, besides chunks of rusted iron, we came up with some extraordinary find. The two best things we discovered on our first dig were two ancient, and I mean old, old brass hand-held oil lanterns. Theo said they had to be Spanish or maybe Egyptian or old world pieces, extremely rare and very valuable. My mind went to California history and the missionary guy named Serra and the California missions. The lanterns might have come out of an old mission or church, but we would know better once they were cleaned up.

Then Theo struck paydirt, finding an old broken box, about the size of a boot box but still sealed. When we pried it open, there were two duelling musket pistols, still sitting in rotted velvet. They were rusted from the moisture but all the accompanying parts, such as the rammers, the lead bullets and what appeared to be a container of old fine gun powder was right there. No doubt, this was worth big bucks. More than excited, we immediately took it back to the cave.

As we dug into the mound we found more frames. Some were silver and many were brass, but most of them were broken. Several of them had pieces of painted canvas still attached to the frames. This spurred us on to dig deeper so that we were not paying attention when we heard the whacking noise of a helicopter just on the other side of the point. We dove behind a log and lay quiet, hoping that the disturbance of the sand would not give us away. The shadow of the chopper swooped right overhead without slowing down and continued south. "Wow, was that a near miss!" Theo whooped.

We immediately became more cautious to the air patrols going on around us. We still whooped and awed when we found old clocks. Of course the things were rusted solid, but they were old. Entangled in this mess, were hundreds of rusted horse shoes. The further we dug into the mound, the more curious we became. We found brass buttons, odd badges or what we thought were badges, until we hit a stash of small swords bound wrapped up in a leather pouch. The handles were ornate and each sword or dagger was of the best steel.

These finds just kept on and on. By the time evening came and we were back in the cave with our acquired treasures, we estimated that we might have several thousand dollars worth of antiques. I was elated, but soon became concerned about how the heck we were going to get this stuff out of here and… what if we were caught?

That evening JJ sent a text message, "joker! part had to be ordered. deliver to shell station near castle tomorrow. staying at friends house."

Over the last few weeks, we had adapted a code system using—yes—cards! So when JJ sent the message beginning with "joker" we knew something had gone wrong.

I replied with, "ACE! Hire Shell mechanic to bring you and part to van and pay him to repair it-make sure it is done right-stay out of trouble."

The ace gave JJ authority to work things out as he saw fit.

The best part of that evening was all the speculation we did. With me being a research freelance writer, this was a fabulous story in the making that appeared to be bigger than it looked on the surface. However, reality brought us to the possibility of selling the stuff, and actually making some needed money. The next day, bright and early, I spent an hour before the sun came over the hills digging into the actual gully and found what turned out to be an old bell, really rusted. At first I thought it to be part of a wood stove, but as I freed it, it slowly became a bell measuring about eighteen inches high and sixteen inches at its base that still had the clapper inside. Theo helped me pull it out and put it on a rock where we cleaned off the mud. There were some engravings cut around the rim of the bell and what appeared to be a Spanish name "San Bella" and a date—1895.

"Now, that might be a ship's bell and if those names can be traced, we got one heck of a treasure here," Theo excitedly proclaimed.

"You know, I'm wondering why old man Hearst would have all this stuff just dumped," I conjectured.

"It is possible that he didn't, but maybe some of his workers were stealing from him and hiding it out here as if in the dump, but with the intention of collecting it later," Theo added his two cents.

"That could be, because some of this stuff is just too valuable to have to have been considered junk," I surmised.

Theo sat back and began to recall something, "I read a book one time about Randolph Hearst and his castle-building obsession. It took many years and there were hundreds of people and crews of men working day and night on its construction and its furnishing. The Hearsts traveled all through Europe, buying up entire castles and old churches, having them dismantled and shipped back to be used in his personal castle. As they arrived, any one of the hundreds of workers could have slowly bled off some prized objects and hid them in this gully.

"That could have been," I nodded my agreement. This sparked an idea and I decided to call my good surf buddy, friend, old time editor and now my lawyer, Dustin Arrow, back in Huntington Beach. I decided to use a few bars of my low battery cell to get off a call to Dustin. When I finally got through, without any fancy explanations I told him that I needed him to do some research for me. Dustin and I had been long-time friends going way back to high school, and through college, then he became my editor when I decided to become a free-lance writer. I found his lawyer connections to be valuable in many of my personal ventures into news-worthy articles. He would send me out in all directions to investigate and see what might be gleaned out of unusual events and differing situations. With his encouragement I had begun to earn a serious reputation as an investigatory journalist. He would also glean new clients from some of the situations I discovered. We formed a good team and worked well together.

Still though, I had learned that journalism was considered a financially risky career, due to periodic droughts in income. He also had to bail me out of several unpleasant troubles over the years. This investigation thing often took me into areas where the light was not the brightest, and certain elements did not want it turned on, especially on them! We had a special bond, not only as my friend, but as my struggling companion in life, and now my lawyer.

My grandparents, Steward and Gladys Mitchner, had been killed in an airplane crash several years back, in the Canadian wilderness. Through this tragic event, I had inherited a considerable-sized fortune. As good as the inheritance went, that was fine, but my grandparents were some of the greatest people around. Not just because they were my new adopted parents, after my own parents' drowning at sea on their sail boat, but they were high quality people and I missed them. When this tragedy had struck my life, Dustin and Theo had been there for me; our friendships were sealed in and through these events.

However, within this sorrow, my inheritance had attracted the wolves, and now there were hoards of unscrupulous lawyers lined up trying to get a cut. All this had been tangled up in Canadian litigations for the last few years with a multitude of low-life, will-chasers, trying to get their piece of my endowments. But with both Dustin, and myself, near broke, we were left somewhat ineffective to simply hire the right people to deal with a supposed twin sister, totally unknown to me, and a hundred never-before-heard-of relatives. So in the meantime I kept up my free-lance work to pay the bills. Besides, I loved the work, the travel, not being tied down and always into something new. Who knows, this find might add some very much-needed funds to our struggle to set things right!

Theo continued talking about what he knew of the Hearsts while I punched in Dustin's number, "There was an actual dock loading facility for Hearst's yacht, and for many art treasures to be brought in. I'm not sure, but it's just south of here a little ways if I remember. Possibly where the state park is now," he pointed south as Dustin's phone began to ring.

I quickly went on with Dustin, giving him as much detail as

I could, while he took notes. I wanted to see if there was any connection with the date 1895 and a ship named San Bella. This might have been a ship that was lost in the early part of the 20th century along the California coast. It might have something to do with the Hearst castle or family. I explained that my cell was low and that as soon as he found something, call me or text me or send an email.

He agreed, laughed and said, "Mitchner, sounds like you're on a hot one again."

"Not sure yet, but it could become a royal blaze soon," and I shut down, thinking I heard something off in the distance.

We both heard the blade-chatter of the helicopter off in the distance. Immediately we stood up to listen. I told Theo we better toss some sand over the mound and get hidden in case this was the patrol again, buzzing the beach for trespassers. We worked frantically tossing sand over the areas we had uncovered, then laid behind some of the larger boulders that had crumbled off the cliff. Just in time, for the chopper appeared around the northern point, not far off the water leaving us with no doubt that someone was patrolling the beaches. The chopper slowed and seemed to take a double look, but thanks to a high tide, our prints were erased. Soon the chopper was on its way.

Theo said, "Sure enough, they got the beach covered. Make note of the time, maybe there's a pattern to the flights."

"Hey, that's a good idea," and I marked the time as just a little past nine in the morning.

"We better pay closer attention here, be ready to cover up and hide," Theo said as he scanned the sky.

"OK," I agreed. We went back to digging through the back side of the mound, preventing someone from seeing the sand

and grass disturbed from the front.

The morning wore on and sure enough, the beach chopper came back from out of the south about two hours later. It did not return again until the late afternoon; still though, why was it constantly checking out this cove? We realized that the mound itself was compiled from many iron and metal objects. The bad thing was that the weight of the pile had slowly pressed all the objects down deep into the sand. We had dug down about three foot at an angle and still kept finding things. Our thoughts about how we were going to get this stuff out of here became an on-going discussion. We cautiously took another hoard of interesting discoveries back to the cave and took a rest from our fascinating labors.

While we sat there nibbling on some over-the-coals fish my ear was alerted to what I thought to be voices. At first I thought it might be JJ calling out for us, but it was female voices we heard. Both Theo and I moved to the opening of our cave and slowly looked around.

"Check that out," I pointed beyond the waves.

"Those are kayakers," Theo said.

"Yeah, looks like they might be coming into the cove. What you think?"

"Looks like there are a few of them, and they seem to be headed in, we better lay low for now," Theo stepped back out of the light.

It was about noon and there were four kayakers that rode the waves into the cove and beached their rigs near the northern point. There were two guys and two girls, and we were holding our breaths that they were not in any exploring mood. It became apparent that they were taking a break when they opened up a parcel to share wine and sandwiches.

We could hear them talking and laughing and hoped they would soon get on their way. Our worries grew when the boys spread out their blankets while the two lovelies went walking, most likely looking for a place to do their thing and they were headed our way. Good old Theo had to take notice of those two well endowed girls, and they did not escape my eyes either, but this was no time to make goo-goo eyes. I jabbed Theo in the ribs, "Now calm down boy, calm down."

Fortunately there were plenty of boulders and driftwood logs for them to hide behind before they came to the cave area. They were finished and just about ready to continue our way when we heard the chopper pounding the air out of the north. They heard it too and stopped to look around. The chopper came over the point and immediately saw the kayaks sitting high on the beach. We could clearly see the pilot and another passenger in the helicopter as the chopper swooped down and came to the beach cove right above the shore break.

A harsh voice came over a loud speaker announcing in a not so pleasant tone, "Attention please, this is a restricted area. You are trespassing on private land. Please get into your boats and go your way. Get off the beach." The chopper moved around as if intimidating the kayakers, with the wind blasting up the sand, and it did the trick. The girls hurried back to the others and they stood there for a while, not sure if they should go. Then the voice repeated the demands in a serious voice. I thought it was a little over-kill already, but that was just the beginning.

The kayakers got into their rigs, pushing out through the waves and turning south. The chopper swooped down at them like a fat pelican diving after sardines, as it followed them out beyond the waves, beating up the water around them. Then again, the chopper went out of its way to cause them trouble by buzzing them. It was near enough to blast them with the chopper's downwind and I shook my head, saying that this was not necessary. I took note of the number on its side, HC-7. Theo said, "Man, that pilot is pretty good." We could see the kayakers paddling for their lives while the chopper took its time and continued diving at them like a hungry hawk, swooping down, nearly touching the paddlers' heads. We saw the co-pilot lifting the megaphone, blasting out near-insane phrases over and over. The scene was unreal. These men were sadistic; there was no call for this extreme action. We were wondering why.

When one of the kayaks was flipped over by the downwinds, the group began yelling and shaking their fists at the hovering chopper. It was one of the girls that had flipped, but recovered with the help of the other kayakers. The chopper continued blasting them; this scene had became more than just a game. After a few more near-misses the chopper certainly put a scare into the kayakers. Soon it lifted, then departed.

"Wow, guess we know that this place is really patrolled, and not by anyone over-friendly," I spoke out as the chopper disappeared, following the kayakers around the southern point.

"Yeah, best we be on guard and figure out what the heck we're gonna do to stay out of their view," Theo delivered his concern.

"Think we could work, maybe in the dark, a little?" I offered up a suggestion.

"No more body surfing for me. Maybe later in the evening we can dig around a little bit with the flashlights we got now, but that ain't much," Theo answered. "It might do us well to use our flashlights to move some of this stuff up the beach to that hut and store it there. Then when the van is ready, we can hustle across the field and carry the things to the van."

I said that this might work, but let's think it over first, "That sounds like a good idea, but we can't be taking too much stuff with us, the van could not carry it all anyways."

We both agreed that it had been a close call and a warning not to be too casual about freedom in our secret pirate's cove. I nodded and turned my ear to the outside to listen for any further voices or disturbances. It was quiet other than the shush of the low tide waves

We made our way back up the beach, using the boulders
and cliff area to walk in, trying not to leave footprints. We
decided to climb up the crevice, through the shrubs and take
a look at what might be further up in the junk site. We soon
found that we were well hidden under many of the shrubs
and eucalyptus trees that had grown up along the top of the
cliff area. This gave us a whole new idea about how to get
our newly acquired treasures out. The grove of trees, thick
old pines and eucalyptus trees, ran clear to the fence along
the road. It was dense and well tangled with bushes and
shrubs and we could carry our finds up near the fence and
keep them hidden under the bushes. Then when the van was
ready, we would drive up to the treed area and park alongside
the fence pretending we had a flat tire. Then we could load
up the van from there.

We thought for sure that JJ would be back at any time, but
the day wore late as we kept an eye out for him. I suggested
that Theo continue to dig in the upper trench area, while I
went down to the cove and did a little more digging around
from that end.

"If you do, you'd better really pay attention. We just lucked
out the first day."

"No problem, if I hear the chopper coming, I'll hide out like
a salamander, and you do the same."

"Not a salamander, but a chameleon lizard," Theo corrected
me, but I loved to tease him with such oddities.

"We could sneak back to the van tonight and grab a few

things, including the camping shovel," Theo said.

"That's a possibility. It might be a good idea to check on the van anyhow."

I made my way back down to the beach mounds and began my exploration. Sure enough, about two hours later I heard the chopper off to the north as it grew louder and louder. The chopper blew by, headed south without a slow down. I waited to see if the patrol kept its schedule, and again, just about an hour passed when it came back, flying low, only right above the cove this time. I was hoping that Theo was well hidden, for the chopper seemed to be scouting the upper area.

The day was on its way out when I got back to him. "Hey Theo, are you there?" I half whispered through the bushes as I climbed up the trench.

"Keep coming, all is clear so far. Just don't stand up," I heard Theo answering.

"What's up doc?" I inquired.

"Oh man, you won't believe this," Theo spoke excitedly as he pointed to several long objects lying under the bushes a little ways out of the trench.

The first thing I noticed was that he was filthy dirty, from head to toe, completely covered with dirt sticking to his sweaty body. This was unusual because Theo was more of an intellect than a laborer, so something had to be up. "What is it? You must have really found something to get that dirty," I commented.

"I think so. I dug out three really incredible statues so far and it looks like there are more down here," he pointed down the hole he was standing in.

"What kind of statues?"

"I'm not sure, but I know they are polished stone of some kind, really detailed-out nicely, by someone who knew what they were doing."

"Man, they look heavy, how the heck did you get them out of there on your own?" I asked.

"It wasn't easy. But when I put my mind to it, nothing's gonna stop me. Go take a look while I loosen this one up."

I crawled over to the objects lying under some leaves and rubbed my hand over what seemed to be a female face. No doubt, there was fine detail showing through the dirt. There were three stone statues created on their own bases. They could have been those kind you see set around a pool or in an ancient Roman palace. They were exquisitely carved from what I could tell, but I was no expert in this art stuff.

Theo's voice called over to me to come help him with another one. I scrambled down next to him so that together we could lift out another strangely shaped statue, only this one was made of what seemed to be bronze.

"Now this is incredible, what the heck happened here? Why would anyone dump such things into the ground and walk away?" I gritted my teeth as we pushed this last work of metal onto level ground.

I was on high alert, watching and listening carefully as we sat back resting, shaking my head, saying that this did not make sense. "Theo, did you see any other place where someone might have been digging along here?"

"You know, now that you mention it, just down a ways I did see what looked to be a hole that had been filled in sometime back. Why do you ask?" Theo was looking at me with some curiosity. He knew I often came up with some far-out ideas.

"Because it seems awful strange that they patrol this area so well. Maybe someone knows what is here and keeps the beach patrolled so no one can come along and—well—discover what we have found." I added, "And, put skulls into hideaway huts to freak away strangers."

"Aah man, that sounds pretty far out. If that was true, someone would have already dug all this stuff up."

"True, but maybe this treasure dump had to be hidden for a while, until everyone just thought that these things never made it to the castle."

Theo seemed to sit back, looking up at the afternoon clouds, so I knew he was doing some serious thinking. I gave him a few moments then asked," What you thumpkin, old wise man?"

"You know I told you that I once read a book about the Hearst family fortune and the building of this castle. Somewhere in that book I remember that a ship carrying a lot of his stuff sank or disappeared, right off the shore around here."

"Really now," I exclaimed.

"Yep, there was some kind of an investigation and a search for the ship but it was never found."

My mind went to work now, coming up with a few crazy ideas. Instantly I flashed back to the picture that came to me back at the beach hut: the sinking ship and men in the water; but I did not say anything about that. "What if the ship did not sink, but moved close into this cove and unloaded its treasures? Everything was hidden in this gully and covered over. Whoever did this, waited until the coast was clear. But something happened and the treasure could not be recovered. And so forth…"

"That is a lot of far-out speculation. Without a doubt, all this is a mystery." Theo was looking at me with his piercing eyes, while fingering back long thick strands of hair. He mumbled that this whole thing was strange.

"How's that?" I asked.

"Well, we thought this might have been a dump site, and it could have been at one time. However, these statues were not just tossed into this hole, but carefully laid in their place. In fact the three up there had some canvas cloth still wrapped around them," and he lifted up an old scrap of canvas, well rotted now.

I took hold of one of the pieces, dirty and torn, and said, "Ok, now the mystery does get thicker and thicker."

My mind was racing, for if this was not a real dump, but a hiding place for some of the Hearst Castle's missing treasures, we could be in one heck of a mess, no less in danger, if anyone knew what we had found.

I told Theo, "That is enough statues. Let's look for some smaller things to be able to get away from here with at least our lives, and maybe enough goodies to put a dent into making our surf movie."

"Hey, you're scaring me Mitchner." He would call me Mitchner when his serious mood kicked in, "Do you really think we might be in danger?" Theo's face was not only dirty, but with this statement it showed some sobering anxiety.

The one thing about Theo was that he had been well guarded by over-protective parents while growing up. Any type of trouble or danger would send him into scared-rabbit mode.

He would break into stuttering or exhibit odd behavior patterns when threatened. I had come to know his moods and knew I had to help curb his anxieties to keep him on course, "Don't worry, if we play it right, no one is going to know that we were ever here."

With this, Theo went back to work and I half rolled and dragged the statues into the grove and covered them over with leaves.

I took a moment to sit back and ponder on how this was rather a pleasant place. The ocean breeze carried in the scent of the sea, mixing in with the pines and eucalyptus and the fragrance of the low growing shrubs. The leaves on the trees sang their song and a peace lay hidden in this cove of many mysteries. However, the discovery of old statues, pottery and iron as well as the dragging of ancient statues through the grass and into the trees was a strange contrast. I wondered how many people had walked over this very place and never suspected that there would be hidden treasures just a few feet under them. The entire setting had to be worth a good story in the making.

It was a cold but clear evening, the sun had just gone down and we were not wasting any time in our search. Theo was getting excited; I began calling him Mr. Archeologist. He was digging up brass fixtures that seemed to be from old sailing ships, handing them over to me. I was hidden under a low-growing pine, going through a full set of silver utensils, tarnished but old and extremely intricate in design, when a noise from down in the cove caught my attention. I scrambled over to where Theo was bent down in the hole to alert him, "Theo, shut off your light and get out of there, I think someone is down in the cove. It sounds like something is going on down there."

Theo climbed out, shoving the brush into the hole, and together we crawled along the gully and lay still under the shrubs. Looking out and down, the night was not yet set solid, but a partial moon had risen. We could see what seemed to be a fishing trawler sitting about 200 yards off shore, just a silhouette against the faint night sky with no lights on. Then, strangely, we saw a blinking signal light aimed at the shore. Soon we noticed up on the north point another signal light answering back.

Straining to see, until several flashlights went on, down on the beach. A large crowded rubber raft appeared with ten or more people making its way into the cove. The rubber raft rode the low tide waves and swooped onto the beach. Three men who had made their way from the north point along the beach were carrying what we were sure were weapons. Loaded down with back packs, they stood waiting for the boat load of people.

The tightly packed group came alive scrambling out of the raft and gathering on the shore. We could see about ten men, a couple of women and two young children. Two of the waiting figures held their weapons and flashlights on the group, while the third was speaking Spanish to one man left standing in the rubber raft. The man still in the raft bent down and began tossing up a number of smaller bundles about the size of footballs out of the raft. Two of the men set down their weapons on the sand before they began catching the packages, quickly fitting them into two of the backpacks that were sitting away from the waters edge.

As the light of the moon increased, I thought the men seemed familiar. They might be two of the Hearst Castle Security guards; one looked like the pilot of the chopper we had seen running off the kayakers. Both Theo and I knew that we had just witnessed an exchange of some kind, and we were sure it wasn't some high priced tea leaves.

"What the crap is going on with this?" Theo whispered.

"Well, I think we named this Smuggler's Cove just right. It looks like these are illegals being smuggled in, and this cove is a near perfect place to handle them, along with some contraband—most likely drugs!"

"But where are the patrols when you need them?" Theo asked.

"I got the feeling that those two were the guard patrol, the same ones off the everyday chopper patrol!"

Beyond the darkness of the night, after the initial exchange had been made, it was evident that someone else was still in the raft, lying down. The larger group stood off to one side huddled together for safety, maybe to keep the night breeze from cutting them down in the cold. We could see some type of exchange taking place between the head man and the one in the raft, while the other two stood with weapons ready. An intense discussion could be heard, with the words sounding up the cliff to our hiding place. It was part English with more intense words in Spanish. The group from off the boat were looking around, speaking low in Spanish. It seemed that the newly arrived group of men and women were scared, not knowing what to do, just waiting.

Within a few minutes the man in the raft made a cell call. Soon he barked out several commands and waved the group to get going, move up the cliff to the highway. Immediately the group of men and women headed our way.

Soon the group of Mexicans, we assumed they were Mexicans, since they were speaking Spanish, moved towards the cliff, weaving themselves up and over the rocks, climbing up to the top of the cliff, coming out just a short ways from where we lay. The first thing I thought of was—what if they stumbled across our stash of oddities in the cave? Or worse, what if they decided to come up the gully trench we were lying in? Just then my phone bonged, and the passing group stopped dead, beginning to murmur.

"Ah sheet, shut that off. What if they hear us?" Theo jabbed me in the side, nearly fainting as he whispered, when the group halted about 10 feet away from us. The men down on the beach stood still, looking up to see what was going on, scanning the cliff with their flashlights. Oh man, was I ever happy we looked like piles of dirt, stained and splattered with mud and grime; as the lights actually went right over us. When one of the kids started crying, they looked around in fright but quickly disappeared into the trees. Soon we heard a vehicle's brakes squeaking slightly on the road above us, then it stopped for a few minutes, and we listened to a gear-shifting truck drive away, and they were gone. Never before did being a dirt clod feel so great and a crying kid sound so good!

We lay low, still and quiet. I could hear Theo breathing and muttering under his breath. This was something serious, way more than anything we had bargained for, but there was nothing we could do but stay hidden. I told Theo to carefully try to get a few pictures. Even though it was dark, maybe something would take, and please, do not use a flash.

We watched. Soon the man who was standing in the boat arguing with the third man on the beach lifted up somebody else from the bottom of the raft and shoved him over to the waiting men on shore. The person seemed to be hurt and needed help, he was practically carried to shore. Whoever it was, his hands were tied behind his back and he stumbled to his knees in the back-wash of the tide. The figure fell to the sand and lay there in the shadows of the night. One guard took several larger packages out of another pack, then a second exchange took place with the waiting figure standing in the raft. It was quiet, other than the swishing of the rise and fall of the tiny waves.

After this, the one man left standing in the boat flashed his flashlight out to the waiting trawler beyond the waves. Immediately a long line drew taut and the rubber raft was pulled out through the surf and back to the waiting vessel. We were amazed and dumbfounded; this had to be a smooth-running operation.

Fear set in, but there was nothing we could do. It was obvious that the three gun-toting guards, having a prisoner with them, were not going to find favor with us if we were discovered. It was also obvious that this was some kind of a drug exchange, tied into some kind of a cross-over smuggling operation. But who was the person lying bound on the sand?

We lay there quiet, listening and watching. The main guard or leader bent down and cut the bindings loose from the hands of the figure quietly sprawled on the sand. It was hard to hear but we both thought we heard a woman's voice, crying and asking questions. She was told to be quiet and they helped her up as they put their packs on and moved along the beach back towards the north point, just below us.

As they moved along, I heard Theo's camera clicking, and we could hear the woman's voice asking questions. Her voice was not young but not old; she had to be around 40, and no doubt: she was defiant. The camera clicks must have caught the ear of one of the three. They halted. Suddenly one of them called out, "Who's there?"

I grabbed Theo's arm and pulled him back away from the open edge. Their flashlights scanned the cliff across the area we were lying in. One of the three lifted up his weapon and the next thing I knew—flashes of flame were bursting from his gun and bullets were snapping off branches and thudding into the dirt around us. Theo let out a little screech as one of the bullets hit his shoe, blowing off the heel. "Oh my God, holy gobs of royal gun drops!" he cried out a mixed-up metaphor, half his father's and part from his own immediate descriptions. Apparently they did not hear his cry over the blasts of the weapon. Then we heard a voice yell, "Drake, you idiot, stop! That is enough. You're going to wake up the whole damn coast with that racket."

Another voice said, "It's only a damn seagull, you trigger-happy jerk. Let's get the hell out of here."

They moved on, shoving the woman along, soon disappearing around the point near the rocks. Then we heard a noise off in the distance that sounded like a sand buggy start up and move north until it was gone.

Our little adventure had just turned into a full fledged nightmare. We lay there looking up at the stars, talking about what the heck we were going to do with this information. Should we report this? What evidence did we have of the exchange? Who would we report? We could be dragged into some personal gang exchanges, and what if it was part of a deadly South American cartel?

Theo's teeth were chattering as he stuttered, "I don't know about evidence but I know one thing, my-my shoe is-is shot to pieces."

I looked him over to see if he was OK while he was rubbing his foot and holding up what was left of the heel of his shoe.

Just a few minutes ago we were happy-go-lucky adventurers with our little find of antiques, but now there was a whole new level to this Hearst treasure cove adventure. Then just as a falling star streaked overhead, my cell phone bonged again. The frightful moment was broken, and we both laughed at this reassuring coincidence.

It was JJ, "Yeah, whats up? Is all OK?" I whispered, knowing it was JJ, Mister Flash himself.

"Yeah, all is OK. The part is here at the Shell station in San Simeon and good old bearded Barney wants fifty bucks to bring me out in the morning and replace the pump."

"Does that include the cost of the pump?" I inquired.

"No, the pump was around forty dollars and I already paid that."

"So do you got enough left to give him the fifty?" I asked.

"Yep, just enough, as long as he doesn't decide to charge more."

"If he does, try to bargain something out with him, maybe a later payment when we get home." I heard him groan in frustration as I added, "Use a bit of that new-found wisdom of yours, if need be," I expressed my confidence.

"Then what?" Jason asked with a tired attitude.

"After the van is done, test it out. Fill it up and go down to the San Simeon State Park and get a camping spot to wait in. We're kinda stuck here. Sleep and stay out of trouble, we'll be calling you as soon as we're ready. I'll give you further instructions on meeting us, or Theo might, my cell is nearly dead."

I heard someone talking in the background; JJ was interrupted, "OK, got to go and meet a few of his buddies for a game. He's ready to close up and he's got to go."

"Hey, where you gonna stay tonight?" I asked.

"Got a few surfing buds that are anxious to hear about the surf flick." I heard him clear his voice a little before he finished, "Anyhow, I told them I might get them a part in it."

That was JJ, wheeling and dealing, already selling off our movie to strangers. But I had to laugh—at least he got himself a place to stay for the night. I just hoped he didn't lose my van in one of his midnight card games. When I heard the word "game" I had the feeling that good old Barney was going to end up paying for the gas pump and his time, with some of his own out-of-pocket money — sorry Barney!

We worked our way back up to what we now called the dig, and refilled the hole with debris and brush and made our way back to the cave. We had to clean up; both of us were filthy with dirt and debris. Watching carefully that the boat had gone and the night was clear of patrols, we stripped and ran into the surf. The water was more than cold and time did not allow us the pleasure of enjoying the waves. We dried off, came back to the cave and tested the fish. The coals were burned low so we fed the fire some small dried sticks to keep the smoke down. The smoke rose up into the ceiling and found its way out through the cracks in the rock to drift along the grass into the trees and away into the night.

Theo asked me if he might go to the van and grab some clean clothes, another pair of shoes, along with some grub. I was hesitant but he soon persuaded me that he knew plenty on how to be cool as a ghostly shadow unseen. "After all I have seen every James Bond movie ever made," he made a sneaking gesture and I laughed and nodded, but pleaded for him to take precautions to make sure no one saw him.

While he was gone I began to go through the things we had piled in the cave and put as much as possible into our back packs to get things ready to move the next day. We would have left that very night but the van was not ready. We were trapped here for at least one more day. Evening in the cove brought an offshore breeze which carried the scent of eucalyptus trees while the sea breezes brought in the scent of salt and sea. It was rather a pleasant moment alone, but a good hour had gone by and my worries for Theo's escapade had just about reached peak when I heard the whispering alert that he was back. "Man, Theo, I was damn well worried for you. What took you so long?" I spoke a little harsh as my worries were released.

"Oh Mr. Lukas Michener, you ain't gonna like this," he immediately began to talk with serious sarcasm before he was all the way into the cave.

"What, what? It's not JJ is it?" I exclaimed.

Theo slumped down onto his sleeping bed and said, "No, no, but the van was broken into and our boards are gone. I think they got your laptop and a few other things."

"Ahh crap, that is a shitty deed by some idiot. Why us?" I nearly yelled.

"Yeah I know. That was my main display board, the best one ever, sort of a sweet long-time friend," Theo was nearly crying and pounding his fist into his palm.

"Hey, think about my laptop. All my notes and interviews from the show were on there," I shook my head, just now realizing for the both of us what this meant, "Whoever it was, knows that we were in the area if they read my materials."

"You think so?"

"Sure, I keep a lot of data on that laptop. Even though there's no banking stuff, there are notes about all my articles and who and what we were doing in the last few weeks."

We were silent for a while as Theo tossed over a bundle of clean clothes for me, saying, "Why the heck didn't we just stay at the van in the first place?"

"Listen Theo, don't worry about your board. I got insurance

and we'll get you one of those really fancy-dancy ones you can refurbish with your sonic beam thing." I wasn't sure if my insurance would cover this and at this moment didn't even know if I still had insurance, but wanted to make Theo feel better about the loss. I added, "It would have been shitty staying locked up in that van, and besides, the patrols would have made us tow it away right then."

"Sure, no problem, I feel better already, just like winning the big lotto and then finding out I got a month to live," he shrugged sarcastically. He went on, using his chosen lists of politically correct statements, "Do you think it was one of those government-sponsored vehicles we heard stop to pick up the new American Vine Dressers union members and saw the helpless van there; then thought to enrich their lives at our tax payers' expense?"

"Don't really know, could have been anyone, maybe the governor himself."

Then he blurted out, "Oh yeah, guess what?"

"Don't know, what are you asking?" I replied.

"Your side mirror was back in the van, just lying on the floor."

"Whoa, that is weird. What the heck?"

Just then Theo remembered something and dug into his pocket, "Here, I found a wallet lying near where you hid your lap top, it must have been dropped there by the guy who was in the van. And take a look at this, it's your note that was under the windshield. It was sitting on the front seat and it has something written on it."

I took the note and held it up to the flashlight and read the message penned in under mine.

"Warning. Due to our tow truck being repaired we were unable to remove your vehicle. We have given you warning that within 24 hours this vehicle will be removed. We will be in touch

Hearst Castle Security Services - CAT"

"Holy Moly, the whole stinking neighborhood wants to know everything, and I bet they're going to hold our boards and laptop for ransom until we show up!"

"Yeah, that's what I got from it too. Looks like it was the guard patrol after all. Whoever it was, really trashed the van, looks like someone is telling us something. But at least we got their wallet."

With that I opened the well-worn wallet up to a California license. It gave his name as Charles Anthony Trimmer, age 35, height 6 foot, weight 220 with black eyes and brown hair. There was a San Luis Obispo address and a really mean-looking character staring out from his photo. I showed the picture to Theo asking him if this was the same guy that we saw on the beach. Theo was not sure but thought for a moment and responded sarcastically, "Charles Anthony Trimmer sounds like a cat to me."

At first I didn't get it but then saw the title in the initials, C-A-T. We were curious enough to scan through some of the business cards and we shuffled through them. Theo read them off aloud; a few were from arms companies and several export firms out of San Francisco. Going through the wallet we found eighty dollars in cash, a few business notes, several receipts from a supply yard and a tiny phone book. The book was nearly full of assorted numbers, and I noticed many of them had foreign country codes, like 94 for Sri Lanka and

618 for parts of Australia. That's weird I thought. There was also a key tucked into one of the side slots. I put everything back into the wallet and put it into my pack for sorting out later. I thought this might come in handy in getting our things back later.

"Well, we ain't gonna do anything as of yet, not until we get our treasure out of here and my story is secured and we figure out what to do next," I rambled on with anger brewing under my skin.

"I'm tired, let's talk tomorrow," Theo stretched out and was asleep in minutes.

Morning was cloudy and overcast with a slight breeze out of the north. A haze hung in the sky but the early summer weather still kept the air warm. I was really concerned about my laptop being gone. What if the Hearst security had it and now, they could read my emails. And if Dustin had sent his research to me, it would be on my server and this was bad, really bad. I called Dustin and asked him if he had sent me an email as of yet. "Yeah Luke, you asked me to speed things up so I did, sent it just this morning. Didn't you read it yet?"

"My laptop was stolen out of the van yesterday and anyone who has it can trace me through that email."

"Aah, not so good my friend," Dustin rebuked me with a harsh tone.

"I know, I know, is there anything we can do to remove it before anyone might read it?" I almost pleaded.

"It is a possibility. But the email I sent was packed with your San Bella ship wreck, or the lost ship story. So if anyone reads it, they'll figure that you definitely are aware of the missing wreck," Dustin poured out his bad news as my worries doubled in weight.

"So there was a San Bella ship wreck that took place?" I became curious and asked him.

"Yes, it was back in the early 30's when this small steam freighter disappeared. It had come from Europe and it might have been loaded with rare treasures of all kinds, previously purchased by the Hearst family on one of their buying expeditions."

I absorbed this news while my brain began to connect the dots, but first I asked Dustin, "Please get hold of my server. Do something. Get hold of Wally if need be, but try and get my email messages erased, like now, my friend!"

Good old Wally. He and I had been tossed together a time back at his ranch house up in the desert at a place called the Pitt Stop. He was a hi-tech programmer and together we had cracked a nefarious government plot to create a massive data base using a strange bump in the road experiment. His computer skills had opened the door to this military experiment and together we had narrowly escaped at the last moment on the back of his huge Harley. He was an old friend of Dustin's and he fit well into our team of oddball characters. Wally was a huge hairy character who had proved his worth many times over.

"You sound desperate Luke, what's up this time?" Dustin inquired with some concern.

"This is big time stuff here. Real treasure in a smugglers cove, mixed in with some heavy duty bad guys. And we have just touched the tip of the iceberg." I hurried along, explaining with frustration in my voice.

Dustin came back on the line, "Hey, is Jason gonna be all right in this adventure of yours? I send him off to a simple surf show with you two bums. Now you're involved in smuggler's treasure with maybe the Hearst Foundation after you. Good grief, why can't you guys just ever do something ordinary?"

"Calm down Mr. Arrow. All is not that bad," I paused, "not yet at least." Then went on, "JJ is out chasing a fuel pump for the van right now, and should be back by this afternoon, but I cannot guarantee his well being unless he follows our instructions. You might call him, just say you want to know how he's doing."

"Just get that kid home safe," Dustin insisted.

"Will do. Got to go, phone fading out," I cut his tirade off and finished up as another bar in the charge icon on the phone disappeared.

We knew it was time to go. Theo was concerned that our calls might be over-heard, depending on how sophisticated these guys were. We began to arrange and pack the items we had in the cave. The chopper made its routine patrol but seemed to linger over the cove a little longer than usual. We were just hoping that the Hearst Security Patrol had not put two and two together as of yet. If so, they might be sending a team to take a closer look for us. The only hope was that if they did read the research email from Dustin, they would only suspect that, as a journalist, I was probing for some insight to the rumor. We decided to make a few stealthy trips up to the fence area and prepare our departure this night. The rest of the day went without incident as we crawled back and forth through the brush and brambles up to the stash along the fence area.

Finally JJ sent a text to my phone saying, "Joker: van broken into and things missing but everything else went well. van gassed and parked in camping #22. far end facing the ocean - waiting!"

Theo texted him back letting him know that we were aware of the break-in and not to worry about it, just wait and be ready for our call—soon!

By late afternoon we had eaten and rested. By nightfall, we

began the final hours of crawling back and forth, transferring our new found treasures up near the fence. Jason was waiting at the San Simeon State Park for our call. We waited for the night to take hold and most of the traffic to slow down.

Then it happened. It had to be near midnight when we heard the helicopter blades beating the night sky. We laid down under a wind torn pine and wondered why the chopper was out at this time of night. It drew closer out of the north. Then suddenly a bright search light flooded the entire area from the trees down towards the cliff. Our hearts sank. We thought for sure that they were searching for us—somehow we had been found out. I thought maybe they had intercepted my call to JJ, but no matter what, we were caught!

"What do we do now?" Theo was grabbing my arm as he lay there pleading for some way out of this mess.

"I don't know. Just be cool, stay hidden here and see what happens."

The chopper moved in closer with its eye-blinding flood light scanning the ground. At first I thought it was searching for us, but as the light moved back and forth, we could see that it was looking over the gully area. Then suddenly, the main light went off and a smaller ground light came on, while the rotor blades thrashed the air, scattering dust, leaves and debris over us. The chopper slowly set down on the grass next to the trench area. Theo wanted to run but I held him back, "No, just stay still, something is going on here. If they were looking for us, they would have moved their flood over the trees and they didn't." We hugged the ground and watched; I could hear Theo's teeth chattering.

Soon the engine shut down and the whirling blades slowly came to a stop until it was quiet. Immediately the chopper door slid open. The three same guards that we had seen on the beach the night before jumped onto the ground, carrying what we first thought were rifles.

"Oh sheeeet, I did not sign up for this," mumbled Theo in pure fright. His eyes were so big I thought the light would reflect off them and give our position away, so I shoved his head down and told him to shut up and lie absolutely still.

We were like deer hiding from the hunters, only as they moved towards the trench we could see that they had shovels, not guns.

"What the heck?" I whispered. Within a few moments, two of the guards had pulled back a large area of brush and moved some dirt around and then rolled what looked like some tree limbs and a few timbers until they rolled back what looked like a carpet. Then they jumped down into a hole which barely left their heads showing. A brighter light began to glow down in their working area and soon we could see things being set up on the grassy area, with the pilot guard loading things into the chopper.

At first there were a few canvas bags, then some wooden boxes, crates and several smaller things we could not see. After about twenty minutes of stacking up stuff, we could hear them discussing if that was enough for this load. One man climbed out of the hole and began helping put the larger crates into the back cab of the chopper. Soon the cab area was full and together the two guards laid out the logs and timbers, pulled the limbs back in place and then reset all the brush over the pit they had just climbed out of. They dusted themselves off, lit up cigarettes while looking around talking about someone named Buck and the fortune they were going to make. Finally they climbed into the chopper and within a few minutes, the blades were thrashing the air and the beast in the night lifted off and flew north.

"Wow, what the heck did we just see?" Theo expostulated in relief.

"I am not sure, but it looks like someone knows about this hidden cache and is slowly removing it."

"Yeah, now we know why they are watching this beach with such strict patrols," I reasoned.

"What now? I am scared shitless," Theo expressed his real concerns. "Let's call JJ right now to come get us."

"I don't think we have to worry right now, this behind-the-scenes landing cannot be seen nor heard from the road or anywhere else around here," I looked around as I speculated.

"So, what good does this do us? We're dead if we are found out!"

I slowly rose up to my knees and said, "We are going over to the pit and take a look for ourselves. We might remove a few things from there and stash it with what we have over by the fence and take it with us."

"You got to be kidding me, Mitchner. I think you've been hit in the head too many times with your surf board or held under water too long. You go, I'll stay here and guard my life!"

"Listen Theo, this is one of the greatest stories I have ever come upon and there is no way that I'm not going to take a look." I knew I had already missed our scheduled meetings with those bully lawyers at home and had no intention of leaving here until I got something for my time and loss. I started moving and whispered to Theo, "You can call Jason on the cell and let him know to come get us, tell him to park right at the burlap strip next to the fence so we can just hand things over. You start moving things up closer to the fence while I go take a look at this treasure pit. But stay low."

A cool night breeze was blowing and the only light for now was the stars. I felt my way over to the brush area, pulling back a few shrubs, all the time listening to Theo grumbling forth his escape plans. Shoving some dirt back with my feet, I pushed the logs and timbers back just far enough to allow me to flip the rug over them. Shining my flash light down into the hole, I was astonished. The entire area for about eight foot square had been cleaned out. There were all kinds of odds and ends strewn or stacked around. I slid into the treasure pit and started looking around. Knowing that I didn't have much time before JJ would show up, I began randomly lifting up some of the smaller boxes and chests. They were sealed, some much heavier than others.

I slowly lifted them up to the grass area and piled as many as I thought we could handle. I tried not to disturb the boxes and bags which were well stacked, running down the trench towards the cliff area. If this trench was full, there had to be thousands of dollars worth of antiques and unimaginable treasures. I noticed that nothing was set on the bare ground but everything had been piled on cedar planks. This was no dump site, it was a cache site for someone's stash and it had been here for a long time. There were roots from the euca-lyptus and pine trees sticking through the side of the cliff wall. You could also smell mold and could feel the dampness. If it wasn't oak chests, steel or iron, this stuff would not have lasted for as long as it did.

Suddenly, a whispered voice came down. It was Theo's, he must have changed his mind and came creeping up on me. "Hey, I got everything ready for JJ and it looks like no one is around. I think only one car went by in the last twenty minutes. So what do you want me to do?"

I laughed under my breath, knowing that even sure danger could not keep Theo away from this adventure, "Start hauling those boxes and bags over to the fence area and stay low, I want to look around just a little more and then that will be it."

Theo stuck his head down into the hollow and exclaimed, "Oh my gosh, this is not real!"

"Yes it is, and get moving. We got but a few minutes once Jason pulls up."

"What is down there? You mean we're gonna take more?" he asked.

"I don't really know, everything seems to be packed in chests or boxes. But I took a variety of things, so whoever is hiding this stuff won't realize someone was in here. And damn right, we're going to take a taste of real adventure with us! We'll look at what we get later," and I added, "Don't worry though, I'll pick out something nice for you. Now get going but keep your light off."

Theo replied, "Hey take my phone and shoot some pictures with it, it still has some battery power left," so when he handed over his cell, I began shooting the stacks of boxes and took some close-ups of exposed writings. I gave his camera back, "That was a good idea, wish I'd thought of it."

"Remember, I'm a photographer. I like those unusual shots, and this is a million dollar picture if there ever was one."

I cracked up, thinking, a million dollar picture, huh? How about a ten million dollar picture? It was time to move, not waste time pondering. Regardless of the few bars of power left in my phone, I marked the exact site on its GPS, then took a few moments to shoot down through the piled boxes until I knew it was time to go, in case the guards returned for a second load. One of my ideas was to find some kind of a date sealed into one of the boxes. There was plenty of faint writings on many of the stacked crates but all in foreign languages. Many of them seemed to be in Greek or maybe Cyrillic.

Theo had already made several trips carrying things away and moved them into the trees. He was on his way back for the smaller things when I handed the last of the thick canvas bags over and picked up the last few boxes and carried them into the trees. I thought I heard something, maybe it was a car on the highway, so I stopped to listen. Oh sheeet, it couldn't be, but yes, it was the chopper still afar off. I began to panic. I had to get back to the hole and make sure it was covered properly. I warned Theo, telling him to hurry and toss leaves over the pile of stuff now lying near the fence, then to lie down under one of the pine trees and stay out of sight. I added, "Call JJ and hold off his return until we call and don't crap in your pants, they might smell you out!"

Scrambling back to the pit, I kicked leaves and grass back over the area we had been walking on. I quickly pushed back the main covering and slid back the cross timber and began to reset the shrubs when the chopper appeared over my shoulder just rising up off the beach area. Its searchlight had not yet come on, but it was too late for me to run back to the trees. The hole was not quite covered and if this was the guards making a second run they would know for sure that someone had been in there. I had no choice, while yelling out for Theo to be cool and stay hidden, I slipped under the brush and slid down into the pit. Straining from below I pushed back the planks the best I could and tried reaching up to pull back the rug and shrubs, while a ton of dirt fell into my mouth and eyes. Just then the floodlight went on and I had to figure out what to do next.

In pure panic, spitting out dirt and wiping the dirt out of my eyes, I flicked on my flashlight for a second, took my bearings and saw that I only had one choice—to climb up and over the piles of bags and crates and wiggle my way out of sight, finding a place to hide among the crates of treasure. Up and over I went, immediately entangled in dust and cobwebs. I slipped or fell into a tight crevice barely beyond the open area, just as I heard the upper planks being moved back. I only hoped that my noise would be canceled out by the shutting down of the chopper and the guards own efforts to get back into the pit.

Immediately I ran into a dead end. Several large crates blocked my way. I frantically felt around, pushing my way further along, and slipped into a small opening. But while wiggling back into the unknown I knocked something down. I heard something break and everything went quiet. I thought, there goes a Ming Dynasty Vase! I hung breathless in suspense while the guards were dropping into the pit and I heard them say, "Probably just a rat trying to get away from us, we better bring more rat poison with us next trip. Come on. We ain't got all night."

CHAPTER ELEVEN

NARROW ESCAPE

One of Theo's idiotic phrases popped into my mind, 'Now we got ourselves neck deep into a barrel of camel spit!' This is insane, I thought as I lay there with my upper body jammed between a barrel and two canvas bags while my legs were wrapped around a crate. Everything seemed to be shifting under me, while I was wedged tighter into the black space. I only prayed that nothing would slip loose and call attention to my hiding place. I could see the lamplight moving through the parted crates and over the top of the bags and held my breath hoping that the guards would not look too close and see my raggedy beach clods, or decide to start removing things next to me. My thoughts were everywhere. Here I was again, in another crazy fix. This was not my only time for being caught or trapped in some strange situation, but at least I was lying on a million dollar treasure and not in a dirty Mexican jail.

I had the feeling that if I were caught this time, I would end up an empty skull-head sitting on a shelf along the San Simeon coast line. The rat comment flashed into my mind—I felt something scamper across my back. I so wanted to move! But I knew that one tiny noise would draw the guards' attention, so I bit my tongue while the furry creatures used my back as a runway.

The worst was yet to come. I was crammed into what felt like a communal nest of cobwebs and soon I felt spiders trying to figure out what unknown creature had just destroyed years of their hard work. One monster spider, at least I thought it was a spider, with more hairy legs than Waikiki Beach in tourist season, crawled across my face, stopping right on my eye-lid looking for the trouble that had come its way. I knew I didn't like spiders, have always lived near arachnophobia, but there was nothing I could do—only try blinking my eyelids to freak it away. Wrong. That ignited its curiosity and the damn thing latched onto my flickering eyelid, sinking its teeth into my only weapon. My arms were jammed downward and it took every thought and emotion that I possessed not to move, or release that scream now caught in my mouth and in my eyes. Again, the image of the lonely skull in the beach cave flashed into my brain and kept me silent. On top of this, I could feel several of the companion spiders calling a meeting to visit the open skin on my neck, to feast. Sure enough, one or more of them began biting me, and I was helpless to stop anything from biting or crawling on my exposed neck and face. Whatever had bitten me, it was painful—to say the least—it hurt like hell. As if a drunken nurse was giving me a long needle shot in the eye, prepping me for a laser operation.

Oh wow! I did receive some relief when another rat scurried across my back, forcing the spiders to run for home. I had to play dead while the tunnel rats and beach spiders spread the news that a great feast had fallen into their camp. I only prayed that these spiders were not poisonous—I might survive them.

But the worst thought came to my already over-worried brain, my cell phone: it was on! And what if good old JJ decided to call and inquire about my well being? I knew if I moved an inch, I would give myself away and even if I could reach the stupid phone, it would beep when I shut it off. At this moment, I was hating technology and all that went with it! For the first time, I begged all higher-authorities that JJ was waylaid in a hot card game and had no thought of calling me.

Just a few feet from my head, my first nightmare was alive and well. Their conversation was interspersed with grunts of lifting things up to the pilot above. Apparently they knew what they were after, for one of them said, "Buck told me to load up some of the smaller boxes, they had better things in them."

"I like that idea, lighter things. I'm tired, and it's getting late, been a long night for me," one of them retorted.

"Yep, me too, but let's get done here. A cold beer and getting in the last take of Molly on stage sounds good," a deeper voice replied.

"Hey George, you think that we could snatch a few coins away like the other time? That was easy pickings. Buck wouldn't miss a few coins if we snatch them from down here."

"Man, Drake, keep quiet, Tripper might hear you, but go ahead, grab a few from that broken box under the bags. But damn well make sure you keep them hidden, if we're caught, we can count on a chopper flight out to sea with no return flight," the deeper voice, apparently George, hushed up his companion named Drake.

"Do you think that's what happened to Montie? Wonder if he became fish food out there," the questioning voice of Drake intimated.

"Don't know, but it was strange how he just disappeared one day, right after that fiasco with the delivery up to Frisco," George replied.

Things were quiet for a while as they worked, but it was George again, "I think Buck found out that he was tapping into those midnight deliveries," then went on, "That's why if we take anything, it better be from down here, not yet inventoried."

Then I thought it was over for me—a light flashed around and over the crates that I lay behind. I felt someone's probing hand digging around under the canvas sacks I lay on. Whoever it was, he had to be hunting around for an open box, previously left behind and within a foot of my belly. The bags were pushed up, I could hear Drake grunting and stretching his arm deep among the bags, then a sigh of relief in finding whatever he was searching for. I heard metal clinks and a hushed murmuring between the two guards. "Man, nothing like a ton of spider webs back in there, but got a few coins for our troubles."

Another voice from above spoke into the pit, "Hey jug heads, it's starting to get foggy up here, get going with that stuff." That had to be the pilot named Trimmer, I'd heard him called, and he did not sound happy.

While bent crooked around crates and over boxes trying to keep my legs from cramping up, I intently tried to determine what might be going on only a few feet from my twisted body. Through their broken exchanges I heard something being said about a woman. Then a piece of the puzzle came to my ear. They were talking about the woman that had come in on the boat, and how she was on her way up to San Francisco where someone named Buck Skullkin would be making the exchange with her.

I caught the name sweet Ruthie, being tossed around. Sounded like she was being held captive or traded off for some reason. I missed most of this part of their conversation,

I was so freaked out at the spiders now gathered on my neck and in my hair; but even so, I was left with more information than I wanted.

After about twenty minutes of grunting and small talk, the voice from above told Drake to come on up and help with the larger boxes. Shortly thereafter, Trimmer called down to George, saying that was about it, the chopper was pretty well loaded and everything was getting soaked. I could hear them climbing out, the light went off and they covered the opening. Time waited.

The night was silent other than the surf breaking easy off in the distance. I lay there listening intently, with the choppers engine creaking as it cooled down. I could smell cigarette smoke and guessed the three stood around smoking while talking. "Yeah, I thought I saw some foot prints back up the beach yesterday," one voice stated.

"Well, as soon as those lines are all fixed, the cameras will be back up online and we'll be able to see every square inch of this whole beach."

"We better get that van towed as soon as the truck is ready, Brookstone is gonna get pissed."

"No problem, the cameras being down gives us more flying time. We can make several more trips before they're repaired," one voice added in. "That quake did us a favor."

"I got a feeling those surf bums were down on the beach. We better keep our eyes peeled for them, they could spell trouble."

"Man, I hope that weird noise I heard last night down on the cove was not any of them watching our operation," one voice expressed his concerns.

"If it was, you must have scared the living crap out of them with those 30 rounds you blew off!"

"I hope so. Don't need any witnesses around to tell our story."

"OK, let's get out of here for now. We got to drop this load off. The truck will be waiting for us. Let's go."

After another ten minutes, I heard the helicopter start up, then move up and away. I waited until, in the pitch-black dark, I could twist and work myself free to begin my revenge on the spiders that had been feasting on my life. Ah crap, my neck had lumps beginning to swell. It felt like a layer of bubble wrap had been tied around my neck. And, Oh great, my eyelid was swollen up the size of a half lemon and it hurt like heck. I carefully worked my way back to the open area in the hole and turned on my flashlight to see that another section of the crates and boxes had been removed. I ran my fingers through my hair, patted and slapped every part of my body that I could reach. But there was no way to get all these crawling things off me, so I began to dance and shake and rub my back against the crates. I reached up and pulled back the first plank, when suddenly a light glared down into my face. I knew for sure they had laid a trap for me, but then Theo's voice was muttering down, "Luke, you OK?"

"Shut that damn light off or at least get it out of my eyes. I'm blinded like a moose on the railroad tracks at night and you're the on-coming train."

"Sorry, I was only worried for you," he paused then gasped out, "Oh donkey turds, what the hell happened to your eye?"

"It's a short story, too long to tell. OK, OK, sorry back. Glad you didn't have the heart to call me a few minutes back. And no, I'm not OK!"

He was looking at my swollen eye, "What's the matter? Are you OK?" he inquired again with all sincerity. But I knew he was thoroughly happy that it was not him that had been trapped down in the pit. I was glad too, for he would have been screaming out for help no matter who was in the pit with him. No doubt, spiders, bugs and creeping creatures were not in his agenda. But I didn't say anything to upset him even more.

After that nightmare of an experience, no way was I going to leave this treasure pit without at least a taste of whatever those guards were risking their lives for. There was a dream forming in the back of my mind. I was not sure about the ownership of this long lost treasure but that answer would have to come later. The answer would not matter if we were caught, for our fate was sealed if we were caught knowing what we now knew. I wondered what it would be like to become fish food.

My mind went to my greater predicament. Dustin and I were living on the edge of economic crises and unless we could come up with the finances, the legal entanglements involving my grandparents would take years to be resolved. By then, the lawyers and never-before-heard-of relatives would have eaten most of my inheritance in fees and lawyer costs. I was well on my way to give it all up and let the blood-suckers have it. This unexpected adventure and our fall into this trench of treasure just might hold the key to finally settling up the long dragged-out battle. Hoping that this dream would not turn into a nightmare.

Bending down, I reached my arm under the bags on the dirt floor and felt around. Ah ha, I felt a wooden box with its lid partially ajar. With one finger I pried it open and felt around and sure enough, there were large what-seemed-to-be coins and I took hold of four of them and tucked them into my back pocket, then stood up. I lifted my arm up asking Theo to help me out. But just before he reached for me, I thought, hey, for all our troubles, I'm gonna take one more box with me. Reaching over I lifted one nice box about the size of a loaf of bread and set it up on the grass ledge, then climbed up and rolled over on my back. I was a little woozy and getting dizzy, but I just lay there breathing in the scent of eucalyptus through the mist and the scent of the sea, staring into the night sky. Oh man, was it ever good to be alive!

"I told you I'd get you something special, so for being so quiet and not getting caught, here take it," I handed Theo the box. Then I told him to call JJ and tell him to get over here!

Just then my cell rang, it was Jason telling me that he was about a mile away, and what did I want him to do? "Just come on by, do not stop as you pass us, but go a few miles up the road and turn around and come back toward the trees and when you get near to us we'll signal you with a blink of light. Make sure there is no one on the road, slow down, pull in at the burlap patch on the fence and pull right next to it. We got to load up some things. Open the slider door and we'll hand over some things to you. Do not turn on any lights. All this has to be done quietly and fast."

His voice was fading out, "What the heck you guys up to this time Luke?" he asked with some concern.

"It's a long story. Just be careful and if for any reason someone stops while you're parked, just tell them that you have to take a leak."

"Dustin called me this morning and told me to get my butt home and fast. This is sounding like some clandestine mission, and it's beginning to give me the worries..."

I cut him off and told him, "Just do the job as given, my young friend, explanations will come later; you're safe and sound as long as you obey." I hung up, looked around, checking if the treasure pit had been properly covered. We hunkered down and found our way to the fence where all our things were piled.

Theo kept glancing over at my face, shaking his head in concern. Then as we got things ready, Jason came pulling up. I waved for him to shut off the dang headlights and move in close. It's like the kid just could not follow the rules. After a few minutes, I banged on the side of the van and finally the side door slid open, Theo barked out some instructions to wide eyed Jason and started handing boxes over to the stunned partner in crime. "Stack everything in the back under the bunks, wherever they'll fit," I told him quietly.

JJ stood there like a petrified dummy and finally choked out a question, "Luke, what happened to your eye? Are you going to make it?"

My left eye was now fully closed and swollen over. I nodded that I needed to hurry and get out of here and I'd be OK, maybe. Theo and I together lifted the bell and the statues up and over, shoving them into the van while Jason grumbled and tried asking questions, especially about his missing board, as he dragged things into the van. Soon we had everything jammed into the canvas bags and loaded up. I went back and scattered leaves and twigs over the area where we had crawled and walked, pretty well covering up our trail. Theo took down the cloth, shined his light around to see if we had left anything behind and all seemed clear other than the trampled down grass. One last touch just in case, I asked Jason to hand me a good amount of toilet paper, which really floored him, and went over to where we were hidden and half buried it near the trunk of the tree as a bodily function decoy. Theo was now in the drivers seat when I got back and within a few moments, we were headed south on Highway One.

Theo and I were wet and dirty, exhausted and quiet, as Jason jabbered on about his experience in San Louis Obispo and his outer space experience with bearded Barney the mechanic; and something about winning 200 bucks from him, but we barely heard. My neck and eyes were on fire and it seemed that I was getting dizzy and nauseated; the pain in my left eye began to let me know it was not a happy eye. It was late and I did not want to forget any details so located my digital recorder and began to make notes. We drove on until we found a rest stop on the outskirts of Camarilla. We pulled in to shut down for the night and crashed dead to the world.

Theo got up first, put on some coffee and after a groggy start we were on the road. From our first aid kit, I had sloshed on some anti-itch cream of sorts, which helped bring down the swelling. But now the eye was turning a weird purple color and I was still somewhat queasy. I did not want to be found anywhere in the area, just wanted to get this stuff out of the van and hidden away until we figured out what to do and have my eye taken care of. JJ had already started asking questions, but I just mentioned that whatever got my eye was in one of these boxes. There might be a snake or rat or two found in them, so be careful. Immediately he jumped onto the upper bunk, put on his head phones, pulled the curtain and that was it. We did not hear from him the rest of the way home.

However, curiosity got the best of me. I slid one smaller box out from under the side-bunk. It was bound with two iron bands, nearly rusted through, but it still took a pair of wire cutters to break the bands.

I carefully pried open the lid, for it was well sealed with what seemed to be wax turned to glue. The lid finally opened and there lay before my eyes, something that would put meaning into the word Treasure! A gust of astonishment escaped my mouth. There were neat rows of gold coins. There had to be at least twenty-five to fifty coins in each different row, neatly set into long wooden slots. Each row had different sized coins. After my heart started beating again and Theo's voice broke through my dumbstruck brain, I managed to pluck one of the larger coins out of the tray it set in.

I held it in my hand, rubbing it for a while. No doubt, it was heavy. It was a five sided coin—strange I thought, and thicker than any coin I had ever seen, ornately decorated with odd symbols, but it was gold alright. It had to weigh at least five ounces and made those few coins I had put in my back pocket seem like play money.

"Come on man, what you looking at Luke?" Theo twisted his head, talking into the mirror, trying to see what I had in my hand.

"I am not sure, but you better not drive off the road once I hand this up to you." He laughed and I told him to hold out his hand as I placed the large heavy coin into it.

"Oh hebephrenic-schizophrenia nutullbockers, this is outrageous, unbelievable!" he blurted out. Sure enough the van began to weave all over the place.

Immediately JJ yelled from the back bunk, "Hey skid-Oh-thumpski, you guys smoking those camel turds again? What is going on up there?!"

I poked Theo, "Hey, get yourself under control or I'll get JJ up here and let him drive. All we need is to be stopped for drunk or reckless driving."

Theo slowed down and got into the slower lanes so he could hold the coin up to examine it as he drove. "Do you know what this is?" Theo demanded.

"A coin that might be gold," I replied.

"Sheesh, it's more than that. It's a Spanish gold doubloon from way-back-when, I'm guessing from around the sixteen hundreds," he stated factually but with great excitement.

"How do you know that?" I asked.

"Hey, my parents own an antique shop in Balboa, I have seen a few of these pass through our shop, years back—but nothing this nice." He went on, saying that his brother Jay dove on a few wrecks off the coast of Peru and Mexico and had come home with a few of these five sided babies. This is how he bought his schooner, the Serendipity, the one he lives on."

I went silent for about a mile, afraid to even mention, then decided to ask, "What do you think they might be worth in today's market?"

Without much hesitation an escited Theo shocked me with more news, "With gold prices today as they are and with the intrinsic value involved, and if it is from a certain era—one coin, depending if it is pure or mixed with other metals, might run an easy five to seven thousand dollars."

I sat there in shock, and finally said, "Until we know what is really going on with this whole Hearst thing, we got to keep this under wraps. This is too much!"

"How many coins are in the box?" Theo asked. In reality, he wanted to know how much trouble we were in.

"Well, just in the row of the larger coins there has got to be at least twenty five of them. Then a second row of smaller coins must hold fifty, and the last few rows look like silver dollars from long ago and there has to be maybe one hundred of them."

Theo's mathematical brain started ticking, then he whistled under his breath and said, "Wow, you do realize that just in that one box, there must be well over a hundred thousand dollars in coinage." Theo smiled while he surmised the value in this one box, as he placed his coin into his pocket.

I slumped back in utter shock, and felt the coins that were still in my back pocket. I saw my dream turning into hope. But then again, what if we were found out in all this? Should we tell anyone? It is strange what gold can do to a person. My eyes were locked onto this exclusive collection like a pack of Rottweilers and Dobermans sinking their teeth into me. I was smitten! My mind would not allow the thought of trouble to enter my dreamy adulation of sudden wealth.

The idea of being transported from near poverty into a realm of riches dazzled me into illusionary bouts of triumph. The dream was real, as my hands ran over the rows of coins. This was only one of the boxes we were carrying home. I did not want to wake up from the thrill of this tremendous feeling of new found riches. I double checked the moment, the time, the place and marked the feeling of thrill and excitement, in case I did awake and found this all to be an illusionary episode of psychic trauma—all this nothing but a paranormal delusion!

Our phones were well charged now and I called Dustin to report in. "We are safe so far, on the road and a few hours out. Your Jason is fine, sleeping soundly in the back. We got some pretty heavy stuff going on here and if those Hearst Security guys got my emails, we might be in for some trouble."

"As far as we can tell, no one has got into your account, and I had Wally get in and erase everything," Dustin let me know.

"That's good. For now please set up a secure place to store about 20 boxes and canvas bags of rare items. I mean rare, big time!"

"Rare, rare you say, certainly my friend. Anything interesting for me?" Dustin laughed and was curious but I told him he would have to wait.

We dropped off JJ first, with a promise of reward if he remained silent about this adventure and our smuggler cove discovery. He might find himself in trouble if someone got wind of what he knew. He promised and asked if he could still be part of our team and we said for sure. I sweetened the deal by promising him a new board to replace his old one. We would stay in contact.

We then found our way over to the secured rental storage unit that Dustin owned in Huntington Beach. Dustin met us there and a guard allowed us in. This was a high security storage for the rich—a perfect place for us to unload our newly acquired treasures. The secured unit was walled in with its own camera, safety locks and alarms. We first unloaded everything in rows, inventorying the various boxes and canvas bags. Then with shaking excitement we began to go through some of the boxes that were not sealed.

There were several boxes that held still more coins and small golden icons, surely rare. It looked like an ancient Spanish or Orthodox Church had been robbed of its wares and found their way onto the San Bella. There were exquisite Greek vases in near perfect condition, still packed in fine cedar chips. Dustin had done a lot of research on the lost San Bella and actually came up with a ship's manifest telling what the San Bella was supposed to be carrying. There were hundreds of boxes, chests and rare antiques which had to be worth more money than I could guess at. We only had a tiny drop from the treasure stash. Just in rare coinage, Theo estimated that we held several hundred thousand dollars. The statues and other pieces of art and ceramics had to be researched and identified.

Dustin was no dummy to these things. He just shook his head, wanting to know the full story. As a lawyer he knew there had to be ramifications. No way was the State of California going to let anyone get away with a treasure of this enormity without due taxes or outright confiscation. But we were not going to allow that to happen, no way! I had gold on the brain.

I let him know, that in no way were we going to give up any part of this treasure to money-hungry California to fill their coffers and support another ten million interlopers. Then I remembered the boat load of illegals that had come in that night and speculated that Hearst Security might be involved in allowing this to happen. No matter what, we were going to hold onto our share for now, and be silent until we figured out what to do.

We had our own plans for helping others and for charities we knew. I suggested that we at least divide up one box of coins among us, right now, in case anything were to happen to our stash. Dustin and Theo agreed with the promise to exercise all caution in their distribution and so we took our first share of this incredible treasure to do with as we so wanted.

The first thing was to get old Betsy, my traveling van back up to par. Then I'd go back to San Simeon and retrieve our surf boards and my laptop. This had to be done as soon as possible so I could finish up my pre-assigned articles that were soon due. In the mean time, Theo would begin his research into some of these treasures using his brother Jay, and through his parent's antique shop. We agreed to do more research first on the Hearst fortune, Dustin trying to damper some of our excitement but we agreed that we would come back again and go through the rest of the sealed boxes and bags.

In the meantime, we were tired, dirty and hungry and wanted to catch up on our lives. My first concern was a visit to the doctor to look at my new purple eye and the bubble wrap neck patterns. Blood test results showed a low dose of poison but a heavy dose of antibiotics would soon clear it out. The eye, well, that would have to heal on its own.

I told Dustin about the woman that we had seen being removed out of the boat on the beach—that maybe her name was Ruth or something close to that. He suggested that we put Wally, our computer whiz and researcher on it. In the meantime Dustin would do some further investigation on the treasure and look into the missing person's department. But for now, there was not much we could do about it.

"You're not really thinking of going back and dealing with that security outfit are you?" Theo asked incredulously.

"Listen Theo, it would be better to go and play dumb and retrieve our things rather than stay away so they'd think we had something to hide and then come looking for us. I'd rather be the cat than the mouse in this one," I reasoned.

"Hey, these may not be such nice people. You do remember the guys in the chopper and how they treated those kayakers, don't you? And, Oh yes, have you considered what might have happened to us if we were caught watching the drug and Mexican flotilla thing on the beach? Perhaps you forgot those bullets zipping over our heads and shattering the rocks around us that night. And, Oh yeah, how about your close call in the pit? Imagine if you were caught down there." After a pause he reminded me, "Oh yes, do you remember the wonderful skull, by the way? Who did it belong to? Maybe some crazy journalist riding on a hot story, ha."

"Sure, I thought of that. But if we went as surf bums and a starving writer we might throw them off the path if they are looking for anything. In the meantime we might learn something."

Theo looked at me as though I had lost my mind, "You're sitting on maybe millions of dollars and your worried about your laptop? You're beside yourself man. What the heck do you want to come to know—anyhow?"

"Not really sure Theo."

Theo glared at me and asked, "Do you want me to actually go back up there with you and stick my neck into those chopper blades? Become fish food and crab farts bubbling up alongside you?"

"Nah, don't think so, if you don't want to. But for me, I got to see this story through all the way. Besides, I'm not asking you to come along, unless you like the idea." But I knew that he would go with me. He had the curiosity bug in him and could not allow such an event to pass by without him, even if it was rife with danger and risk. He might have been telling the truth, and arguing with himself, but somehow he always ended up giving in and tagging along with me, then returning home with more tales than I did about our strange adventures.

Theo realized my seriousness and mellowed out his remarks, "Let me ponder over it. Maybe I'll get bored and tired of life and decide to go with you. Or I just might stay behind and guard the treasure all the way to the bank, right?"

Finally I made it to my own home, my castle in the sky, the only three story apartment unit on the Newport peninsula. It wasn't anything fancy but it was unique, with a killer view of both the ocean and the bay. A quiet out-of-the-way place, always filled with a cross breeze, with only one way to it—up a zigzag stair leading way up to a tiny porch, high above the surrounding rooftops.

After a good rest, I made contact with an old friend, Thortin

Mayhurst, the editor for the San Luis Obispo Tribune News, to ask him if I might come in a few days for a visit and travel stopover on the way back down to the Hearst Castle. He was happy to hear from me and invited me to stay with him and his wife as long as I wanted.

In the meantime, Dustin and Theo were thoroughly involved with treasure and antiques. It was hard thinking that there was millions of dollars worth of treasure just sitting in a storage unit down the street. Plus, we hadn't gone through the heavy bags yet. I was also considering what Theo had said about me being crazy. We had possession of wealth beyond our imagination and I wanted to go get a near-obsolete laptop and three well-worn surf boards, maybe he was right—was I crazy?

Ah, but it had to be the true and unquenchable journalist in me, or maybe my adventurous spirit gone mad. I really didn't know, but good old Theo was next to me in the van, still calling me crazy, as we pulled into San Luis Obispo and the Tribune's newspaper office a week later.

Chapter Thirteen

Thortin Mayhurst

It was the same old enthusiastic Thortin I knew back in college who greeted us personally as we entered the spacious newspaper office. He was considered tall, dark and handsome back then and he managed to add a great politician's smile to his appearance. The sun had taken its toll with early wrinkles, but he still sported his well-groomed handlebar mustache. He waved us into his private office while asking his secretary to bring in some coffee. I introduced Theo and before we even sat down, Thortin Mayhurst, in his deep chocolate voice asked Theo, "Are you the photographer that shot those incredible pics in last years Waimea Bay winter surf contest?"

Theo waved his hand out dismissingly, "I did shoot some photos and a few of them were published around."

Thortin pointed up to a large walled book shelf where a picture was posted of an incredible thirty foot wave curled over, not one, but two riders. He said, "Like that one, hey? Those were some great shots. You don't see photos like that much any more. Nice work and glad to meet you," Thortin stuck out his large tanned hand to seal their personal acquaintance.

Theo's moment of glory was broken when the secretary came whisking in with the coffee tray and set it on the desk. Thortin thanked her and asked us how we liked it. After a few moments of old times talk and exchanges, we were warmed up; I began to make my inquiry. "Thortin, do you ever do any news stories about the Hearst castle, or anything about the beach area that runs up to Big Sur?"

He leaned back comfortably in his high-backed chair,

seeming excited to talk with someone from out of his past; yet he also seemed curious over my inquiry. He hid his excitement by taking up his pipe and carefully packing the cherry-blend tobacco into the bowl. His gold rimmed glasses were tinted light blue, a carry-over from our hippie days. The glasses sat down on his long straight nose while his ponytail hung down to his neck, wavy and thick. He was a typical California coastal transplant, moved out from Ohio, who had made it good. We had attended UCLA together and I remembered him as a caring person, firmly honest in his ways, always looking for adventure. I knew him to be an honest soul. Above all this, he was forever looking for that special story that might one day win him a Pulitzer Prize. He did not know it, but I might have the story that would, or could, win that journalistic prize of a lifetime for him.

Above and beyond the significance of our visit, Thortin was staring at me, then gestured to my eye. He had to ask, "Now Luke, this might not be any of my business, but where the heck did you get that purple-black eye? It is a real conversation piece."

"Just part of the job Thortin, that is all I can say for now."

"Sure thing Luke," and there was a notable pause for reflection.

Thortin gestured his pipe through the air to let us know he liked to smell the aroma of the tobacco, more than to smoke it. With some caution he answered, "Sure, I'm forever doing stories on the coastal areas, its development and everything that might create or generate interest in keeping our area pristine and safe. I live along the coast, so I am forever interested in its well-being."

The word safe caught my attention and thought I might ask,

"Thortin, what if I told you I had a story that might shake up this area, maybe actually cause an earthquake for California and all the coastal regions around here."

"Oh no, not another earthquake, we just had one." With this he laughed but he sat up, putting down his coffee mug. Chuckling at his own statement, "It would have to be bigger than the one we just had. It would have to be a really strong story in order to wake up these 'leave me alone hippified people' who live all along this coast. And what might this story be?" He leaned forward towards me with interest as he moved his glasses up his nose and began chewing on his pipe.

"Perhaps there might be some danger in it to anyone who gets their hands on it. It might not be a good idea to say too much until my lawyer finds out more."

For the longest time, he puffed his pipe, looking at us with a reporter's curiosity. "You mentioned the Hearst Castle area and the coastal beaches…that is a very hard nut to crack. Since the Patty Hearst situation a few decades back, the Hearst family has shut their doors to journalists and reporters."

I pondered on how far to go, and thought to be a little more discreet until I knew where Thortin might stand. If I gave him this story, he would have to swear to never release its source or we and the treasure could be in big trouble. But I knew that it would take a newspaper to stir up enough flack to get the ball rolling. I just did not want to be in the way of a storm that was sure to arise from the news; we had our treasure and did not want to draw attention to ourselves in its place. The San Luis Obispo newspaper just might be able to set things in motion without us being in the light.

I moved ahead and took another small step for mankind,

carefully laying out another possibility for his curious mind, "If I did give you this story Thortin, it might involve the State of California, your sleepy little beach town for sure— and consume your life in ways I cannot say."

Oh man, did this statement make him bite: he took sinker, line and hook. "Listen Luke, I'm already involved. I'm on the San Luis Obispo city council and I've got my eyes on a state legislator position, so, involved I already am."

"Really. I didn't know you were into the politics thing." Now I knew where that flashy political smile had come from.

"Yes, for the last four years now. Been working my way into the real world of money, crap and gods."

Thortin could see that I was holding back, so he broke the moment with a friendly invitation to come out to his home and stay there for a day or so, enjoying the area. I looked over at Theo who was scanning the book titles, distantly listening, but saw him nod his approval. Thortin mentioned that his wife was out of town on a book tour so we would have to fend for ourselves for a day or so.

I replied, "Hey, no problem, let's do it."

He buzzed his secretary, telling her he was leaving for the afternoon and to hold down the fort. He laid down his pipe, grabbed up his beach cap and told us to follow him out to his place in Cambria about six miles south of the castle. I asked for his address, telling him we wanted to pick up a few things and then come by a little later. He said that would be fine. I punched his address into my GPS and we shook our goodbyes and left.

Theo and I drove out to a well known winery and purchased a gift pack of wines, cheeses and olives as a gift for the

Mayhursts. I then bought some thick steaks and a few other items that we might want, finally arriving a few hours later. We were well surprised to see that Thortin had a nice home sitting on a bluff overlooking the Pacific. The beach rolled up to his property and we could see why he wanted to protect this pristine area. The blue Pacific lay at his front door while the mountains of the Santa Lucia range spread out in the distance behind him, but it was the Nitwit Ridge that led us up to Moonstone Road and to his house that made us laugh. "Wow, Moonstone Road, now if that ain't a throw back from the sixties."

Thortin warmly invited us in; I handed over our gifts which really surprised him, "Nice taste you have Luke." He set our gifts down in the kitchen, walked us around and showed us to a guest room that was nicer than my castle in the sky apartment. He told us to take showers if we wanted, while he prepared a salad for dinner and got the coals going for the steaks.

We enjoyed a great dinner. Thortin was well capable of entertaining and explained that his wife was a teacher and an author who had published her second book with Amazon, a book for kids. She was now on tour for a week or so. We finally finished up with all the touching base and catching up, when Thortin asked, "OK, Mister Luke Mitchner and Gentleman, what kind of a Pulitzer surprise story do you have for this hungry newspaper man?"

I was still not sure how to approach this, for once I opened the door, there would be no stopping anyone from digging deeper. I only asked right up front, that Thortin, under no conditions, would reveal or expose us as his source. I explained our reluctance to get involved and our hope to retrieve our surf boards and my laptop.

He agreed whole heartedly to my request and I felt then, that we could trust him with the story. I began with our van breakdown on the beach stretch, finding the skull, going through the entire episode step by step, stressing the overly serious patrols, the landing of the illegals, the possible drug connection, the woman taken off the boat, and then got into the nighttime removal of the stash out of the treasure trench. I told him that the only thing we took was the San Bella ship bell and a few items from the beach mound.

I explained the night landing of the HC-7 helicopter and the shooting of serious weapons towards us. I went on, telling of the men who opened up the gully and loaded up the chopper with crates, boxes, bags and chests. I told him that we had gone and taken a look for ourselves, and we took a few cell-phone photos. I concluded with the San Bella research: we knew that a ship of this name had disappeared off the California coast early in the 1930's. The loss of these rare items was kept under hat by the Hearst family. We suspected that old man Hearst did not want the government or the public to know about his purchases of Church property and European castles and would not publish the full story in his newspapers.

Before I got half way through the telling, Thortin was up and pacing, had got hold of another pipe and was listening to every word. He asked to see our photos. He studied the pictures carefully, and finally looked up, "The faint writing on the first few crates is Cyrillic. It is Russian, sure thing."

"Oh wow, that might tell us something. We thought it was Arabic scribbling," I admitted.

Thortin went on, "Whatever all this is, it sounds almost beyond imagination. It is nothing less than a 10 point earth-quake, or should I say a full fledged cruise missile attack!"

He stood there looking out his windows at the sea, began nodding his head, "I will say that this could easily become a Pulitzer Prize story."

The sun was setting a beautiful watermelon red with a delicious blend of lemon twist. Thortin just stood there, calmly smoking his pipe, either in shock or in deep contemplation on the ramifications of such a story. After about a half hour I finished up with explanations about wanting to retrieve our things from the Hearst Castle Security headquarters, and possibly determine who we might notify about all this. The treasure is there; it could not be removed easily, but it could be taken in a day or so if someone had to remove it, or wanted to. I explained that this is why we did not want anyone to know that we knew of the treasure, or it would be taken away, and maybe lost again. We were guessing that a part or the entire shipment which existed inside the San Bella cargo was fitted into that gully and covered over. So one might imagine what else might be in it besides the few boxes and bags and statues we saw removed that night. There had to be millions of dollars worth of treasure still in the gully, and maybe more skulls.

"So why did you come to me about this?" Thortin asked. "Oh don't get me wrong, this is almost too incredible to believe. I am honored to have been the one you told."

Theo spoke up, "We discussed all the points and realized that it is too big of a story for two surf bums and a freelance writer to tackle. We had two choices, that is to tell someone who has a reputation in the newspaper business, someone with the right contacts, or we would have no other choice but to contact the State Attorney General and the Hearst Foundation."

"No, no, we do not want to do that. Not right now, not

until we get things figured out a bit. Believe me, I know how government works and they'll screw things up worse than the tax codes." Thortin ran his thick fingers through his long hair that was being tossed around by the evening breeze, "So what do you guys expect from this extraordinary discovery?"

"Once all this is settled and we know we are safe from whoever is running this treasure stealing operation, I would like to write a book about the whole matter. I have a few connections. It could even be made into a movie."

"No doubt," Thortin nodded and waved his pipe to emphasize his agreement.

I went on expressing my concerns, "There is the possibility of drugs being brought into the country which really turns this little adventure into a serious and dangerous challenge, and then there is the illegal worker part of the equation."

Thortin looked out the window below and asked us if we wanted to take a walk on the beach. Soon we were strolling along the tide line discussing various points. There were both legal and danger components to all this: the treasure as part of Hearst property, and the security company. Who are they and what are they doing with the things they extract from the gully stash? We may have to involve the California authorities, maybe the FBI, in regards to this sophisticated operation.

The memory of the night down in the pit, when the guards were talking about someone being turned into fish food, really brought the lethal aspect of our dilemma to the forefront. We covered pretty well everything we could think of. I told Thortin that we could put him in touch with a trusted officer in the FBI using Dustin Arrow my lawyer, but to use extreme caution in keeping this under wraps.

"I would like to get out there and take a look for myself," Thortin said.

"No, absolutely not, this is exactly what we do not want, that would be too dangerous. We brought along the San Bella bell and you can use that as proof and a starting point for your story. Theo has taken some very nice photos of the bell that you can use in your first story. Besides we are not sure on how the HC Security Company is going to deal with us. We are hoping it will just be a simple matter of playing dumb— give our apology and we get our stuff back."

"Yes I see that. You could be right. If we are dealing with millions of dollars and tons of treasure and drugs, any leak could bring down some serious consequences on anyone snooping around." Thortin was looking out to sea and went on. "That San Bella bell had to come off the ship. That means that the ship must have gone down somewhere off the cove area. If that is true, there still could be a lot of treasure inside the ship. Now once I publish the story of the bell, there's going to be a lot of people asking questions, and for sure, doing some serious searching."

Theo acknowledged with, "You got it. Treasure hunters up the ying-yang!"

I gave over my GPS positioning for the site on my phone and told Thortin to use them to go on-line and zoom in on the area to keep a birds-eye look out, but keep a safe distance at the same time. We also advised Thortin not to publish anything about where the bell had been found. The idea of the San Bella lying at the bottom of the ocean off the Hearst cove added further intrigue to this story. For if it were out there, we might put a dive together with Theo's brother Jay and maybe, just maybe, hit the jackpot all on our own.

We spent most of the night going over the journalistic aspects of how such a story might be released through the newspapers. We decided that the first thing was to contact Dustin's friend Max in the FBI and bring him into the story so we had a backup in our corner, just in case things went wrong.

The first introductory story through the San Luis Obispo Tribune would be the unexpected find of the San Bella ship bell on one of the San Simeon beaches. We all agreed that it would not be wise to publish a specific location of the bell's find, that would certainly cause a thousand people to head for the cove and all hell would break out. The San Luis Obispo coastline had some 80 miles for treasure hunters to begin their hunt, which we knew they surely would. We also had to laugh that this episode might bring in the tourists by the tons, all looking for treasure!

Thortin's eyes lit up at the ramifications concerning his place on the city council and his upcoming effort for a state legislature seat. But it was that hope of one day maybe, just maybe, attaining a Pulitzer Prize, which finally painted him solid into this picture.

I suggested that Thortin place the bell in safe keeping for now and just use the photos Theo handed over.

Thortin would begin his own in-depth investigation of the San Bella shipwreck and see how it might be tied into the new-found treasure. I would get hold of Dustin and fill him in on our discussion and ask him to make contact with his FBI friend. In the meanwhile, Dustin could also do some legal research on where we stood in the discovery of the trea-sure. We unloaded the San Bella bell into Thortin's back shed and finally fell into bed. The next morning we had a great goodbye breakfast and cruised down Moonstone Drive and up to Nitt Witt Ridge, headed for the Hearst Castle Security compound.

Thortin explained that the HC Security operations were located on the north end of the Hearst property next to the mountains on a 200 acre ranch butted up to the Santa Lucia mountain range. He had been out there once, for a news item when one of their helicopters had gone down. Their helicopter hangers and landing pads along with all their personnel were housed there. This was going to be a little spooky for us, giving ourselves over to these guys, hoping for the best from our act of innocence. And so we went—like sheep unto the slaughter!

It truly was a pleasant day, perfect for catching a few good waves, warm and fresh, not a day for putting our necks into a noose! We drove by the entrance to the Hearst Castle and came to the long stretch where we had been stranded. We learned that the area where we had found the skull was a fourteen mile coastal stretch which had been given to William Randolph Hearst by his mother Phoebe Hearst in 1919. Of course, we named it Skull Beach. It was one of the longest privately owned beaches in the United States. Then there was 240,000 acres that rose up to the mountains on our right, all part of the Hearst ranch property.

Soon we came to a small inconspicuous sign with HC Security printed across its face. We turned onto a long well maintained gravel road that took us back about a half mile. Pacific pines lined the road with fat cattle grazing out in the pastures, a peaceful setting. The road came to a football sized cement pad, which had three large circles painted on it. These must have been designated landing areas, for directly behind this were three large hangars. Two helicopters were parked in the first two, the third held what looked to be two sea vans in the back, and at least four new Hummers were being polished by two workers. Nice ranch, really nice ranch, I thought.

We had studied the complex Hearst property maps from Google and I thought to drive around in back of the large hangers to take a better look.

I slowly turned alongside what seemed to be an outdoor gymnasium or work-out area, littered with hanging nets, towers, tubes and every sort of obstacle. Theo pointed out rows of human-shaped targets and several cement bunkers. Off to the left beyond the paved landing area was a cluster of fairly nice homes set in among the trees. These must have been living quarters, for we could see clothes hanging on a line out back. Off some distance there were several barns and out-buildings surrounded with corrals for animals, and there rose a high, what Theo explained to be, radio tower. Just on the other side of this tower we could see what looked like a small compact landing strip with another hangar at the base of the rising hills.

Several rough looking characters stopped to take a look at us, while we passed through this undeniable military training area.

We finally made a turn back towards the first helicopter landing pads and moved along slowly taking in the general layout. I parked, rolled down our windows and waited; immediately we could hear guns firing repeatedly. These were no ordinary beach pistols, but sounded like high powered weaponry. Off some distance beyond the outdoor equipment area we could see several guards shooting at moving targets down range. The whole place took on the feeling of a military complex.

Off to our left was a long, low office type building with a tall flag pole, the American flag flapping in the breeze at its top. Several sand buggies and jeeps and a couple of motorcycles were parked off to one side, with a few men in jungle type uniforms standing around talking and smoking. They had their attention on us as we pulled up to what we assumed to be the main office. One man held a radio up to his mouth, nodding his head while observing our van.

I got out first and went around to Theo's door and helped

him down from the high camper van. I had decided to turn Theo into damaged goods, with crutches and a pronounced limp. I had a reason for this, just for some insurance if need be. Sometimes crippled is good.

We had notified Dustin and told Thortin of our whereabouts and suggested they call every so often. We also had our GPS tracker on so they would know where we were at all times. We had only taken a few steps from our van and barely begun our approach to the main office when the guard who held the radio stepped forward, asking us who we might be looking for.

I looked up at the first guard and his buddies standing in the background. They wore camouflage pants with high laced jungle boots, each sported side guns and their arms were laced with muscle overlaid with a variety of tattoos.

These were not ordinary beach guards, nor renta-cops; they were the real thing you read about in Tom Clancy novels: mean, tough and not so friendly. They looked like something you'd see in a military training movie—strong, outdoors, live in the jungle, kick ass, and cut your heart out for fun.

Their spokesman had sharp confident eyes, pushed so far back into his head, they looked like they were trying to hide, overlaid with thick brows. I saw a pronounced squared jaw, shaved clean, and a well defined scar across the back of his hand.

Then it became clear, this was the man whose wallet we had found, this had to be Charles Anthony Trimmer, the Cat himself. The two other guards watching us intently were the ones we had seen on the beach that night. I saw beads of sweat break out on Theo's forehead, as tiny flashes of fear radiated out his eyes. Fear went through me for Theo, hoping he would take hold and survive this face to face meeting. We were sure now that the spokesman was the chopper pilot and he had to be the same one who had landed that night to remove some of the treasure. This first guard was staring at me while I got the feeling he had been looking forward to our arrival.

Then I realized that he was looking at my oddball purple-black eye, considering its source.

I cleared my throat, as I might be somewhat afraid and said, "We want to talk to the chief or boss or someone in charge."

"About what?" snapped the one front man, who I definitely recognized as Charlie Trimmer the CAT from his wallet picture, who stepped up closer, barring our way to the main door while demanding an answer.

I cleared my throat again, not too sure how to answer this stern faced intimidator, "A week or so ago we broke down on the highway and had to leave our van." I pointed to my dungy looking van and continued, "We had to hitch into town and hustle up a fuel pump and when we got back, the van had been broken into. A note made mention that our surf boards and my laptop had been taken by HC Security, as for what reason we do not know, but we would like to get them back."

"Really now, you think we took your stuff?" Trimmer, looked over his shoulder, smirked at his two buddies and spoke up mockingly.

"If this is HC Security, and according to this note, you did."

"Let me see that note," Trimmer stuck out his callused, scarred hand.

"Nah, I don't think so. Not unless you're the boss or the man that has the authority to return our things."

This short exchange blasted visible tension into the air like an exploding volcano. Things were happening too fast I thought. We stood there waiting as the two guards behind Trimmer exchanged words and stepped out, flanking their front man. I could almost read his mind: his expressions were a billboard with large printed words scrolling across it, "Who is this punk kid who dares challenge me, the killer, the biggest and meanest ravager around!"

Strange, I could hear him saying something, but my attention was drawn to his eyes, where suddenly I was looking into an apparition of strange shadowy enigmas. Something dark was conjured up within those hollow orbs, becoming agitated while watching me from out of their gloomy nests: I was reminded of the spiders coming out of their hidden places. It chilled me to see what I thought was a mocking skeleton floating from out of its grave.

For an instant I was being pulled into a cavern of death, but Theo, seeing that I was lost to the moment, tapped me with his crutch. Somehow his intervention rescued me and the death watch switched to a concern for danger. I managed to keep my wits, and finally lifted my eyes to the blue sky.

A few endless moments crawled by while we could see this trio flexing their fingers, their arms, and even their faces, as if getting body parts ready to break brick walls. It was like standing near broken high-tension wires, releasing flashing swords, dancing knives, and red hot rocket bursts of electricity—all aimed at us.

I uttered one of JJ's odd ball expressions, with no idea of its meaning, but it sounded good at the moment, "Hogoronians." Only five minutes into this visit and we are already facing death or something close to it, I thought. Again, good old Theo broke the time warp and began poking me in the leg with his crutch. He seemed to be begging—'Back away, let's get the hell out of here, forget boards, computers. Let's save our asses!'

Simultaneously, we stepped back into what I call a wise retreat. I really did not see any reason for a war to break out, since we were officially card-carrying pacifists, at least for the moment. But this guy's gunpowder testosterone was boiling out of his pores. With the electricity in the air, we were within seconds of a flammable combustion. A strange thing was, I could detect a desperation emitting out of his being: there was something really bothering this man. He was not going to let us escape his realm.

I was ready. Ready to run, to say the least. But the front man was diverted from his attack as he stopped, looked at Theo— barely balanced on crutches, and slowly rubbed his chin. We could see the muscles in his arms flex while his tattoos continued dancing around as if begging for action. But he seemed to check himself, perhaps deciding how exactly to attack, to get in the first death strike. He had to be a psychopath, a full fledged war machine, loaded with enough hate to bring down pain on an entire city, no less us two little virgin peace lovers!

The only thing I could think of was to throw him a first punch of diversion. Diversion is a great tool if you know how to use it. So I unexpectedly and boldly pointed to the 'dancing skull eating a snake' tattoo on his forearm and said, "Wow, that is a really fantastic tat, man. Where did you get that one?"

He proudly glanced down at what had to be a thousand dollar tattoo and was about to answer when a commanding voice broke the tension as it came through the screen door at the office, "OK Trimmer, back down a little, show the boys in. I would like to talk with them before you kill them."

I sighed with a casual relief when the voice called out the name Trimmer, the same name that had been used in the treasure pit that night. So this was Trimmer, I thought. The one thing that struck me the most when we came was the fact that, without any reason we knew, an instant wave of anti-us, or of evil, rose up against us, for no reason at all, as far as I could tell. Then I thought of this guy's wallet being lost. If he suspected us of having found it, that meant we might possess important information about him, or him and his friends.

Hey, no problem I thought. We had photographed every printed word in his wallet, including his little phone book (but he didn't have to know that) and I would give back his wallet, and even his eighty bucks, if things went right and we were left alive.

Theo finally managed to squeak out in a high pitched doom-filled voice, "Kill us?"

Charlie Trimmer looked at us in disgust, tossed down his hand-rolled cigarette, crushed it into the ground, grunted and gave us a dirty look. Then he did a quick rough search making sure he hit my genitals, looking for what might be considered weapons, then stepped up onto the porch, opening the screen, and waved us into the security office.

Before we even entered, the aroma of fresh-brewed coffee hit our noses. The large office was well lighted; we immediately noticed a beautiful Persian carpet, covering the floor, almost the size of the office. A long window framed a view of the mountains, the light giving even a better view of two young ladies sitting at their desks below the window, bathed in light. Their keyboards clicked away, but our entrance interrupted their work as they looked up, pretending surprise. I knew they had been watching the entire episode outside the window. While holding back laughter, they gave us a welcoming smile. We noticed right up front that they were nice-looking women; 'Wow, I am impressed' came into my mind.

All I could think of at the moment was 'What a contradiction.' We just stepped out of a military environment, battle field and all, and now we stood in what was almost an art museum. Instead of jagged edges of combat, we were in a room of soft curves and excellent works of art. I knew Theo was feeling the same thing; we actually felt safe for the moment.

My eyes, or at least one of my eyes, moved on and roamed the office, where I saw a huge world map set off to the left. Various shaded markings and colored pins were scattered around it, this was not a simple coastal beach map, I mused.

The opposite corner held a large glass display case and both Theo and I were casually taking in its contents: a nice collection of vases, bowls, a variety of utensils, and interestingly enough, a number of smaller boxes with one just like the one I took out on our final escape from the trench. However, what really caught my attention was a row of computer screens which were linked side by side, forming a large media square on the back wall. Oh sheet, I thought, they were all on and I could see that they were security camera systems for surveillance. My heart sank, for if these cameras were somewhere along the beach we had surely been seen. But then my thoughts were that if we had been seen, surely the troops would have come out and rounded us up.

I tried to see what they were scanning, but the head man, who I assumed was the security chief, by the way he took command, lifted up his large hand and casually waved us over as he finished up a phone call. As we moved into the main part of the office, approaching his desk, he was giving one of the secretaries a message. He was turned sideways to us, punching something into a personal hand held device while leaning back in his chair with his legs crossed, not yet giving us his attention. He sat there for a moment tapping a gold pen onto his chin, taking us in with his right eye, as if giving us a moment to focus our attention on him and get our eyes off the office decorations, especially the secretaries.

As he finally leaned forward in his large comfortable desk chair, immediately I could see several scars lining his face. One was faint, running from his temple downwards fading out mid cheek. Another one was smaller but much more pronounced, just along the jaw bone. It seemed as though everyone around this place was scarred up, changing their name to Scarville would have been fitting. I was hoping that those two lovelies over there didn't have any scars on them. Then the chief or general, or whatever you would call him, still not fully facing us, simply announced with a no non-sense voice, tinged with authority and just enough gruffness to let us know he was The Man. "My name is Brookstone, chief security officer for Hearst Castle Security. May I see the note you mentioned?"

Handing it over I saw that the little finger on his out-stretched hand was missing to the joint. No doubt, I thought, this guy has either been in a terrible accident or was once a lumberjack that had fallen onto his chain saw; the name Scarville came back into mind.

Interesting I thought, he didn't even ask who we were or

what we might want. Theo and I stood there as he scanned the letter. When he swiveled in his chair putting his leg flat under the desk, the real surprise hit us. His left eye stared icy cold, dead and direct at me.

At first I could not understand what he was so intense about but then I realized that this was no ordinary eye, it was a glass eye that was aimed at me personally. Behind his gruff and serious face I could see a tiny smile forming, apparently he enjoyed letting his glass eye intimidate people.

Besides the scars and glass eye he was not only rugged looking, but somewhat handsome, as if he were made up as a movie actor ready for a war scene. His appearance was neat, and no doubt he was very fit. It was as though every movement was casual but an action of planned harmony. This guy could only be described as ruggedly handsome, suave, and seriously dangerous. If anyone ever had a square face, this was the man. A close cut haircut created the top of the square, but his jaw definitely defined the full square of his face. His side burns were tuffs of light grey, defining his age, I guessed around forty.

He did not inquire of our mission or offer his hand. I was suddenly thinking military and wanted to salute. However, there was no doubt, his staring emerald eye intimidated me, and the matching live eye told a cold hard story in its piercing examination of two shabby surf bums.

I saw that this meeting was going to be more than we thought it would be. With a little hesitation and with all humility I handed the note over to him. He was reading it aloud and began to laugh to himself.

—Warning, due to our tow truck being repaired we were

unable to remove your vehicle. We have given you warning that within 24 hours this vehicle will be removed. We will be in touch—

Hearst Castle Security Services

While he was reading, my eyes were taken to one of the walls where there were four beautifully framed paintings, somewhat familiar to me, like ones out of the beach gully. The frames were highly polished silver but the pictures were of that old darkish quality that you might see in a museum somewhere in Europe. Off to my right was a heavy door that had to be a walk-in vault. 'Oh man, would I like to see what was stored in that place,' I thought. Then Brookstone coughed a little and got my attention; he had seen me looking at the paintings, then the vault door. I felt another layer of suspicion rise up to meet me.

"This had to be written by the Cat," he said aloud to himself.

I inquired, "The Cat? Who might that be and why so?"

"Charlie Anthony Trimmer, we call him the Cat for short, because he's cunning and fast. He's always giving out too much information." He tossed the note onto his desk, "Ah yeah, I remember this, it was a week or so back. Right." He acted overly casual.

I edged into our story, "Yes, our fuel pump went out and we had to leave the van there while we hitched into town to get another one, but they had to order it so it took a day longer to arrive."

His one good eye moved between Theo and myself, while his glass eye kept us locked into its depths, almost as if being watched through a gun scope. His good eye scanned my face and I knew he was considering my plum colored eye for a moment then asked, "Wasn't that the same day as the quake that hit the area?"

I nodded that it was.

"Weren't there three of you?"

"Yes, we were baby-sitting a surf kid, a nephew of a friend of ours. We sent him ahead and then we hitched out, it's too hard to get a ride with three. He came up with the part, but it had to be ordered. The part was sent out to the Shell station in San Simeon and the next day or so, good old bearded Barney brought Jason out to the van, did the repairs and charged us an arm and a leg. This is when Jason found that our three surf boards were gone, my laptop with a few other smaller items, and the note was left on the seat."

Brookstone seemed to be considering this information and laughed at the mention of bearded Barney, the garage mechanic, and casually asked, "Where did you and your buddy go?" Brookstone nodded towards Theo while asking me.

"We met a few old surfing friends and hung out with them for the night. We told Jason to get the van fixed and gassed up, and we would meet him at the San Simeon State Park until finally everything came together, and we hit the road.

Again, Brookston was scratching his chin and leaned back in his chair, contemplating what seemed to be some major gaps in our narrative. He asked, "You sure you boys didn't climb the fence and head down to the beach and hang out there?"

"I wish," I said. Then I pointed to Theo's leg, "My bud here was hurt up at Half-moon Bay a week or so earlier in a surf contest, and he could barely walk, much less climb a fence and go tramping across a half mile of grass and weeds, then play around on the beach. I was upset enough, that we had to hitch into San Luis Obispo. And that was not easy with this cripple."

Theo grunted his protest at my calling him a cripple. But real nice like, he began to play his role, "Sir, would you mind if I sat down, my leg is really bothering me. I don't want to fall down in your office."

The one secretary laughed at this statement while Brookstone waved over at an office chair as if to say 'Go for it.'

I got an idea while watching the surveillance screens scanning the beach and the parking lots. "I'm sure you would have seen us on your beach through your surveillance camera system, wouldn't you have?"

Brookstone paused before answering, "Well we had a bit of trouble with our systems after that quake knocked out several poles along the way, so we were not sure who might have been on our shores."

This was excellent news for us and I breathed a sigh of relief. In perfect timing, my cell phone went off, I looked at the number, it was Dustin checking up. Brookstone went on, "So you're Luke Mitchner, that's a pretty cool name. You are the free-lance writer and your sidekick there must be Bontempski."

There was only one way he could have known that: he had been into my laptop and read my stories, notes and files. I had to laugh at the sidekick reference for which Theo at the moment had no retort. But with his bum leg, he was, at the present anyway, a sidekick. I nodded, "That's right, and how did you like my articles?"

"He smiled, and seemed to lighten up a little and gave his more-or-less approval. He pointed over to a desk where I saw my laptop sitting.

"One of my chopper crews loves to surf. And I hope you don't mind, but they used your three boards this last weekend on the north point. And well, they may have gotten banged up a little, it was a nice swell."

Theo spoke up this time, "No big deal, we can do some repairs, we're used to it. We're happy to get them back; they sort of have sentimental value for us."

While tapping his pen on his chin, the boss asked, "That one board is rather unusual. What is the odd vent that looks like a little speaker, in the back by the fin?"

I nodded to Theo, suggesting that he might explain. Theo sat up, "That is a sonic admitter which sends out a high intensity echo that will irritate sharks or whales to the point of discouraging their approach." Theo paused and saw that he had caught this Brookstone character's attention, and went on. "It's one of my new inventions—now being tested. It seems to have gained some acceptance here and there. That's one of the reasons we were up north at the big water-sports show."

"I'm impressed. Sounds interesting."

I wanted to move on, so decided to ask the obvious, "Why would your security police take our things to begin with? What was the purpose?"

"It's our way of checking you out. If you were screwing around on the property or doing something illegal, my boys would own a few nice boards and your laptop would have a new home. You would never have come after your stuff."

Great answer I thought, glad now that we had come for our

things. I had to accede a few points over to Brookstone. This left us in the clear, honest as new born babes. "But what if we had gone to the police?" I asked.

Brookstone laughed, saying, "Sonny, we is the police out here!"

We saw the two secretaries laugh at this statement. They seemed to be having fun just listening to this exchange.

I knew this not to be true, or I thought I knew, but just nodded, played dumb and waited.

"I'm wondering why you guys didn't come right up here after your van was fixed, why did you wait ten days or so?" Brookstone asked.

I was taken aback by his ongoing questioning and was glad I had made Theo our scapegoat, "Theo's bum leg was in bad shape and I thought it best to get him home for some proper help."

Brookstone nodded as if giving me points for this answer. Then he said, "You guys were lucky that day. With that quake, our tow truck had a little accident. It was out of commission for a week undergoing repairs, or your van would have been towed that same day."

I instantly thought of my van's mirror being shaved off by the tow truck, maybe by some idiot in a hurry to get to the happy hour at Jug Heads bar, "What happened to it?" I played dumb and tried to switch the subject a little.

"Some drunk ran our driver off the road and tore up one side, adding to our loss of power by snapping another power line and screwing up our surveillance for a few days. This was during the time your van was supposedly broken down," and with that answer he shot us a suspicious look.

This was pure bull. The way that driver had been hauling ass, no wonder the truck went off the road. I also smiled, thinking, this is too much data Mr. Brookstone.

I began to wonder about hidden motives going on here. For we knew that these guys were dealing with illegals, possibly drugs, and the removal of a most valuable treasure that had been hidden for many years. And then there was that skull. Did Brookstone know what we had done, but was playing around with us? For what reason?

Theo was getting brave, waving his crutch upwards he inquired, "Why all the 'no trespassing' signs every fifty feet and the constant chopper fly-overs? What is the big deal with just a long stretch of desolate sand?"

Again, Brookstone waited before giving his answer, "Well, we get thousands of tourists passing this way every day, especially in the summer. There are those types that have no respect for anyone else's property, and leave their beer and wine bottles broken on the beach. They've started huge bon-fires that spread into the dry grass, costing the Hearst Foundation big bucks to clean up. We have caught punks shooting cattle, seagulls and even seals that come up on shore. So we have to be tough. The signs are our first line of defense and a good place to start."

That seemed a reasonable answer. We couldn't argue with it. Brookstone definitely made some points.

As he gave his explanation I noticed a reflection of movement outside on the glass display case. In a moment I saw the three guards walking around our van as if checking it over. For what reason? I pondered.

I thought I'd ask out of curiosity, "Sir, you know that I'm a free-lance writer, you've got me wondering if it would be possible to do an interview with you, a story on your efforts to keep this coastline sacred."

He smiled at the word sacred, but said, "The Hearst Foundation would not allow that, they always try to stay out of the limelight. I would probably lose my job if I gave an interview."

"OK. It never hurts to try," I gave my reply in an approving voice, as if giving him back a few points for his answer.

Brookstone called the Cat back in and told him to go fetch our boards, then pointed to my laptop and said, "Mighty strange that all your email was deleted just an hour before my tech got into it."

At this statement, I saw one of the secretaries glance up and smile at us. She was lovely, and I saw that Theo had been checking her over for the last five minutes and I didn't have a crutch to get his attention back to business.

Brookstone was tapping his pen on a writing pad, watching me for my reaction. I thought I would up the stakes a little and answered, "Mr. Brookstone, I keep important information on my computer and deal with some meaningful characters through interviews and emails. They trust me, and as soon as I found out my computer was taken, I got hold of my high tech friend and had him scrub it. In fact, because of the tracking device inside my laptop I knew exactly where my computer was from the time it was taken."

His pen stopped tapping, this blew him away. He just sat there looking at us two surf bums, trying to figure out who the hell we were, and if we were playing games with them. First, this sonic sound-emitter thing, and now a tracking device in their laptop? Maybe these guys were more than what they appeared to be, he was considering. After all, it was his business to know.

"Well, well, the two surf bums really got it together. So you knew where your computer was…my techs somehow missed that, aah," was his reply and he had to give up a few points in our favor.

He stood up, leaving no doubt that he was a well groomed man, heavily built, and way taller than either Theo or myself. He definitely had the bearing of a military man, and as he turned, the light revealed not just his facial scars but several other scars etched down his neck. I thought, for sure this guy has been around. I don't think I'd want to mess with him, nor his guards. I think he did this to add the final touch of intimidation. I smiled and had to give back a few points for his smooth on-going game.

He told me to gather up my laptop and we followed him out the door. Just as we got to the door, Brookstone said, "By the way Mitchner, I liked your stories. And your efforts to secure people's personal information is admirable." He had a strange smile being held in check while he finally asked, "And by the way, where did you get that most colorful walnut-shaped eye?"

I was first impressed with this admission and reminded him that his interview would always be held in the utmost confidence, if he ever decided to give me one. Then I decided to play his game a bit and asked him, "First tell me about your eye and I'll tell you about mine."

Without hesitation he stated, "From a terrorist bomb—and yours?"

He totally caught me off guard. There was no way I was about to tell him that a little old spider had bitten the crap out of me after he said he had been wounded by a bomb. And with the girls listening, I had to come up with something other than a lousy spider story. So I casually but humbly said that I got the big bad eye from a flying surfboard on a twenty-foot steaming wipe-out!

I heard the girls laugh, knowing I was doing some bragging and trying to impress someone with some macho bull.

Then, just before opening the door, he turned to us and said in a low voice, "By the way boys, your little punky surfer—JJ, I believe you call him—well, his card skills are questionable."

We were shocked, how the heck did Brookstone know about this? But he soon divulged the answer. "Those two buddies of Trimmer over there," he gestured towards our van where the trio stood waiting, "They are friends with the guy you called good old bearded Barney and your poker playing kid took them all for a few hundred bucks that night."

All I could think of was, "Ah crap, JJ, you did it again!"

Brookstone went on, "I don't know how he did it, but he managed to escape a near-death experience that night. Maybe it was the Tequila they were drinking or they had hot dates that distracted them. But they were quite amazed at the kid's skill at cards." The corner of his lips lifted just enough to indicate a smile of admiration. He added with a touch of warning, "It is not often that the Cat and his buddies are taken for anything. You better not let them find your smart-ass poker-playing surf bum! And, by the way, Good Old Bearded Barney is one of San Luis Obispo's deputies."

Theo and I stood there dumfounded, but somewhat proud that JJ had got a good lick in for our side. Another variable had just been tossed into the thickening mix. We knew now that Trimmer and his buds had connected us to JJ and realized that this is what might have set off their wrath. We also wondered what JJ might have told these guys. Oh well, too late now!

The two other guards had come up on an electric runabout with our three boards in the back. I loaded them into the van and with a lot of dramatics, I helped Theo up and into the passenger seat. He got even with me for calling him a cripple, overplaying his part by leaning all his weight onto me while he added in a few groans. I knew we looked like two fumbling dorks.

But I couldn't let the moment of opportunity pass. I turned to ask one last thing, "Bob, do you think it would be possible for me to get a job on your HC Security team?"

The three guards heads snapped around at my casual use of Brookstone's first name. Theo had done his homework the night before so there was little that we did not know about the HC Security Company and its registered and accredited employees. We had downloaded satellite maps of the entire compound and had an in-depth file on the whole ranch and surrounding areas. My lawyer friend Dustin had his number-one man, Wally Justin, doing the bookwork on every penny coming in and going out of this company. And good old Bob Brookstone was the first one we checked out.

Bob, or should I say Brookstone, stood there dumfounded and was obviously pissed red. He finally answered in a low, defined voice, "We'll get in touch with you, we know your names and addresses and your phone numbers and if we need more guards, we'll certainly call you." He certainly put the accent point on the fact that they knew our names and where we lived. This was not good, I thought.

The other guards laughed aloud and seemed more than ready

to get in touch, or at least touch us. The Trimmer guard still had his evil eye fixed on us and there was something that really bothered me about him, as if he were Brookstone's hit man. The feeling was both strange and strong. I was sure he had something up his sleeve while walking around our van, checking it out. I did not like this at all; an odd feeling was stirred within me.

Again, I couldn't let this moment go by. Thinking to smooth some of the wrinkles out of our first official meeting, I looked to the side of Brookstone and asked Trimmer and his buddies if they were regular surfers. There was some hesitancy but the Cat took a puff on his cigarette, all cool like, and let it be known that they had surfed all over the world: Africa, Indonesia, Australia and both US coasts.

I looked up at Brookstone's face and saw that irritated look concerning Trimmer, about too much information going out.

I was impressed and again, tried to take some of the sting out of these wasps, so I tossed out a hook of friendship, "That's fantastic. You know Theo and I are planning to produce a high quality surf flick in the nearby future, and we are looking for some—well," I paused here turning my head to the side, and squinting up at Brookstone, "Well, some different, out-of-the-ordinary surf types, those with experience, and plenty of tattoos. You guys might fit the bill."

One of the guys in the back with the deep voice (it sounded like George from the treasure pit) asked, "You mean like in that 'Endless Summer' flick?"

"Yeah, you got it, but way better, and higher-quality photography, with underwater shots and all."

"Sounds interesting," Brookstone cut the exchange off.

I got the message. So I thanked Brookstone and nodded to Trimmer and the other guards and smiled, "Thanks guys for taking care of our boards," thinking again that it never hurts to be friendly, "Sorry for the inconvenience." With this I gestured over to Trimmer saying, "Oh, by the way Charles, here's your wallet." And added, "Thanks for returning the side mirror your truck broke off when you nearly clipped us a few weeks back on the highway."

If there were ever a look that could kill, I just received it. Those bones that I had seen earlier all jumped up and came to attention, locked and loaded, ready to go to war. Trimmer's hand shot out like a serpents tongue and snapped his wallet out of my hand. At first I thought he was going to strike me and I flinched a little. Nothing needed to be said, I felt that a target was painted on me, to be used in the near future. Trimmer went through his wallet, saw that everything was there, including his eighty dollars, but said nothing. Brookstone stood there, taken back by the news of our mirror and the near miss of the truck. He shot a stern look to Trimmer, who burned red but remained silent at this unexpected disclosure of what really happened to the truck on earthquake day.

At that moment, I felt that the unity or camaraderie between these men was not so secure; there was a lot more going on behind the scene than we could know. I moved to the van, took another look around and climbed up, then fired up old Betsy. Her muffler was rather worn. She sounded like a B-57 ready for take-off, with smoke and dust blasting from underneath. It was a nice touch for what two really stupid and crazy surf bums would do, right?

Who cared? We were out of there; we were hoping never to see these security jerks again. We could see the two lovely secretaries looking out the front window at this farewell meeting and I thought I'd add a special memory to their picture. Just for fun, I spun the wheel and made two large tire squeaking circles on the paved landing pad, nearly tipping the van over while Theo screamed at me that I was crazy. Then, like a bat out of hell, we shot down the long gravel road, weaving from side to side, honking the horn, scaring the grazing cattle along the way in celebration of our escape.

Theo yelled out for me to slow down and shouted, "What the hell did you think to even mention our surf flick to those creeps, no less offer them a possible part?"

"No worries friend, I was just trying to smooth out our path to escape by dangling a zucchini out for them."

"You mean a carrot don't you?"

"Not in this case, it had to be something larger, the only thing would be a thirty pound zucchini!"

Theo had no choice but to laugh as we headed back to Highway One.

CHAPTER FIFTEEN

BIG BOOM ON THE VAN

With a high intense voice, Theo half yelled and half asked me, "What the heck was all that about Mitch?"

"Ah, just a little mind game we had to play, I was probing emotions and digging for a tidbit more information. And letting them know to leave us alone, but I think now we have been tagged with a tracker or something like that," I said as we drove south along the beach.

"Come on, how do you know that?"

"While you had your eyes glued onto those two babes and we were talking in the office, I saw a reflection in the display window of the guards walking around the van, figured they were up to something that I didn't like."

"Um-hum, very observant. And the crutch thing too, was brilliant, it might have saved our butts," Theo admitted. But he failed to mention his eyes being glued onto those babes. He went quiet for a few miles then spoke up, "Old Brookstone sure hit you with a good one when you had to ask him about his eye. And where the hell did you come up with a twenty foot steamer here on the west coast a week ago?"

"Hey, did you want me to tell them that I was crawling around in their treasure pit and a lousy sea spider bit me?"

"Nah, that wouldn't have been too smart."

Actually I sort of liked Brookstone and hoped he was not mixed up in all this treasure rip-off deal. Those guys looked like something out of Rocky Del Gotto, or was it Balboa movies? Tough and mean. But with those four rare paintings hanging on his office wall, along with the collection of vases in his glass cabinet, well, he had to be mixed in the plot somehow. I knew that my computer had been gone through and everything downloaded, but the one thing they did not know was that inside my computer was a sound activated recorder. It had recorded everything that had been spoken in the surrounding area since its theft. The recordings would go on as long as there was battery power. That information had been transmitted and was now housed on my main computer back at Dustin's office.

This was a little trick that Wally Justin, one of our associates and one of the top computer programmers in the country, had set up for me. It was one of his specialty projects designed for the military, but he shared it with a few of us.

Yeah, good old Wally, a great friend to have, I flashed back on our meeting at a place called the Pit Stop, but that's another story. Together we had been working on a few unusual projects and this was just a drop in the bucket. It was one of the reasons I was so adamant in retrieving my laptop.

Without doubt, as we drove south I was watching my rear view mirror with a feeling I did not like—very uneasy. We made it to the San Simeon State Park, which was nearly empty. Turning in we saw Thortin parked in the day use area at the far end, isolated from the other areas, waiting for us. We parked next to him and real quick like, we transferred our boards and belongings into Thortin's pickup. I pulled out the awning on the van and set out a couple of chairs and put on some music, covered up a few pillows on the back bunks as if someone were sleeping there. We were leaving the whole scene as if we were kicked back to relax inside.

Theo kept asking me what the heck I was doing, but I told him to put down his stupid crutch and help, and hurry, so he knew that I had something up my sleeve. After loading up our gear we jumped in Thortin's pick-up and left the van behind. We were not taking any chances; I had pre-arranged for Thortin to wait for us at the park. We could not trust the HC Security people to leave well enough alone, and sure enough we were right–but how right we did not learn until a few minutes later.

Just as we had gone down the road, Theo was looking back up the beach and saw, off in the distance, a pin spot that might have been one of the patrol choppers hovering over the beach area, somewhere near the State Park. Then suddenly there was a flash of orange light, and a boom sounded all the way down to us, now a quarter mile away.

We pulled over, and all piled out to take a better look. Theo's face went white and he was looking at me, now realizing that I did have something up my sleeve. I told them of my suspicions when I had seen Trimmer messing with our van and did not want to panic Theo, but knew we better not take any chances. Less than an hour after the explosion Thortin got a call from one of his friends, the park manager, telling him that a patrol helicopter had hovered off a ways and then suddenly our van burst into flames with a boom. It was gone; pieces of the van were lying all over the place. If anyone had been inside, no way could they have survived. The San Simeon police were on their way and what should he tell them? I told him to just say that the butane tank must have blown and we were fortunate enough to have been out to lunch at a friend's house. I gave my phone number to contact us.

Theo was freaked out, his teeth were chattering; he had been shaken to the core. Now, all three of us knew that this was no game. We had walked into a maze of danger and we were now alert and fully aware that this adventure could lead to a real plot, called a grave site! Our concerns now focused on our futures and how serious this threat was going to be. Once the HC Security team found out we had survived the blast, would they continue to search us out, or would this suffice as a warning to forget our suspicions?

The van was one thing but not really worth worrying over. I would report its destruction by a butane leak, just an accident. With all its dings and scratches, probably the most expensive part of the van was the new fuel pump we just got.

Besides, a new compact RV was being prepared and fitted out for us. It was going to have all the latest goodies and more. Our friend, Wally Justin the highest tech around, was going to work his magic from one end to the other. The funny part of this was that we were going to use some of the Hearst treasure funds to bankroll our new ride; the sky was the limit. The proof that we deserved this had just been revealed to us when our van blew up!

Before Thortin hung up I added, "Tell your friend at the park he is more than welcome to go through the van and take anything he wants if there is anything left."

I flashed back onto Trimmer's erratic state of desperation. Maybe, when I gave back his wallet, he realized then and there that we had gone through it and seen his international contacts. The only way to cover his mistake in losing the wallet was to make sure that no one had any knowledge of his contacts. Thus, the reason for the destruction of our van and our lives became clear to me.

There was no doubt now. The explosion of our van, the Hearst Castle treasure and the Smugglers Cove events had to be tied into the HC Security force. We had stumbled into the middle of a snake pit. This was beyond an article to write; it had become a real crime mystery.

We moved on and spent the day and that night at Thortin's beach house, laying out our plans. We went over all the information we had collected and noted it all into our computers. There was not much more we could do for now, so Thortin took us to a car rental where we got ourselves a nice SUV and headed home. The drive south was a time of reflection and of serious contemplation.

After a well-rounded weekend, allowing us a day of surfing, a day to rest up and time to spend photographing and inventorying the treasure in greater detail, we were ready; but for what? Having passed the danger we had experienced, we began to realize the extent of the wealth we now possessed. In one of the canvas sacks we found another stash of smaller boxes, each of which would fit in the palm of one's hand. These were small, exquisitely carved and well-sealed treasures in themselves; they looked like the same type of boxes we had seen in Brookstone's office.

Theo expertly opened one, revealing individual tiny carved-out cups, each one holding an absolutely beautiful stone. There were twelve and more stones in each of the five small boxes. Some of the stones were the size of robin eggs, and there were no words to describe the beauty that sparkled there before our eyes. Theo examined several of them, nodding his head in acknowledgment that many of these gems had been plucked out of icons or from settings in ornate pieces of fine jewelry. My mind kept taking me back to the old story of a beach bum stumbling along the beach who kicks up an ancient buried lantern. Upon opening it, out comes an old genie who offers the beach bum a wish for setting him free. The beach bum is suddenly granted instant wealth and untold riches. Here we were, right in the midst of this old tale come true. After all, didn't we accidentally kick over the magic sand pile with a mighty thankful genie hidden therein?

We sat in our storage vault trying to determine what we were going to do with this incredible discovery. Our treasure had just doubled in value with these five boxes alone. The remainder of the canvas sacks held what seemed to be a variety of museum or old church icons, some made of pure gold. They had a Russian or oriental appearance. There were two most beautiful vases that had to be from the Ming Dynasty, Theo speculated. Theo, the more scholarly mind among us nearly went around the bend and over the falls when a wooden box revealed two leather tubes, both containing parchment scrolls that opened up nearly four feet long. It had to be Hebrew writings etched into this old parchment. This became his baby, there was no doubt. He asked to be given the task in determining what it might be.

An idea began to form. We were now wondering if old man Hearst had not reported his loss, because maybe, just maybe, much of these things had been plundered out of museums and churches in Russia during the revolution and he could not say that he had possession of them or the Soviets would have demanded them back. We were going to have to hire someone to begin a worldwide search for these individual pieces to see if there were records of them, if missing, and from where.

We wanted to bring JJ-Jason into this work, but felt that he was a bit immature to handle the magnitude of what we were involved with, so we decided to bring Theo's older brother Jay into our confidence. He was another one of those quiet recluse geniuses hiding behind his thick glasses, forever reading and selling old stamps, relics and pieces of antiquity on eBay. We took many of the finer pieces of framed art, along with a few tiny scrolls and one of the vases over to his live-aboard sloop anchored in the quaint Balboa Island refuge. We let Jay handle the research to figure out where they might have come from and if they were worth anything. He was ecstatic about this new work, and we knew we could trust him to keep things quiet.

Jay was soon made a member of our team and now we had five trusted members. It was not planned, but the concept of a working team just came about. We talked this idea over, and a united team seemed most fitting for the various tasks that were appearing on our horizon. We explained that once we had ascertained the historical relevance and a value on these artifacts, we would then decide what we were going to do with them.

We might distribute some of the relics among various museums and maybe have Thortin hold a charity auction to raise needed funds for an orphanage or a clinic of sorts. We had all agreed that we would use part of our new found wealth to help others. For so many people had helped us when we were in need, starting with my own step grandparents when my own parents had been lost at sea in a boating accident.

I was impressed with Jay's forty-foot, two-mast sloop named the Serendipity, a crude but nice sea-ready vessel. Theo had told me that Jay was an excellent diver and often took out diving groups to explore the waters around Catalina Island and along the Baja coast. He had chartered his services out twice to groups back and forth to Hawaii. I mentioned to Theo that in time we might hire Jay to take us up to San Simeon, off the smugglers cove and do some diving off shore; we might come up with the lost San Bella, who knows?

We took all the coins, stones and smaller bags of rings and jewelry and divided them into different safety deposit boxes in different areas. Our dilemma on what exactly to do with this treasure was set aside for a time as the work on our new RV came to fruition.

Wally, one of our new and important team members, had called us to his work shop and his most interesting lab. He was excited to show and explain what he was doing with the new vehicle while we shook our heads, thinking that the new mode of transportation was going to be like a whiz-bang James Bond spy wagon! The 28 footer was a Mercedes Benz rig, well built by their bus department, and named by Wally — The Tripper!

It was a total outdoor rig, rugged but having the comforts of home on the road. It was equipped with a satellite dish, well hidden into the roof, a full satellite phone system that could be charged by solar power, a complete wireless computer system, an alarm system that could discourage the best of bandits, its own safe for weapons and goodies and a beyond regulation GPS system. It had radar this and radar that, including a power-up radio jammer, and with night vision windshields if needed. It was just too much for me to comprehend all at once.

Its tinted windows of course, were fully bullet proof with imbedded electronics inside the windshield. An extraordinary night or day camera system, unseen to the human eyes could scan 360 degrees and show all on a dash-top screen. A heavy duty dual wheel system could take us just about anywhere, especially with the four wheel power drive. It had a long-haul fuel system, more than enough power to really get around, up and over. It had so many gadgets and things on it that we were worn out just listening to his explanations.

Still, there was more to come, but for now we just sat in this roomy RV, not too big yet not too small, taking it all in. What we liked was that it was not conspicuous or gaudy, but rather a simple looking mode of transportation. This was great. Plenty of room to sleep four and even six if need be, storage for our boards, an inflatable raft, two fold-up bikes, chairs, and a special hiding place that you could get to from inside to make your get away from under the vehicle. The beauty in all this was that the entire RV was still compact; no one would ever know it was an electronic laboratory on wheels. Best of all, it had a fantastic kitchen, a design marvel that would easily serve our needs, and one of the best sound systems available.

With all these fantastic devices, the thing that Theo fell in love with was a built-in cup by cup coffee maker. No fuss, no muss, just hit a button and voila! you got a fresh brewed cup of top-end coffee in a minute.

While listening to Wally point out the various features in our new vehicle I began to have flash backs of the love I had lost on my journey across the country to the Florida International Triple Moon Launch. It was her again, called Bib, for Brady Ivory Brewer, an incredible FBI agent who had come into my life on that investigatory trip. Like a lovely ghost that kept following me around, it was going to be hard to forget her. We had been brought together under strange circumstances, joining forces to solve and prevent a terrorist attack against the international moon launch. She had been assigned to follow a suspect named Etroid who was traveling in a green bus with a few young people that I had caught a ride with. At the end the Agency had asked her to transport a new FBI lab on wheels back to headquarters. I got the story of my life but lost the Pulitzer Prize named Bib! As much as I thought she was the woman for me, it became evident that she was in love with her Agency. The electronic van Bib was trans-porting back to Virginia had many of the features that Wally incorporated into our new Tripper. I would love to look her up and show her our new mind-boggling lab on wheels and make her jealous. Maybe she will look me up one day and we will find a new life together, but in the meantime, I wished her the best. I knew I had lost more than a rare jewel… goodbye Bib, I started feeling the loss all over again.

I broke the trance and finally asked, "OK Wally, could you tell me how much this incredible magic wagon is going to cost?"

He looked up through his thick burly beard and smiled as he continued adjusting some gauges, "What I am going to do is to hold some of the treasure items as collateral, as me and Dustin already put up the funds for this new buggy of yours. We are only going to hold back twelve larger coins, a couple of those Church icons, and one bronze statue. That is it, my young friend. You won't even miss them."

At first I was taken back. For we had not yet decided how we were going to use these pieces of the treasure, but I guess the decision on this part was made. Wally figured that since the HC Security Force had destroyed my van, it was only right that they be made to replace it. But at ten times its value? Oh well, I'd deal with it later and exclaimed, "That is it, for all this?" I waved my arm around.

"Listen, Dustin and I tossed in a few things to make sure you got the best, you're always cutting corners so much you prob-ably would have ended up with a dented fender and a broken headlight." He concluded their plan with, "And besides, this electric wizard on wheels could be used by the entire team as time goes on."

The team, I smiled, now we were a team? I nodded to Wally, admitting the truth of the matter. I was rather conservative, especially in these last few years of struggle, trying to make it. I understood that Dustin knew that in time I would receive something from my grandparent's inheritance and he could return the artifacts and collect any difference from the inheritance. I thought this at least showed some confidence in the future victory in the upcoming Canadian court decisions.

I thought back on how this bulky genius guy and I had come to know one another, no less to end up on a newly formed team of dubious existence. Wally was a long time friend of Dustin's. I had met him under peculiar circumstances out on the edge of the Mojave Desert several years back while on assignment in a tiny 'hole in the wall' called Pit Stop, an abandoned mining town, making a peculiar come back.

Dustin had asked me to investigate an unusual happening out there and Wally and I were brought together under even stranger circumstances than these. I'll call him little Wally, now and then, just because small — he was not! I still remember our first meeting, I actually snorted out a laugh at my first take on this huge biker, thinking what on earth is a guy that big and hairy, doing named Wally? He should be named Gorilla or Grumbler, but Wally — no way.

My first sight of him was of a giant hulk, dressed in leather, slowly throbbing along on a big mean Harley. Any part of him that was not covered with leather was covered with hair. He rumbled into the little town called The Pit Stop, made a smooth circle, idling up to the cafe where I stood waiting for some guy named Wally. Thinking, with a name like Wally, he would most likely be some skinny ex-flower-child peddling a three wheeled bike. Boy was I surprised!

Instead he was this enormous rider sitting astride a powerful Harley. The apparition seemed to be one massive hair advertisement: with a split braided beard hanging down his chest while thick mustaches curled back, melting along his face, then joining into the mass of long shaggy hair. Heavy brows bushed out behind large mirrored goggles, while worn pants ran down into leather boots swathing the rest of his body. I stood there in shock, totally proven wrong in a match-up with a name. The title, Biker-Boss-Gang-Killer followed him like a spotlight in a prison yard; he looked to be nothing less than a massacre ready to happen; I thought a gun battle was soon to begin right there in town.

This gigantic aberration pulled up in front of me, shut the throbbing bike down, spit out a few bugs and lifted his goggles onto his head, then said in a voice thick as wet cement, "I'm Little Wally."

His smile was as big as an oncoming Mac truck's grill, shining bright in the midday sun. His watching eyes were large globes set back in dark canyons. I held my peace for a moment, realizing that Dustin had not prepared me for such an aberration, until I finally managed to get my wits about me, jerkily asking, "Are you, uh-huh, you must be Dustin's friend. Is that right?"

"Sure am. You got to be Luke Mitchner, right?"

And that is how I became friends with Little Wally. He turned out to be one of the greatest people I've ever encountered. Super genius computer programmer who was on a sabbatical, living on a ranch for a few years, in good old Pit Stop, putting the final touches on some extremely technical software. He was no one to mess with, but yet, a gentle giant who became part of our team. Our friendship grew into an exchange of serious trust which shortly thereafter saved both our lives. I soon sub-named him Gigabyte!

The only thing that had changed in his appearance was that

he had trimmed his thick eyebrows to keep them off his eyes. I was impressed again on how he had used his own funds but held some of the doubloon and icons as collateral, and assured me that things would work out fine and not to worry about the funding or costs for now. "Hey Luke, no worries. I got friends out there and they were more than excited to know that I could provide them with some real treasure, especially the coins and other little goodies. I can get top price for them, if need be, no sweat."

I just shook my head, more than pleased that we were turning some of this long lost treasure into something useful, and I knew that this wizard wagon would add to our adventures. There was no doubt, Wally had put all his expertise into this work of electronic art on wheels. He loved this type of job and even if he had spent all his own money on it, it would not have mattered. He loved the opportunity to create and use his abilities; money to him was not an issue.

Wally told us to climb onto the roof of the Tripper. He had set up a collapsible rail system on the reinforced roof. It was arranged so Theo could do his filming from a higher level, with camera storage and all. Wally informed us that within a few days we were going to take the little buggy for a test drive. We needed to learn how to apply all its security systems. We agreed, and thought it a good idea to get away and do some thinking about what our next move was going to be. We had no idea what awaited us in our magic wagon called the Tripper!

Dustin called a meeting on Monday of what we were now calling the team. Our first serious meeting. Dustin had asked if he might invite one of his old FBI friends, Max Colton, a man of many talents; someone we would come to know as a man with many faces and long reaching hands. Strange, that name seemed familiar to me. Interesting enough, Wally knew Max from earlier days and there seemed to be a oneness of mind, and some old time camaraderie. We would learn more about this in time.

Dustin, Theo, and I had come to an agreement that we would not reveal or speak of anything about our part of the treasure, other than the bell and a few antique keys. For we had already begun to make plans on its proper distribution and how we might want to use it by helping others in various ways. Our decisions in this matter were as of now, not yet set for action.

Dustin's research as a lawyer discovered that there was no record of a Hearst treasure being lost and not recovered. Dustin found only a ship's manifest revealing numbers of crates, boxes and various barrels. This was strange, but it could work in our favor. For such a find might not belong to anyone, other than the original owners, if ever they could be located and could prove their ownership, which would be nearly impossible. The Hearst family apparently had hidden the fact of the incoming treasures due to Hearst's financial problems during the 1930s. In fact, this treasure might have been up for grabs. For sure, we knew that California would have hundreds of their hungry man-eating lawyers all over this find if we were to announce it, so we left well enough alone.

With this, Thortin pleaded with us to keep the entire event out of the public eye. We had decided to allow him to introduce the story through his newspaper, just a bit at a time. For thousands of treasure seekers would have swarmed the beaches and caused a ton of troubles for all of them. The San Simian coast line was not ready to deal with such an invasion. This all made sense and we assured Thortin that we would try to keep all this quiet for now. Enough was enough! I was already experiencing cut-throat lawyers through the Canadian judicial system at its worst, with my inheritance tied up in years of court and lawsuits. We all knew that if we even breathed a word of 'treasure' every government lawyer and official money-stealing agency would be all over us like, well, stink on dead fish!

Dustin was now representing us, and had explained to Colton, his FBI friend, that in no way were we to be dragged into this unfolding drama. Max had let us know that this entire situation was way bigger than we might know, and agreed that we would be left out of it. We explained that Thortin Mayhurst would be the first individual to begin releasing the story. Colton would be in touch with him and would keep him informed on the progress of the investigation. So far, there were several issues that had to be watched.

After revealing the episode on the beach that night with the illegals being brought in, it became a different matter that was not ours to deal with. Dustin had told the story to Colton, who had notified the immigration department who had already found the means by which the cheap labor forces were being brought in to work on the wineries along the coast. Apparently, the HC Security Force was not involved directly in this illegal immigrant exchange, as far as they could tell.

The most upsetting part of this situation was the drugs, if that was what they were. Max assured us that this was well under investigation and for us not to be concerned in the matter.

When I came into the office and saw this Max character I got the feeling that I knew him from somewhere. He was a rather quiet individual, friendly enough, and very business like. I kept looking at him trying to recall if I had ever met him. I had rubbed shoulders with many people in my journalistic journeys and just wondered if I had ever run into him before. I was forever curious as usual and had to put my attention back onto Dustin's discourse.

The next issue was to either go in or confiscate the entire treasure, which would pretty well give all the suspects time to depart. Or, put a sting operation into existence and allow the FBI to trace down all that were involved and eventually round them all up. Things got more than complicated here and we began to suspect that the HC Security Force had its fingers into more than just the Hearst Castle security concerns.

Now for some strange reason, the HC Security Force had found out that Max the FBI guy had come to learn something about the Hearst treasure and there seemed to be some type of agreement set up between them. This bothered both me and Theo but Dustin asked us to stay low key and not ask too many questions. The HC Security Force was not going to let anyone touch the treasure for now, not even the FBI. Not until certain agreements could be made. In and through all these behind the scene negotiations the secret of the treasure in the trench was still held confidential. How long this would last, heaven only knew.

During this unusual meting Colton explained in vague terms that several most interesting events had taken place just in the last month since Dustin had given over my recordings off my laptop. The FBI had done some digging into the HC Security Company and had found out that Brookstone and all his security forces were active mercenaries with connections all over the world.

This sent my mind reeling. Wow I thought, I knew there was more to the HC gang than anyone knew. Then I recalled the layout of the training facility out on the ranch. The world map in Brookstone's office with its many pins stuck into it came back to my thoughts; Theo shot me a knowing look.

Colton, saw our puzzled look and went on in the simplest terms. He seemed to be dancing around the main issues but explained that it was possible that they, the HC Security Force had somehow come into the knowledge of the treasure, either by accident or by someone in the Hearst family. This could have been Patty Hearst, back in the 1970's when she was kidnapped and became involved with the Symbionese Liberation Army (SLA). She had gone through some serious brain washing and it is possible she mentioned her grandfather William Randolph Hearst's lost treasure to someone.

This was almost funny to me. It was before my time and sounded like the story of Eliot Ness and The Untouchables hunting for Al Capone during the gangster times of the 1930's!

Now here we were, somehow being touched by strange events of the past. Most of the SLA gang members were killed in a shootout, but the rest were sent to prison. The original gang leader escaped and went into hiding, James Kilgore, an urban terrorist. He lived all these years in a middle class lifestyle hiding in a Cape Town suburb alias Charles William Pape, who became a university economics lecturer. The investigation in Cape Town of the Symbionese Liberation Army founder, James Kilgore, now 55, finally located him, but he was not yet apprehended after an FBI tip-off.

Colton looked over at me, mentally answering, yes, that tip had come by means of my computer recordings; as he made the comment that whoever set my bug into place, really knew their stuff. Of course, he was referring to good old Wally.

He went on telling us that two of the calls recorded on my computer were made to Cape Town and this put the FBI on the trail so that a long hidden terrorist had been flushed out. The HC Security Force had been making deals with James Kilgore for several years now. With all the restrictions on international banking they were exchanging art works and rare antiques for information, instead of large sums of money.

Kilgore still had connections and was able to locate and secure the exchange of various hostages for art and collectibles. Either a government agency or a large corporation would contact the HC Security Force, explain the situation and then Brookstone and his team would begin determining how they might make contact and create a plan of extraction.

 Once a plan had been made, a dialogue had been established, Brookstone, being the head honcho, would send a team with a shipment of preferred artifacts to Cape Town. After the captives were released from the pirates or cartels, the HC Security Company would then negotiate and extract their fees from the families before they released them. It was well understood that kidnapping and the taking of hostages had become a very exclusive means for groups, gangs and cartels to enrich themselves for near nothing.

In fact Max said that America just last year had paid out nearly 400 million to Mexico for the release of some American captives. The HC Security team had actually extracted a good number of those hostages. Some were released with an exchange of art and treasure while others had gained their freedom by brute force with a high cost to those who decided to play keep and steal! This treasure was being used as the means of exchange instead of going through a banking system. For most of the big cartels and rogue gangs actually had hay bale size bundles of cash stored in hidden warehouses. But moving cash was a problem for many of them and great art works and rare treasures could be sold, or used to enhance one's self-importance. Max made it known that this was pure genius at work and seemed to be taking sides with H-C Security, which seemed to be taking on the fuzzy outlines of a Robin Hood character.

This was all a hypothesis for now but a slow accumulation of facts were pointing in the direction of exchange for treasure for hostages. The facts had come from my laptop record-ings taken while it was in their office. I had given it over to Dustin to give it to Colton and they had extracted various international calls, several informative conversations, which led them to more pieces of the puzzle. All the dots were not yet connected, but it seemed as though one of the gang members a few years back, while still in prison, had bartered information about the hidden treasure to someone who was getting out of prison. This man's name was yet unknown, one of the key names yet to be discovered.

Max got up to refill his coffee cup and went on. "Some of what I am going to tell you is pure speculation, mixed in with some facts as we know them so far. The FBI thinks that this treasure story found its way to the HC Security group but was discounted until maybe they put two and two together. They must have had an idea of where it might be stashed and finally found it buried in the cove trench, proving the trickle down treasure rumor. Within a few years they realized its further potential beyond a cache of antiques, and began trading off the treasures to various weapons' dealers or negotiating with terrorists for the release of captives with treasure."

Max was slowly pacing back and forth as he talked. He would wave his coffee cup through the air to emphasize certain points. It was obvious that he was excited about this intriguing find. I was thinking that this little discovery must have made him some real points back at headquarters. He went on, "In reality, it is brilliant how they put all this together. It was working so well, until you guys, two surf bums, or well, at least one free-lance writer and a photographer, broke down on that lonely stretch and stumbled into the lost treasure of Hearst Castle."

Theo and I just sat there stunned. I was thinking of that skull and how easy it would have been for us to have disappeared if we had been caught. This was more than a story, it was unfolding to be a super Pulitzer Prize winner for Thortin and a future book deal for me.

Colton must have seen the concern scrolling across my face and said, "We have sent in a forensic team to take a closer look at that skull and dig around to see what they might find."

"Oh my gosh," Theo finally said something, "That skull, I forgot all about it!"

Dustin cut in, "When will you know more about it?"

Colton hesitated but decided to say, "We have already found out that there were three skeletons buried under that driftwood hut."

Theo jumped up running his fingers through his long hair saying, "Jason was right, Jason was right on, that punk kid knew, he really knew that something was wrong and made us get out of there."

I gestured to Theo to calm down, and asked, "Who were they and how long have they been there?"

"That is what is strange, they have been there for a long long time. But as far as who they were, we don't know, other than they were possibly sailors or from a ship's crew."

"How do you know this?" Dustin inquired.

"We found several things that indicate they came off a ship."

"Like what?" Theo asked.

"One still had a partial uniform of sorts, indicating he was an officer of some kind and he had a rusted cross around his neck with a partial name of B- Esca... etched into it. The others must have been deck hands, by various objects found in what used to be their clothes."

Suddenly, the memory of that flash picture of the old iron ship turning over in a storm came to mind. Was that a vision of the real event I wondered. Nothing like that had ever happened to me before and the coincidence of seeing a ship go down and then finding three skeletons of sailors buried on the beach was nearly inconceivable. But I kept quiet.

Then I began speculating out loud, "I'm wondering, since it looks like most of this treasure was taken off a ship, possibly the San Bella, could this have been the captain and two of his deck hands that met their fate one dark and stormy night?"

"That is a possibility, but we might not ever know, for it was so long ago," Max gave some information over about the lost freighter but it was Dustin who added the most insight to the ship that had disappeared. "From what Wally and I discovered, this coastal freighter was a service supply ship owned by the Cunard Line. It was a small two hundred ton runabout freighter built and commissioned in 1895 by the Cunard Line. It was a delivery and transport vessel specifically designed and equipped to transfer supplies to the Cunard Liners and larger freighters at their ports of call. It made frequent supply runs from Britain to Europe, to America, from Africa to Australia and to South America. It had been lost at sea in 1932 off the California coast," and here he paused.

Dustin was enjoying sharing these facts and kept looking over at Wally as if for verification, then continued. "There were no known survivors. However, rumors of the San Bella being used for smuggling and transporting contraband cargo had been suspected. Its disappearance put into motion a search, but nothing was ever found or discovered."

Wally added further insight about their research, "A connection was made with the Hearst family. They were major stock holders in the Cunard Shipping line. The last known ports of departure were several Black Sea ports, known escape routes out of Russia, Batumi in Georgia and Odessa, Ukraine, Istanbul and a small port used to supply the Vatican in Rome with special works of art. The Cunard Line had several smaller freighters like the San Bella to transport special cargo, machinery, crews for repairs and carry animals and secured freight for their more important passengers and owners."

Dustin got up while Wally was speaking and refilled his

coffee, sat back down and leaned back watching our reactions as Wally continued. "It had made hundreds of port calls according to the records. The crew were mainly Greeks and the captain was a Barnardo Escalante who must have gone down with the ship. The storm that hit the coast during that time was one of the worst ever recorded and after that storm, the San Bella was never heard of again. Strange enough, all types of debris began to wash up on shore for months afterward. It was reported that there were one or two survivors, but it was possible that old man Hearst bought them off and sent them packing."

Now Dustin took the explanation over, "Part of the story is that Hearst never reported the missing ship to his insurance even though he had interest in the Cunard Line. Apparently, whatever the freighter was delivering was either lost when it went down or was hidden away. The men who ran the cargo barge drowned that night, and the treasure must have been hidden in the roadway leading up to the highway. Then the storm had blown sand and debris over it, where it remained until it was rediscovered by the HC Security team, which had been hunting for it for years."

My curiosity went to work, "That is great information. Is there any way to trace down the two survivors by the Cunard records of employment?"

Wally spoke up, "Been searching, but ship hands and crews were often hired for one trip and few records of this was kept by the Cunard Line themselves. I am searching all of Randolph Hearst's diaries and records for any trace of those two mates, if there were really any survivors. He certainly would have wanted to know if the treasure had made it to shore. But if these two survivors did, they could have just been cooks or someone who did not know a thing about the cargo. They also could have been the people who ended up burying the three drowned men in that sand hut. We'll most likely never know the details."

"So you're saying that the HC Security guys most likely had nothing to do with the skeleton thing?" Theo asked.

"Oh no. So far we cannot find or connect them into any violence or even the illegal thing, just the removal of the treasure and the mercenary tie in," Max added.

Theo suddenly spoke out, "Hey, you're saying that the Captain of the San Bella was a Barnardo Escalante and the faded initials on the cross seem to be a B—Esc...? Sort of a match up there I would guess."

This connection by Theo made sense and there was a long silence in the room, for another piece of the puzzle came together and it was an important mystery, rather than just a Hearst junk dumping story. Colton then surmised, "It is possible that these three men had drowned in a storm and were found by the survivors and buried there together. The skull could have worked its way up to the surface and maybe the HC guards put it on the shelf to scare people away, never knowing that there were other skeletons buried a few feet down."

"Is there any way the HC gang can connect us to the FBI being informed?" Theo asked nervously.

I thought back on our visit to the Hearst Castle Ranch and the military stature of those men. They were no easy pushovers—tough, scarred and no-nonsense warrior types. I could see them as mercenaries training rebels out in the darkest jungles. It was best to keep our distance. Dustin knew of the blowing up of our van, but Max did not know the whole story, but had warned us to stay away, stay low and maybe start on the long desired surf movie. In other words, get out of town!

Max concluded, "These are no dummies here, they might suspect a connection, but if you covered your trail as you so said, I think they're going to have greater concerns than two surf bums." He slapped Theo on the shoulder and gathered his things, indicating that it was time for him to leave.

The meeting ended with the thought that our part was done. The relief came knowing that we were not going to be involved any further unless some very unusual events occurred down the line. We said our goodbyes, with Dustin's assurance that we were free, letting us know that things were not in our hands, with real professionals taking the situation in hand. As we departed, I took a second look at a vase sitting on Dustin's desk, holding some flowers and I had to shake my head. Max had been looking it over when we first came in, maybe he knew rare antiques but said nothing. For just in that one vase, if it were a Ming Dynasty vase, we might have enough to hire another round of lawyers to settle up my inheritance. I guess everyone must deal with treasure in their own way! Good old Dustin was having fun with it, for who could tell that this vase might be worth twenty thousand dollars, just sitting there with fifty cents worth of dried flowers in it.

Even though it was nice knowing we had a heavy hitter as Max in our corner, we were still not comfortable with giving out all our secrets to him or his organization. Nothing was told him of our entrance into the treasure trench or seeing the chopper landings and our own bit in tapping into this hidden treasure. For once we allowed this to be known, there would be an investigation against us and what we had taken. No doubt, our lives would then be dragged into court and most likely more lawyers from every corner would come out of the woodwork. Therefore, Max was left out of that part of our involvement and we now understood that it was best we remained silent about our taking a few items from the massive stash still hidden in the trench up in San Simian.

Besides this, for some reason both Theo and myself were left with an odd feeling about Colton. We inquired with Dustin about how he came to be friends with him. Dustin assured us that Max was a decent man and yes, he did have to wear several faces, but he was trustworthy. But for some reason I still was uneasy about anyone outside our circle knowing about our involvement in this situation. This left me uncomfortable.

I still had a heavy weight trying to gain my rightful inheritance, and to be tied up in any other legal circumstances would be way more than I could handle. Dustin knew this and reassured me that things would work out to the good if we were patient. I had to laugh, what choice did we have other than to be patient?

Chapter Eighteen

On The Road To Phoenix

Within the week I finished up two articles about the new sonic sound surfboard technology along with several new products introduced at the surf show. They were accepted and soon to be published. Theo and I invited Jason over to Theo's surf shop, and of course, he came along with one of his surf girls. Theo told him to pick out any new board he wanted.

"Wapperdom! Float me baby to the giant wave in the sky. Incredible. You're kidding!" he exclaimed enthusiastically, while doing a little jig, showing off excitedly.

Theo laughed, waved his hand towards the rows of new boards saying, "No. Because our boards were banged up and stolen, the insurance will pay for their replacement. So don't be shy about choosing something nice."

"Oh Wonko, that's great, but can I still hang with you guys when you head out for shows and contests?" he asked as his eyes scanned the boards.

"Sure, in fact we might be headed for the islands in a few months to begin that shoot and if you stay out of trouble, we might bring you along to test out some of the new boards," Theo offered him this really huge carrot which was meant to help him stay clean and free.

At the mention of Hawaii, his bikini friend moved closer to JJ and put her arm through his and smiled up at all of us.

After a few minutes of looking around, Jason nonchalantly asked, "Hey, how did the treasure thing go?"

I had been waiting for this inquiry and just answered casually, "Pure bummer event. Awh, nothing much, everything turned out to be fakes, probably dumped there after some carnival festival. It was really a bummer for us, we thought we really had something."

Theo and I left him to determine the board he wanted and went and sat down in the back room for some coffee. "Wally called this morning and said that the Tripper is ready for its maiden voyage and wants us to take it out for a few days and he wants to go with us," I spoke up between sips of the thick aromatic coffee that Theo was famous for.

"What do you suggest for a maiden voyage?" Theo asked.

"Well, since we have handed over the gems and stones to Dustin, he has begun his research on their values, and has made a suggestion. He's thinking we might head out to Phoenix to the annual three day gem show that is going to take place next week." I sipped more coffee and went on, "We might then head over to New Mexico, then cut up towards Lake Powell, cross Utah and stop off at a few rock and gem shops, then head to Vegas and Reno to visit a few other famous stone shops and then maybe up to Oregon and then down the coast to visit Thortin."

The phone rang and Theo answered it, listened and said, "Yeah, both of you come on in too. You're gonna be busy for the next few weeks," and said goodbye. Then asked me, "How long will this trip take us?"

"I'm guessing about two weeks, that would give us time to let things cool down while we get use to our new hotel on wheels."

"I'm guessing you have all intentions of taking along some of the stones we now own, right?"

"Dustin is going to send a few of the lesser valued gems along with us. He is saying that if the larger stones are rare and have been catalogued way back when, they might alert the wrong people to us, so we might casually see what a few of the smaller ones are worth. No better place than a world famous gem show."

"All is OK with me. That was Sally and her twin sister Cinder, my sales girls, asking if I wanted them in this week."

Jay, Theo's brother, had stopped over and excitedly told us that so far the items we had left him seemed to be of the Russian Czarist era. He explained in his in-depth scholarly lesson that during the Czars final reign back in the early 1900s, much of the old Russian treasures were being plundered. The revolution was brewing and people were stealing and smuggling things out of the country. Those icons seemed to be from a Russian Orthodox Church or monastery. The few statues were extremely costly and two of them were carved of alabaster. All this was too much for us; we told Jay to just continue on the research, and in time, once we found out what everything was worth, he would be our broker in these rarities.

I asked Jay if he would like to stay in my place for a few weeks and get off his floating home. "Where is it?" he asked.

"You can probably see it from your boat. I call it my castle in the sky. It is the only three story unit on the peninsula—right in the middle. You can look out one side of the apartment and see the ocean and the surf, and then look out the other side over Balboa Bay and the various boat slips."

"I often wondered who might live up there, since it's the only three story structure allowed on the peninsula." Jay accepted my offer, "I'll take it."

"Just no parties. You can use my computer to do your research and have a few of your friends over, but watch my stuff, especially my telescope please." I always tried to keep someone in my place while I was out of town, it was much easier than worrying about someone breaking in. Jay, Theo's brother, might be my answer to finding that right person from now on.

The drive to Phoenix in the next two weeks was filled with interesting developments, becoming more a working trip on wheels than a vacation get-away. Wally had us learning how everything in our new Tripper worked and what to do under certain conditions, and what not to do. I finally learned that Wally was once a specialist in a confidential government entity that dealt with special operations of which he would not say. But I suspected this is where he might have come to know Max. But he didn't say.

Wally was about seven years older than myself, and with Theo a year younger than me, we began to not only gain a greater respect for Dustin's old-time friend as a techno wizard, but we began to see him as a protector, especially once we knew he had all this, well, military ability.

As we were driving, Wally showed us how to make the best of the various systems built into the iron chariot, as we called it. The Arizona sun tested the roof imbedded solar panel charging system, and we learned the codes to operate a secondary computer system which was hidden behind the existing OS available to the ordinary user. That was in case anyone ever thought to search our databanks, they would only find the gaming and common ordinary computer programs up front.

There was a high end military police scanner, and an incredible GPS that could track anyone's cell phone in the world if you knew the number. He presented the latest smart phones to us, all set up and ready to go. He went on and on, punching buttons on several radios, a shortwave and a powerful CB. Wow, it was all fun stuff.

He made us remember the combinations to three different safes, hidden away, each having room for weapons with a good bit of cash already in them. And there was plenty more, including a full camera system that could scan the entire area, above and below the RV alerting us to any movement that should not be there.

There was one outstanding feature Wally had created that I really liked and thought it would become most useful. As you drove along, no matter where you were located, there appeared on one of the screens, a history of the city, the town or the immediate area. An example of this was when we were driving through the desert outside of Barstow California; the screen came alive with all kinds of facts. A voice would read them so a driver did not have to take his eyes off the road. This history went as far back as time permitted. It told of the explorers who discovered the area, the native history, all geological activity, and the population of humans, animals and species. This program was so detailed it told you how many beer cans were found alongside the highway in one year. It gave forth the history of any and all famous persons, events or books tied to the region, mysteries, and the potential of the area. This on-screen history changed constantly as we drove along. It presented so many interesting facts we wanted to stop at every one of them to look for ourselves. One feature was you could press a button and that particular data would be saved into a database which could later be recalled. It was tied into a GPS satellite observation system and you could zoom in on any address or object that was being spoken of or being shown. Another button brought up an up to date address book and phone list of every person in the area. Another database would search any one of those names and if there existed a record or history, we then had access to it. Half this stuff was illegal but as long as we did not abuse it, no one would ever know. I thought this "Historyonic" searcher would be most incredible driving through the Hollywood hills!

We used the satellite phone system to call up Thortin and we had him on-screen and he had us in-person, as we drove along in the Arizona desert. The bell of the San Bella article had already caused a fury of activity. His phone was ringing off the hook and people were stopping by trying to get him to narrow down where the bell had been found. One enter-prising couple had already printed up treasure maps of the coast and were selling them to incoming tourists. He said that he even got a call from the HC Security management inquiring about it. Wally warned Thortin not to say too much on the phone, for once this treasure thing heated up, his phones might be bugged. Thortin went silent over this, then laughed as though this could not happen, but I soon reminded him of our van gone BOOM! Wally came on and stressed further concerns to Thortin, and he listened.

The Tripper ran like a dream, air conditioning and all. We did get to stop at the Colorado River and go for a swim and soak in a little sun, but that was it. Even then, our task master was filling us in with codes, details and all the tricks on wheels we now owned. To tell you the truth, I let half of it go by; it was rather over whelming for my puny brain. This electronic stuff took a very well trained mind to understand. I understood that it would be a learning curve to get just a portion of it. I was still shaking my head at the smart phone in my hand.

Wally had us on the onboard computers doing research on the International Gem Show. Dustin's secretary Nadia made reservations for us at the Hamilton Inn just down the block from the show and we were well acquainted with its every detail. We now knew more about rare gems and precious stones than we needed to know, but good old Wally insisted that knowledge is power and power is protection!

Before ever entering the show, we knew many of the 400 vendors, where they were and who might be honest enough to assist us in selling a few of the stones that Dustin had sent along. Oh yeah, that was another revelation: Wally was connected, by this it was meant that somehow old Wally had various friendships scattered around in all quarters. His surprises never ended.

After check-in at the Hamilton, the first evening, all casual like, we entered the great hall of rocks and rare gems. We spent that first evening walking around among the stations, listening to various talks by gemologists, appraisers, lapidaries and professional geochemists. This was a whole different world from one I knew, but fascinating.

Theo ended up buying a few chunks of fool's gold, at least big as my fist. "What on earth are you going to do with that?" I asked.

"I got this order from the Pacific Surf Club to make a special first prize board for a contest. I was thinking that I might crush the fool's gold crystals into fine chips, adding it to the resin to give the board a First Place Gold look."

This guy Theo, was forever coming up with ideas. I guess that is why we were such close friends, two heads in the clouds. I said, "Hey, you never know, you might start a whole new golden surfboard fad."

For the next few days our conversations were filled with min-
erals, rubies, agates, sardonyx, amber, amethyst, ametrine,
apatite crystals, beryl, bloodstones, faceted citrine, diamonds,
emeralds, jasper, opal, sapphires and investments in new
rare finds. Wally advised us to take our time, look around,
ask questions and lay the ground work for our approach to
selling a few of our stones. By now, we knew this to be a test
from Wally to see what kind of savvy we might have.

By our third visit to the show we could not hold back any longer. In our investigations with various vendors, we came to like one older man named Robbie Kaamin, a dignified gemologist. We thought he was possibly from Eastern Europe who intrigued us by speaking with a twist of humorous but broken English. He stood tall, a grey haired man with an Einstein hair-do, neat in appearance but of simple dress, without the shine of a pushy over-zealous salesman, but yet he had that sophisticated professorial look to him. We had learned a little about the few stones we brought with us, but since we were not sure about their identification or value, we used our casual play-dumb approach that morning.

Mr. Robbie Kaamin stood there chewing on his pipe, carefully observing these two gazers. We were looking over his well displayed collection of various stones, when he asked, "Youngest gentlemens, what mayest I assist you likes with this days desire?"

Looking up at this frail old man, here it was again. It was strange, but something familiar began to register with me. The first thing I noticed was his long face anchored with a square jaw. His eyes were close to being almost precious stones in themselves, a deep sparkling green, a jade or emerald color. His grey, almost white hair was fluffed out like an eccentric old time violin virtuoso. "Well Sir, I want to know if you might take a look at a few of the stones we got from our grandfather."

"My great pleasant work, yes, I loves old grandfather's treasures," he answered with his broken but poetic grammar.

I shoved my hand down into my front pocket, dug around to pull out a hankerchief with five of the stones which Dustin had sorted out for us. I wanted him to think that we were totally ignorant in how to treat precious stones, so I opened the little bundle with lint and all, holding them out to him. He set his pipe aside, stepped forward, looked into my hand and then slowly plucked each stone up, one at a time. Sitting down on a high backed stool, he carefully wiped each one off with a special cloth. Then he pulled down his jeweler's scope, and we waited. We watched his facial expressions change from casual to serious and from disbelief to admiration, looking for a hint of good news. After examining each stone with his keen eye, he took his fine cloth, wiped each stone again and set them under a microscope. We saw him nod his head several times and could hear him make a grunt now and then. After examining each stone, he placed it onto an electronic scale.

He then turned to us, carefully looking us over and asked, "Wheres did you say you get these?"

"From my grandfather, he passed away a few years back and gave me these. He told me that I should set them aside until the time came when I needed some extra cash," I delivered my prepared spiel.

"Do you know where he find thems?"

I shook my head, "Nah, he was a world traveler who worked for some mining company and that's all I know." I thought to ask, "Why, is something wrong with them?"

"No, no, on other contraries, nothing be wrongs with them. Fact they be good nice stones. Plenty good they be."

Theo asked, "What are they? Are they worth anything?"

Old man Robbie Kaamin raised his jewelers scope up onto his forehead, scratched his ear and quietly said, "Yes young men, deas worth some monies." He proceeded to carefully hold up the first larger stone, about the size of an almond, saying, this is a faceted African Malaia Garnet worth good many funds." He then gently set that one aside on a thick piece of black velvet and now I could see the glow in its beauty. He then took the second stone which was more oval but still good sized and he held it between his fingers, with a glow of great pleasure spreading across his face he stated, "This is very nice, good nice, and worth mors monies. Deas one is African Orange Tanzanite, a little bit rare."

He laid the stone next to the first one then took up the third one from my hanky and shook his head a little, then almost whispered, "This one is all the best, very much treasure, call phosphophyllite." From that moment on his language cleared itself as he went on, "Phosphophyllite is one of Holy Grails, you know grail thing, only of rare gems. Very much beautiful, nearly all gem phosphophyllite in world found at Unificada mine in great mountains of Cerro Rico famous silver mining district Potosi, in place call Bolivia. The supply very much gone now to say sadly, over my life times since discover the mineral there. I do not knows who your grand-father was, but he smart man wise, know his stuffs, how pick good pieces."

We waited and finally asked, "How much?"

He turned his head this way and that way and once again examined the stone through his jewelers scope and sighed, "This one worth more than those," he gestured down to the velvet and went on, "I think this is double much more, maybe $900 because so nice. I weigh it to be 9 carets, maybe more, grand dollars!"

The last two aquamarine colored stones became the key for us when Mr. Robbie Kaamin's eyes lit up. His heavy brow seemed to get heavier as if to cloak the sparkle in his eyes until he finally looked up from his jeweler's scope to look at both Theo and myself. We stood there, somewhat bothered at his stare, thinking maybe these stones had someone's name carved into them.

But then he said with a quieter voice, "These are alexandrite stones. Alexandrite was named for Czar Alexander and is very much more special, from Czarist ruler's times. They be discovered in the early 1830s in the emerald mines near Tokovaya in the Ural Mountains, Russia. where many hurting slaves dug in mines. Dese are big much demand because they was owned by the Czar family. Alexandrite best known for color change call alexandrite effect. It sometime be green by daylight but change to red or purple-red color with change light.

Most of alexandrite still from Russia but the end deposit are almost been dug and selled or so kaaputzee, you understand kaaputzee?"

We nodded that we understood.

He was now holding the larger stone up close to his eyes, as if transfixed by its facets and went on as if we were not even there. "Some new deposit they find outside Russia to produce stones but none beautiful like Russian Alexandrite. And these be real beautiful!"

By now we were waiting for the answer we wanted, "How much valuable?" Theo managed to ask almost with the same language slant.

"Because you show respect to me, I tell you truth in this matter and please call me Robbie." Old man Kaamin became more than friendly. Looking around he leaned closer to us and said, "Dese first twos are well worth from five to six hundred dollars."

Immediately we knew he was playing games with us, Theo instantly asked, "That's all, five or six hundred dollars?"

Dustin had done his research and had given us a ball park number to keep in mind and this number did not even enter in. The old gemologist squinted a strange look at us, shook his head saying, "No young ones, dhat is being five to six hundred pers onlys ones carat!"

"Oh, that is better." Theo nodded, and asked, "How many carats are they?"

"Easy, no's problems, to weigh. One is four carats and this larger one be seven and half carats."

I quickly inserted, maybe too fast, "So you're saying that these first two stones might be worth maybe six or seven thousand dollars total?"

"Oh yes, very much so, but you must find correct buyer or you get stolden."

Theo then pointed to the third stone asking, "How about that one?"

Mr. Robbie Kaamins eyes grew bright before saying anything about the third stone, looked around first, "Dhis one is most rare, long time few people own such stones as phosphophyllite, this make me thinking, but easily worth letem says nine grand monies, you knows grands?"

We knew that these stones were worth some bucks, but were not prepared for that amount. Our surprise was noticed.

Now Theo's inquisitiveness took hold, and he asked the old

gemologist if he might take a look at the stone through the microscope. The old man was very pleased in his interest and asked him to step around the corner of the booth and look to hearts content, very much beauty there, you fall in loves. Theo was soon cooing and ahhing and I had to tell him to keep it down, he was attracting people. But he was glued to what he was seeing in the lenses. More wows and awes rose up and I thought that old man Kaamin was right, Theo was making all the sounds of a lover, ready to propose to the stone.

Now Theo was anxious to price these stones out, for it seemed that other vendors were looking over our way, "OK, now for those last two alexandrite stones, the Czar ones, what might they be worth?"

"Ah, he nodded and pushed the two alexandrite stones around on the velvet saying, "These two about same, maybe seven grands each."

"You mean that the phosphophyllite one is worth more?" I asked.

"Yes, very much so, nicer stone, not many around, hardest to finds."

I stood there almost shaking for a moment then asked, "Mr. Kaamin your saying that these five stones right here are maybe worth up to thirty thousand?"

"Oh yes, very much so worth easy that much."

We had somehow attracted a few curious onlookers, for a few other vendors had seen our exchanges and must have grown curious and probably knew that old man Kaamin would not waste his time on nothing. He saw the other vendors gathering and talking and quickly wrapped each stone in a velvet pouch and handed them back to us saying, "Go lock these up in safe place, do no other trade with bad men, call me and I come with monies as you wish, I be honest man, I pay brand new cash," and with this he handed us his card and stood back like nothing had ever happened, all serious with his pipe back in his mouth, but his eyes were aglow.

We were both hooked and elated over our good fortune, spent the rest of the afternoon wandering through the show, asking questions and doing some cross checking. We had pretty well decided to do business with old man Robbie Kaamin but wanted to see what else was out there for us. One well-arranged booth really caught our eyes. Well, it wasn't so much the booth set-up but the two women working in it, "Oh my, how did we miss that? Nice gems I must say," I joked.

Theo quickly pulled me off to the side nodding at the two ladies we had seen somewhere before. I read the name of the gem dealer, "Security Gem & Stone" was the name on a sign above the front counter. But once I read the name, I instantly knew where we had seen those pleasant looking ladies. It was the two fine secretaries at the Hearst Castle Security office. Instantly, warning bells went off, at least I thought they were warning bells.

"That's the two secretaries at Brookstone's office," I whispered in a tone of suspicion.

"You're right. Wow, this is getting stranger and stranger," Theo half mumbled as he spoke while staring through the passing crowd over at the young women.

Theo thought it was best we get out of there, but my curiosity held me in place as Theo tugged on my arm. Too late, the girls spotted us and began to excitedly wave us over. Several of their customers turned to see what all the excitement was about and it would have been stupid to have just walked away. So we hesitantly moved across the aisle and gave our surprised hellos.

No doubt about it, these were some high-class young women, but I guess they had to be, with probably a million dollars worth of gems and stones laid out under glass in the displays before them. We were dressed casual, sort of Arizona surf-bum cool-dude style, and a few eyes turned with reservation to see what creatures could have caused these two beauties to get excited. Some thought maybe we were their younger brothers, come to tell them Mom was waiting outside.

Amber was the first one to speak up while introducing herself and pointing to her associate Crystal, while she finished up with one credit card purchase. "My, my, don't you two get around," she smiled warmly then nodding towards Theo, said, "I remember you are Theo." She looked over to see how his leg was doing. At first I couldn't figure out what she was doing, but then she quietly laughed saying, "Looks like your leg healed up rather nice and so quick, humm."

I felt like kicking Theo to maybe get him to rub the leg or do something but he just stood there, mesmerized by this gorgeous green-eyed long-haired brunette, just his type of dream-come-true woman.

Then she pointed at my eye and said, "Looks like your purple walnut shaped eye seems to have dwindled down to a brown almond."

I raised my fingers up to my eye, actually trying to hide my embarrassment while Theo laughed, getting even with me for making him into a cripple in front of these lovelies.

The other dazzling gorgeous creature came over and held out her hand saying, "Hi guys, I am Crystal. Nice seeing you

again. Hope this time it will be under better circumstances."
She said this as if our meeting here was not just going to be
over-the-counter business, but maybe more. Crystal was tall
and slim, well tanned but for sure she was no surf bunny.
These girls were sparkling gems in themselves, both with the
same emerald-green eyes and nice long hair, and I noticed
some distinct similarities in their gestures and movements.

"For sure these are better circumstances. We were sort of
under unusual pressure the last time we saw you—like
military intimidation," Theo managed to speak up, while
chuckling in mangled stupidity.

"Oh, you mean like nearly getting torn apart by The Cat?"

"That was good for starters, and I hope more than enough," I
replied.

Both of them smiled, nodding their agreement. A few
viewers stopped by to take a look, and I could not say if it
was to see the stones under glass, or the two gems behind the
counter. It was hard not to look; they were dressed to kill,
and many eyes fell victim that day to the weapons of real
women. I finally managed to point out one familiar stone
under the glass, to distract my eyes and get Theo's attention
to something other than warm inviting smiles. I said, "Nice
size emeralds there. They from Brazil?"

Amber had been leaning over, looking down at what I had
pointed to. With a humorous valley girl twang, she laughed
and said, "No dear, I am and all my parts are from San Luis
Obispo."

I looked up embarrassed, thinking that she thought I had
made some off the wall comment about certain parts of her
body displayed above the gems, but we both laughed. I went
on trying to be cool and sophisticated, "Oh, look at those

alexandrite stones, they are beauties!" This time I made sure I pointed off to one side.

This surprised her a little, that I knew what they were called.

They were about half the size of the one I had in my pocket but asked her, "What kind of a price you got on those?"

"Oh, so you know about this gem, Luke? They are a bit expensive," she warned me off, assuming that we were truly two beach bums looking for big surf in all the wrong places.

Immediately I regained my senses and went into my mister cool mode, speaking like I was a professor of gemology, "Sure that is Chrysoberyl, a rare gem first found in Russia in the 1800s in the slave mines of the Ural Mountains, and named after Czar Alexander. In fact the stones were made famous by the Czar's family, and they turn a really neat reddish purple color in different lighting." I only repeated what good old Robbie had told us a short time back, hoping I got it right.

She was impressed, "You really know your stuff Mr. Mitchner."

This took me back, how could she... I thought, but she reached out and touched my cheek with her soft warm hand, stopping all my thought processes. Her soft voice was teasing me while her green eyes were starting fires within my tender dry heart, "Luke, I am the tech that went through your computer while it was with us. Remember back at the HC compound, with Brookstone?"

I mumbled out, "How could I possibly forget."

I could not quite put this marvelous hunk of curved flesh together with a computer geek, but she went on, "I read all your articles, your interviews and also tried to read your voided emails, strange there, umm. I will say that I was rather intrigued and also impressed. You guys really get around."

"Being a free-lance writer, I do find myself getting mixed up in all sorts of things. And seeing places that offer interesting perspectives." I spoke this to her with our faces about a foot apart. Her eyes, those dang eyes, there had to be precious stones transplanted into her orbs; they glimmered and shined and I was already lost in their facets. In that moment, we were on a lonely tropical beach, under the moonlight with a perfect scent and the perfect breeze, the feeling of kissing each other loaded into Cupid's bow. Then Theo's voice broke in like a storm on the beach, asking about rotted seaweed cluttering the sands, as far as I was concerned.

Then I heard Crystal laugh back to Theo, something about the San Bella ship bell." She laughed saying, "Maybe I better leave that subject off the board today."

Paradise evaporated for me as reality came back full force, in the off-shore winds of real life. I was baffled now, but had to play dumb cool stupid. I asked, "Amber, you still have not told me how much those alexandrite stones are."

"You mean those chrysoberyl stones there?" She finally broke the spell by pointing down to the velvet pouch they sat in.

"Yeah, sure, yeah how much might they be?"

Again, it was almost a game going on here like the one back at Brookstone's office, but she unlocked the case and lifted out the velvet pouch. She stepped over to a scale to show me the carat size of each stone. Theo was still running wild with Crystal as the trade show pavilion began to slowly empty. Amber said that they were an average of 3 carets each, and each caret would be about $700. I shook my head saying, "I like them, but because they are smaller I will give $400, tops."

"Luke, you do know that I am saying that they are $700 per caret? Not per stone."

"Let me see one of them." She pinched out the nicer one and placed it into my open palm. I held it up to the light and watched the colors change, just as old Robbie Kaamin had said. "I'll give you $450 per caret."

She was taken aback, and now Crystal had stepped over with Theo, moving over to me. Crystal looked at me, shot a glance over to Amber and shrugged her shoulders as if to say, this is your deal honey.

Within a twinkling of an eye, Amber went into her business mode, "OK Luke, lets make it $500 per caret and we'll call it a deal," she smiled reluctantly as if to bring this kid bartering stuff to an end and get rid of us.

"Great, I'll take all three of them!"

Now she was taken aback a little but was soon composed, realizing that she had a possible serious buyer at hand.

Fine. Smart buy there," Crystal stepped in, taking the three stones and setting them into the velvet pouch, saying, "How do you want to pay for them?"

The way Crystal said this was as if this would be the clincher, knowing if these two shabby surf bums would have any such funds. But I played it cool, real casual like, took out my shabby worn wallet and handed over my credit card. Amber saw my old wallet and was now taking a double look at me, with conflict of interest scrolled across her face, most likely wondering if my purchase would clear. Ah-ha, it went through without a hitch, just under $4500. I was rather surprised myself but it felt good, Oh so good to have monies in the bank.

The show was shutting down and while Crystal handed over the velvet pouch she said, "Hey you guys, we're having a few of our vendor friends over to our suite tonight for dinner and fun. Why don't you come on by, around eight this evening?"

Amber joined in saying, "Hey, that is a good idea, please come on over. It might be an interesting night, you know, rubbing shoulders with real gemologists, and I do not mean stone freaks," and her smile dazzled like a sunbeam through clouds.

I looked at Theo and we nodded our acceptance while Crystal handed over her business card with the hotel and suite number on the back.

We stood there for a moment as the two female gems began to close up shop. Theo was looking down at the card and seemed to be reluctant about something but he very carefully cleared his throat, looked up and inquired, "I'm curious, you know, well, business and all, are those your real names?"

Both of them looked at us and with gracious smiles and a tiny laugh from Amber, Crystal said, "It's a family thing."

We turned and walked away not knowing exactly what this meant but hey, those two could be named after trees and it would have been fine with us.

Theo was still shaking his head and asked one of the most profound questions I have ever heard him ask. "Why do you think God had to put so many curves on a woman?"

I burst out laughing at this preposterous question. But was caught up in his thoughts, and began pondering the idea and gave my answer, "Because, well, they were made like rare flowers, exquisite, and, the curves were so that man would take notice of them, like bees to pollen."

I was not sure what to say at this point, but went on, "A colorful flower, full of designs can call a bee from a mile away, not only by beauty but by scent too."

"I don't know about that but they got my stinger up, searching for the pollen no doubt!"

"Come on Theo, this is business tonight and nothing else."

"Yeah, honey business!

Things had moved along rather fast and Theo as usual was worried. Why in the heck had I bought those stones? Secretly, I myself was going over what the heck had happened back there. Theo was making the wise crack accusations that I had gone stupid under the influence of the Amber Venus Fly Trap creature. I retorted that I had to do something before all his blood had rushed out of his head. He was about to faint over sweet Crystal, fall down and get stuck in thick honey!

We were bantering back and forth about whom, what and why, when Wally caught up with us and with some irritation told us that he had to cut his adventure short. Dustin had called him back, letting him know that someone had cracked their way into their computers and it was expedient that he return. I knew this to be puzzling and serious, for it would take someone very savvy to get past Wally's firewalls and security set ups.

We picked up his things at the room and took him to the airport, all the while bombarding him with questions about what might be going on. He could not say but did make some internet connections through our onboard systems, making sure that our systems had not been compromised.

"Wally, could this have anything to do with the Hearst Castle Security gang?" I asked.

"It could, but we won't know anything until I get into the programs. I have so many chase and hunt programs in my system that there is not much that can hide from me." His voice did have that puzzled twist in it as he expressed further concerns, "I'll tell you one thing, it's got to be a real high end tech to hack into our systems; no ordinary kid could ever do this. And whoever did get in, will no longer be a happy hacker. When I'm done with them, they'll wish they never messed with me!"

We saw him off with time to spare. We asked him to stay in touch and expressed our concerns about not being dragged deeper into the on-going mystery. He understood our worries and assured us that everything would be OK. Don't worry, he smiled his reassurance through his bushy mustache. We waved him off as he boarded and then his plane lifted up, departing out of the valley of the sun, turning into the colorful western sunset, headed back to California.

Our trip had just begun. And for some reason, I had just spent a small fortune, and for what? To impress some girl, to show off? I thought that my purchase would pay off in time, after all, didn't we have a pending sale of $30,000 waiting for us with only a phone call. With this thought, I asked Theo if we should go ahead and make the deal with old man Robbie Kaamin tonight, and hit the road tomorrow. We decided to give him a call and invited him over to our room. I told him that we'd like to settle up with cash in fifties and twenties only, no hundreds.

Wally had explained this lower denomination thing to us. 100 dollar bills were the most counterfeited. Many places would not accept them and it was best for us to ask for 50's and 20's no matter how much trouble it was, unless you wanted a cashiers check. A large check was also a road to troubles, for a deposited check leaves a path a mile wide and we did not want a trail leading back to us. So cash it was. We would push for just a bit more, but negotiations were to be finalized when old man Kaamin would arrive. Wally had been pleased with our hooking up with Robbie Kaamin, he knew of his reputation and said that we could trust him up to a point, but we would have to learn the rest on our own.

We parked the Tripper right where we could keep an eye on it from our room. We showered, changed and sat back for a nice hour's wait until old Robbie Kaamin was supposed to show up. An hour into our R and R, rest and room service, with a variety of snacks and drinks, the phone rang. It was Kaamin and we invited him up to the room. We were nervous and really did not know what to expect. Never had we done deals like this before, no less negotiate for thousands of dollars in cash.

Soon a knock came quietly. Rising off my bed I crossed the room to open the door. I asked who it might be. It was Robbie; I undid the chain pulled back the slide bolt and opened the door. There he was, old man Robbie Kaamin standing there with a serious but pleasing smile fixed on his face, with a satchel tucked under his left arm. However, right behind him stood, or should I say hovered, a very large figure. Instantly I became a little concerned, to say the least, not expecting a second person. Could it be some thief who had followed Robbie and now was going to burst in and rob all of us? All this was racing through my mind when old man Kaamin saw the concerned look on my face. Immediately he pointed over his shoulder with his thumb and said, "This my guard and security man Jaden, and he is also my youngest of sons."

With some hesitation I opened the door all the way and waved them in. Now this dual visit was unexpected, but Robbie asked to sit down at the table and things just moved along, seemedly OK. However, something about this guy

Jaden was rather strange; there seemed to be a familiarity to him. His bulk was one thing, solid—I would say massive. No doubt he was some kind of body guard, at least. He wore sun glasses and it was obvious that he was armed. He seemed to make sure we noticed the bulge on his side as he stood back and watched. Besides this, there was still something that was bugging me about him, but Robbie cleared his throat, calling my attention back to him while saying, "You does understands that I no go around towns carrying so big numbers of cash without someone with me, I hopes you understands, I ams a little mans."

"Sure," we nodded hesitantly and got to the business at hand.

Within a few moments old man Kaamin was reexamining the stones and our negotiations began. Of course we were new to all this but Dustin had given us some pointers and we had at least narrowed the exchange down earlier at the show. After examinations of some of the other stones at the show and our purchase of the three Alexandrites, hey, we knew that we had some really nice stones. Old Robbie got comfortable as he sat back and opened the first round with 28 thousand. Theo started coughing, not from the price being too low but from the sheer mention of 28 thousand dollars. I shook my head saying, "Nah, we got to start at least 32, that is what you mentioned at the show."

His eyebrows shot up. "Start there you thinks, you mean yous want to go ups than that?" he sternly looked at me while speaking.

"Well sure, if you can go down from 30, I can surely go up from there, isn't that fair?"

He smiled, and nodded his head, knowing that we were not going to give ground, but asked, "Young mans, so whats you asking for in final end?"

"I think 32 would just do us right."

His bony hand went to his mouth, he coughed a little and with a smile said, "32 is good price for yous, but not so good for me, I go up to 30 from 28 and that is all cash, just like yous wanted," he padded the satchel and folded his hands as though the negotiations were over.

I looked over at Theo, hoping he would not cave in at the first go round as I spoke, "What you think Theo, does this meet your expectations?"

He stuttered out his words, "Sur-rre, ah, ah, well that sounds good enough for me, sure-ah yes."

I could have kicked him because I felt we could have at least gotten another grand. But with Theo's too quick of an answer, I lost fifty percent of my negotiation powers of trade. I had big plans for a real Eastern European exchange. I had seen those Arabs and Armenians, shake their fists, click their tongues, spit on the ground and jabber wearisome epitaphs to one another over a bag of raisins before a five dollar deal was ever struck. I didn't even get to click my tongue or spit on the floor, when my hopes were dashed as I realized it was all over in a few moments. I saw that old man Robbie knew it too. He sat there with a great smile across his face, his eyes twinkling with the evening lights.

"OK, OK. Let it be a done deal," I dragged my acceptance out in some disappointment.

Old man Kaamin extended his bony hand and we shook on the deal. He proceeded to close up the velvet pouch which held the five stones, but when he went to put it away, I reached out and placed my hand over his, remembering that

Wally said we could trust him, only up to a point. I said, "Excuse me, but maybe you should lay out the cash here first."

"Oh," he shot me a puzzled look saying, "You no trust me now?"

His son Jaden moved his hand a tiny bit closer to his belt line but said nothing. I knew we were being intimidated but there was nothing I could do about it, other than toss out a tiny enticement.

I did not know exactly what to answer but finally I said, "You know Mister Kaamin, this is our first deal and I do trust you or we would not have invited you here to our room. We carry no weapon, we have no guard, but we do not want to be put in any disadvantage with you holding all the cards—or should I say, stones and money too."

I paused and looked over at his son standing like a giant redwood, "I would like to cement our friendship with a good solid deal, starting with trusting each other, for these are only a few of my grandfather's gems and the others in his collection make these look like pigeon droppings."

Immediately I knew I played the first beautiful note to a good opera. "You wise young man, I like more to business with you, you may trust me good, I no do you wrong," and with this he left the pouch in front of me and asked Jaden to bring over the money. Jaden reached down, pulled back his shirt and lifted out a thick flat pouch. This scared the crap out of us, we thought for sure it was a gun to cement the deal. With a huge grin on his face, he strolled over and laid the pouch on the table in front of his father. Old Robbie was almost laughing at our surprise, and pulled out thick well-bound bundles of beautiful green American cash.

It seemed to take longer to count out the monies in twenties and fifties than the deal took to make. But it was all there, thirty big ones and now we really got nervous.

I wanted to seal the deal without knowing what to do. But sometimes genius comes flying off its mountain and swoops down to kiss your thoughts. Yes, that's good, I thought of something—pulled out one of the smaller Alexandrite stones and held it out to old man Robbie, "Here my friend, here is a present for you."

He looked at me, trying to discern my motives, then his eyes went to the stone between my finger tips, not quite sure what to do. However, I smiled and reached over, took his right hand and pressed the stone into his palm, saying "Take it!"

He took the stone up with his fingers, putting it into the light from the windows. Holding the stone, again he examined it as if to make sure it was not some chunk of glass.

"Very nice, very nice, thank yus much. You very very smart boy!" all the while I could see that he was trying to suppress a mysterious grin of delight quivering under his skin. I knew that he knew more than his smile was revealing. I smiled back.

I looked over at Jaden and motioned him over, he moved up hesitantly and then I took a second stone out of my shirt pocket and handed it over to Jaden, the big bad body guard. He stood there not knowing what to do but Robbie nodded his OK, "Son, you knows, take while they givening but always run when they is hitting! This be bary nice bribe for us dis day."

We all laughed and stood up and said our goodbyes and that we would be in touch along the way.

I would guess that old man Robbie Kaamin and his son Jaden left our room with a very different opinion about us two stupid looking surf bums.

"Wow, you're something else Luke. How could you just give away those two stones like that?"

"It was not easy but I got a feeling that the little gift was worth more than just a truck load of cement!"

"Where did you learn how to do that kind of stuff?" Theo was standing at the window looking down at the Tripper while he asked.

"Well Theo, you got to remember, I've been around a lot in my freelance work. Sometimes you got to take that extra step, maybe let others think you're backing down and giving in, but in the long run, things work out better for you."

"Yeah, but that was like, three thousand dollars you gave away!"

"Not really. Remember, just a few weeks back we were sitting in a broken down van stranded on a desolate beach, nearly broke. Right now we are in a nice hotel, with a pile of money sitting right here," I pointed to the pile of cash. "So what is three thousand dollars in the light of bigger things?"

Theo looked over at me and said, "You know Mr. Luke Mitchner, I think your gonna go places, maybe take me along too!"

I patted him on the back a little roughly and said, "You are welcome. But you'd better be ready to hang on for the ride." With this thought, we headed out for our evening's adventure with those two precious looking gems.

We locked up the cash in one of the Tripper's three safes. But we were taken aback to find several specialty items waiting there. Wally had placed a compact stun gun, along with a high powered pellet pistol inside the first easy-to-find safe. I wondered what might be in the other safes and what the heck Wally had in mind. If anything did happen with a need for some protection, these little fire and pellet enforcers could scare troubles away. At least we didn't have to worry about permits.

We pulled out and drove across town to the Hilton, but before we parked, I drove around the area, reconnoitering. Theo asked me what the heck I was doing going around in circles. I explained to him that it is always best to know what's going on around you, to prepare for the unexpected. I added, "I learned that in the Eagle Scouts, and my skills were developed the hard way, through experience."

We located a space for the van next to the hotel, set all the switches and pushed several buttons as well as we could remember, and made our way up to the suite. Of course we had dressed for the occasion with clean Levis and wild Hawaiian shirts, after all, they did say casual.

Upon our entry a brute of a guard approached, asking if he might help us. I said we were headed up to suite 77, as guests of… I turned to Theo, "What were Amber and Crystal's last names?"

"I don't know, they never said."

The guard looked us over, "You're saying that you're invited to suite 77 and you don't know who invited you?"

I explained that we had been to the gem show and had been invited by the security gem sales people for a get together tonight with other vendors; the two sales associates had invited us. He hesitated and asked if he might announce our arrival and took up his house phone. In the mean time he was looking us over like we were some clowns who had just broken into the Goodwill shop and made off with...well, at least some clean clothes.

He finally nodded and pointed out the elevators and watched us walk away. I noticed that everyone was dressed in suits and ties, and wow! the ladies were all decked out with jewels enough to have their own gem show. Theo started getting nervous as we stepped into the elevator and pressed the button for the top floor. As we began the assent, he said, "What the heck have we gotten ourselves into, Luke?"

"What do you mean? It was you who was drooling over that Crystal jewel this afternoon."

"Ahh, come on, I was only looking at that incredible necklace she was wearing."

"Sure, I saw you growing faint as you stood there dumbified, divinely wondering about heavenly curves," I was laughing out loud when the elevator stopped and the door slid open. Thick rich and very plush royal blue carpet stretched out across a waiting area as large as my apartment. We were in a foyer area walled by ceiling to floor windows revealing city lights flickering below. The nicely carved door to room 77 was set back on our left with two ornate palms growing up from heavy cement planters. Looking around, I poked Theo in the ribs telling him to look around and take in the area.

"What for?" he asked.

"Because, already we are on camera. Smile for the viewers."

"You're kidding me!"

"No my friend, this is a high class place, and I think we are a little under-dressed for the occasion, if you look closely, you'll see the cameras following us. But don't look, be cool, no big deal," I reached for the doorbell to the suite.

We heard the concerto from Beethoven's seventh symphony sounding our arrival. Soon what turned out to be a sharply dressed butler answered the door. Again, we got the stare of "No we don't need any room service and no we did not order any pizza!"

I finally spoke up with a tinge of bravado in my voice, "James, please take us to your leader!"

This butler man, whoever he was, turned white then red, and I knew my off the wall remark had rung his bell. No doubt, this was not the smartest thing to open our new experience with, but shortly a voice came from the background, drifting over his shoulder saying, "Dickson, let our new friends in." It was Amber for sure, and James, I mean Dickson, stepped aside for our entry.

All I can say from this point on, is we felt like two Jonahs being swallowed up by a great fish. From the crossing of that threshold we were overwhelmed, and then enveloped with what I can only describe as uncertain astonishment. And… the night would become one of those life-time memories, carved or etched onto our minds.

The huge open room was nearly encircled with glass displaying the city below. The room was lit low with mood lights, and soft quiet music flowed through what had to be enough speakers to supply all the customers for Radio City for a year, yet I could hear ice clinking in glasses. As we stood there, pondering our entrance, it was Crystal the lovely jewel of a female human, who came out of a secondary room and greeted us with one of those smooth flowing voices bathed and overflowing in rare perfumes. I could feel the quicksand slowly rising up around us.

"Oh how wonderful it is to see you guys again. Thanks so much for coming by," she stepped in between me and Theo, putting her arms through ours, and walked us into one of the most mind boggling and stupefying experiences I have ever come to know. With all grace she guided us, leading us into the incredible space. The room alone was all consuming, intimidating: way out of our class. Right there, the trap doors slammed shut. Right on my mind!

The first thing we came to notice was that our two lovelies were dressed very conservatively. High-necked, near calf-length dresses, long sleeves, no cleavage whatsoever and the jewelry they did wear was nothing equal to the gems they had on display at the show. All this was rather formal, something much different from the displaying of themselves at the show. But why? I wondered…it had to be business!

I thought we had been astonished at our entry at the front door, but ohmygosh, I was really shaken, rocked back, and made speechless at what we saw next.

There, and I mean right there in front of us, sitting calmly in one of the larger luxurious chairs was none other than Bobby Brookstone! I had to look twice to make sure, glass eye and all. It was him alright!

To say the least, both Theo and I were stopped dead in our tracks. But what really took the cake was that Jaden, the watch dog for Robbie Kaamin was sitting across from him and Jaden was smiling so big, I thought that his face was going to split open and fall in half. The only thing we could hear at this time was silence mixed with soft music along with the city traffic far below, and the imaginary theme to 'Another World' if there was such a theme. No one said a word, and I must say that I was speechless, dumbfounded— and extremely disturbed.

I could not put it together, everything seemed like a puzzle that had just come apart when in reality it was supposed to be completed. I thought that I had it together until this moment. The realization of things being so much more complex and greater than one knows, not only weighed on my heart but humbled me before Greater Powers. Things were not supposed to be like this, at least that was what I been taught by past lessons. The trap became one of those tiny bamboo cages that a prisoner was forced to squat in for the rest of his life. Certainly, we had just been reduced down into one, specifically designed and prepared for us.

Finally, after what seemed to be the iceberg that sank the Titanic melted, Brookstone without any unusual expression and totally poised, lifted up his drink and said, "Gentlemen, gentlemen, we meet again. How interesting."

Theo slowly moved up behind me as if for protection, while I gathered my thoughts, my cool, and my scrabbled brains. Somehow I managed to utter, for I don't remember if anything I said made any sense that anyone understood, and I was hot under the collar, even though I wasn't wearing one. My brown walnut eye, as Brookstone had called it, began to throb. "Most interesting. Very intriguing and what the hell is going on here?"

Our two lovely sales ladies broke out into laughter as if we were two comedians dressed up in one donkey suit, and had just told the best joke of the year. And that is how we felt. Crystal herself helped us out of our stupor, or one might say our donkey suit, by sitting us down next to her and Amber. Dickson came in carrying a tray of what looked to be champagne and set it down on the glass table in front of us. Crystal carefully reached out and handed both Theo and myself a glass of bubbly and lifted her own up saying, "A toast to new experiences and long lasting friendships!"

Both Theo and I were not drinkers but in this case we both needed some type of medication. I dared not ask for aspirin to help us through this fog of a night. Theo had to do it, how he comes up with this stuff I'll never know, but he casually held up his champagne and asked, "Is this stuff organic?" A ton of rock hard silence fell upon the group, but when it shattered into incredible laughter, the tension turned to sand.

The shocks were not over. Soon the seventh concerto sang out and Dickson went to the door. Without any inquiry, he moved aside for two new guests. I gulped down the rest of my bubbly and sank into the cushions as far as I could. It was no less than the old man, Robbie Kaamin himself. But what almost gave me a heart attack was that in with him walked Max Colton!

Theo actually began to shake a little in confusion or maybe delusion, while his champagne glass swished the beverage over the edge onto his pants. All I could say was "Fantastic, this is the most fun I have ever had. Now, do you have any more earth shaking modifications to our lives?"

Everyone was laughing by now when old man Robbie Kaamin came over to us, waving his hand as though he was saying 'No big deal.' Then he lowered his frail body into another large cushioned recliner, reached over for a glass of champagne and asked us, "Well, Mr. Mitchner and Mr. Vontempski have you met all my family yet?"

Suddenly a few of the chunks, I would normally think of as pieces, but not this time, fell into place. I looked around. Sure, Jaden had reminded me of someone, and now I knew, he looked like Brookstone! And now I saw some resemblance in Crystal's face, and she looked somewhat like Robbie Kaamin, and a bit like Amber too. Now I knew for sure that her womanly charms had distracted me from really seeing her for who she was.

But that was not all. Robbie Kaamin was the father of this crew. These were only a few of his children, as he said earlier. Jaden was only one of his sons, and then there was Bobby or Brookstone, Crystal and Amber who were twins. They were not identical but now I could see the sister similarity. I shook my head laughing, finally realizing the name game here; Kaamin was a Russian or Ukrainian word or name meaning stone. Then all his children so far were named along the lines of gems or stones, but even lovely Amber was precious in more than name. However, I remembered that pieces of amber were famous for having things embedded into them, such as insects, spiders and even butterflies.

Then old man Kaamin introduced Max as a good friend, a new gem and stone vendor, and the fun was just beginning. Max stepped right over and took my hand. It was not an ordinary hand shake, he put feeling into it so that I could tell he was concerned about something and was relaying his feelings into that hand shake. During this introduction, I could see that Max nearly lost his composure on seeing me and Theo sitting there with this family. I knew he was genuinely surprised and I stared at him as though he were a traitor to our cause. I wondered if Dustin knew he was somehow tied into this strange, unusual-functioning family. I was puzzled over the introduction of Colton as a gem and stone vendor. Even though there was a lot of laughter and good humored bantering around the room I caught a look of desperation in Max's eyes. I actually saw a slight but nearly unperceivable shake of his head at me, not to say anything about him being a Fed or that we knew one another. I don't know how I got this message but somehow his body language along with his warning eyes managed to communicate that he was just what Kaamin said he was, a gem vendor. But for sure, we knew that he was just what Dustin said: "A man of many faces."

Within those introductory moments, a whole new layer of strangeness was added to our adventure. As the girls exchanged words with whom we now knew to be their father, I whispered to Theo not to say anything about Max or that we knew him. Whatever was going down here, it was evident that we had a part in it, or at least a trump card to use if we needed it. I had to change the tension of the moment and decided to create a tiny diversion. I ran my fingers through my hair as if I were baffled and could not take this any longer. I stood up and began to pace along the glass wall, "OK, now, you have had your fun. Could someone please tell us what we have gotten ourselves into, and are we going to be allowed to live?"

Everyone burst out in laughter. Then old man Robbie Kaamin began to speak but stopped, he waved over to Brookstone, "Bobby here could probably put it in simpler terms."

Brookstone sipped his drink, shook his head a little and interjected, "Mr. Luke Mitchner and Theodore Vontempski, the next time your van needs maintenance, we advise you to take the time and funds to get it done. You two beach bums have stumbled into something much deeper than we can tell you." He paused, "As for now, we don't know how you're going to find a way out."

I took this as a serious threat, looked over at the girls as if to say, thanks a lot for such a wonderful invitation. I finally answered, with a bit of bravado and shooting a quick look over at Max. "Oh please, I have been around enough to know that there are things that seem too deep for some, but not for all."

The next hour was a Pulitzer Prize winning story. It was true, Robbie Kaamin, whose name translated out to be Stone in Ukrainian, was the father of Bobby and Jaden. Amber and Crystal were his twin daughters and there were three more sons yet to meet. Yes, Bobby or should I say Brookstone which name better fit him in my opinion, Brookstone was the name of the village in the Ukraine they escaped from. His brothers were what we would call mercenaries and they did run a real business for the Hearsts, known as the Hearst Castle, HC, Security Service.

The story of the Hearst's lost treasure in the smugglers' cove was not fully explained, other than they had spent years hunting for it. The knowledge of the treasure was given to them by none other than Charles William Pape, better known to the FBI as James Kilgore, recently captured in Cape Town, South Africa. He was the founder of the Symbionese Liberation Army or the SLA. He had come to learn about the sinking of the San Bella and the lost treasure through Patty Hearst in the 70's. Suddenly the craziest thought shot through my mind—I saw Dickson's strange look when I had called him James. Humm, James? I recalled his reaction and how it was out of line for such a simple comment. I wondered but dare not ask, could this be James Kilgore? Could it be that for some reason he was being hidden inside this crazy family?

This called for more liquid aspirin, and Dickson, or should I think James, as if read my mind, brought out another tray of bubbly. Brookstone went on filling in some of the details. I pondered if he no longer cared if we knew any details, for we were not going to live to tell anyone.

They, the Hearst Castle Security Service, had arranged various connections between covert groups in different parts of the world. Over the years they developed various connections, making deals through their company which became a channel into areas that no one else could touch; or better said Black Opt procedures! They would trade information and handle sensitive negotiations for governmental agencies and others who he did not mention.

Ransoms and exchanges of money and supplies along with art treasures would be transferred for the release of prisoners, once they had located any hostage's held captive. The CIA and the FBI were well aware of the HC Security team and had actually used them on many different occasions. They were not so much violent killers but more or less well trained and well provisioned negotiators. They had many underground connections and had proved themselves to be a useful team for hunting up or down divergent groups, and had already extracted a good number of important people out of jams and jails in distant lands. They were the legal security arm for the Hearst Castle and the surrounding area, but the treasure was a secret bank for their latest covert operations.

From what I could glean. the government was aware of their connections, but did not know much about the treasured art works that they were working with. The government thought they were using some of the Hearst's stored away, lesser works of art or some of the treasure hold from the castle itself. That was one of the main reasons we had to be either silent or—silenced, I thought.

I had to string many of the loose ends together but after the basic story was told, Theo asked about the skull and the skeletons under the sand. Max said that this was still a mystery, the bone doctors were looking into it. But again, this had to be kept secret, for if anyone heard of skeletons out on that beach, a million sightseers would be crawling all over the place—something they did not want.

Brookstone began to explain how we tossed a monkey wrench into the picture by digging up the San Bella bell. The whole stinking country was now swarming over the San Simeon coastline and they had to have guards literally camp out on the north point of the Hearst cove watching day and night. They had been talking with Thortin and were claiming that the bell was a fake and had been tossed into the dump site years back because it was a fake. His story had only caused a ton of so-called treasure hunters to be trampling over everyone's property.

I asked, "Hey, you mean there is not going to be any Pulitzer Prize for Thortin's story of the year now?"

"No story and no prize and for you, there is not going to be any book nor even a word about this situation. We hope you understand this…right?"

My mind zoomed in on all the surrounding desert that stretched out beyond Phoenix, seeing Theo and myself buried in a shallow grave under a prickly pear cactus. "Oh really now," I looked at Brookstone with as much rebellion in me as possible. I saw the scars on his neck stand out a little in the low light as he sat up, leaned towards me and said, "We know you got your hands on some of the treasure, how much, we don't know." He reached out with an open palm and showed us the five stones we had just sold to his father. He went on, "This is proof that you got your hands on some of it, and unless you want us to come looking for it, I think you would be wise to just enjoy the fruits of your adventure, rather than tell a story that might have the United States Government crawling up your butts and on your backs, day and night."

Theo gulped and I went silent, voluntarily crawling into that bamboo cage, pushing down into a suppression chamber. This was not working out like I thought it was going to. I shot a dirty look over to our sweetheart gems who we had been wheeling and dealing with, but they were impervious to our plight at that moment.

Brookstone turned to Max and said, "Tell them Max."

Max Colton was cool about the whole thing saying, "I speak from experience. There was a time when the long arm of the government reached out and shook my tree; it was not a fun time. I am sure that our new friends are not stupid, but if they want the Department of Revenue, the FBI, and maybe even the three other alphabet brothers on their backs, I got the feeling they're gonna be really smart about this whole matter. Especially when the Hearst Castle Security group is dealing with terrorists and strange amounts of monies coming in, right boys?"

Before Max was done speaking, Theo was nodding his head, yes, yes and yes!

I felt like smacking Theo for his instant agreement. This explanation was more a threat than an insight. I could not let this go without poking it a little. "Max, could you tell us what your relationship is with the Kaamin family?"

He was calm about answering, for he knew that we had managed to get the message of not revealing his Fed status. This was a tiny bit of assurance that there was some hope for us. "I am their financial consultant and advise them in gem sales. I also help negotiate some of their larger sales." He looked around to make sure he was not revealing too much and went on, "I also attend some of the international shows in Europe and in the Asian countries and sell off some of the higher end product they own."

Somehow a piece of the puzzle was missing. Max did not mention the illegals or the drugs; now wasn't this getting interesting. I sat up and cast out our last hope, "So you want to know how we got hold of a tiny bit of treasure?"

"That would be nice," Brookstone nodded.

I thought this over. How much should I tell? I could just say that we dug up those stones or found a small box of them buried down in the sand and leave it at that. However, somehow I wanted to let this gang, and that is what I was now considering them, to know that we knew a little bit more than they suspected. After all, knowledge is power. But did I want to divulge all of our most important knowledge? No, not at this time I determined.

"That earthquake must have shaken up the cove trench and forced a few things to the surface. We didn't find any great treasure as you speak of; we only found a few things that were buried in the mound below the trench gully area. This is where the gems came from. We do have a few more but that is it!"

Brookstone just sat there waiting for more; somehow he

knew there was more to all this than we were telling. He had a good sense about hidden matters, but I thought to toss him a hot coal to deflect his inquiry. I would start with a serious accusation, "Why would you try killing us by blowing up our van?"

Now the room went silent, the girls sat up and everyone was looking around at each other, trying to figure out what I had just said. Brookstone asked, "What the hell you talking about Mitchner?"

"Come on now, don't play dumb, you mean that you don't know that our van was blown to smithereens shortly after leaving your compound, on the day we came for our boards?"

"That was your van that blew up over at the state park?"

"Sure was. The same," I replied, while trying to figure how dumb they thought we were.

Brookstone looked over at Crystal, "What do you know about this?"

"Bob, we heard about it, just like you. It was reported that a van had blown up because of a butane leak, and the story warned every traveler to check their tanks for leaks. That was it Bob; we did not make the connection."

You could see the gears spinning in Brookstone's brain, even old man Kaamin was taken aback by my accusation. Then Brookstone began to try to fit into place this new piece of the puzzle. He asked, "Does anyone know anything about this explosion?"

Everyone sat mute, with the girls shaking their heads in perfect twin fashion, saying, "No, only what we read."

Brookstone sat back, rubbed his temples and got serious, "There's something going on here and we better get to the bottom of it," and with this he turned his attention back to us. "If there was an attempt on your lives, this means you guys must know something that you're not telling us, because we have no reason to even consider hurting you. If we wanted to, we would not be so sloppy as to blow you up just a few miles from our headquarters."

I saw Jaden and old man Kaamin both agreeing and laughing under their breaths. This little night out at the Hilton was becoming an entangled puzzle. In fact it appeared that several different puzzles had been dumped into one box and we were now supposed to figure out where all the pieces fit. We slowly came to what might be called a plausible conclusion—that the gang here, really did not know all the details of what had taken place with us, or with their guards on the beach.

I stood up again, walked around in a state of contemplation, not sure what I should ask or tell. I concluded that we had to fit a few more pieces into the partly framed puzzle. I would hold back a few pieces, no way were we going to tell of the extent of our share of the treasure. Apparently, they didn't even know how much treasure was in the trench. I turned to face this family and asked, "I am willing to tell more, but all of you must completely agree that whatever we say here will not ever leave this room or be told to anyone. It looks like our lives, as miserable as you think they might be, just may be in some danger. For what reason I do not know."

Now I really got serious and said to Brookstone, "Before I tell more, I want you to ask Dickson and Max to leave, maybe go down stairs and have a beer or something."

Dickson began to cough with surprise and Brookstone immediately spoke out in his defense. I explained that if they didn't even know what was going on in their own security business, they should not be so trusting about possible leaks in their system. This brought forth arguments and objections, but I held my ground, refusing to say anymore unless they were sent packing.

Old man Kaamin was smiling and shaking his head as he spoke up, "Bobby, I think dis young human is fars more perceptive than we know, no tings will not hurt for Dickson and Max to step away for a time."

The overall feeling floated around the room and it was possible that Dickson was not the man they were pretending him to be. So after everything calmed down, Dickson and Max were asked to take a break. Without much ado, they nodded their heads, gave me a dirty look and left. However, another clue fell into place, for Brookstone nodded at Jaden who was sent along to keep an eye on Dickson. I knew there was an alternative reason for this, but I played dumb as a cucumber.

CHAPTER TWENTY THREE

I waited a few moments. "OK, it was the night of your chopper landing at the trench," I began.

"Wait a minute. What night landing at the trench?" Brookstone sat up puzzled, looking over at his father, the old jeweler.

I caught this and was wondering; I remembered that maybe no one had been clued in on this part of the story. I went on. "The night we finally got off the beach, we were waiting for JJ to come pick us up when your guards in black dropped down out of the sky to land next to the treasure trench."

Brookstone looked agitated, asked Crystal to refill his glass and said, "Tell more please!"

"Theo and I thought we had been busted. You know, we thought that your cameras had seen us and now your guards were after us. But not so. They landed quietly and immediately went to the pit. We had no idea it was even there. Two of them rolled back a few bushes and suddenly dropped down into the pit and began handing up boxes and bags and chests."

"Who were these three?" Brookstone asked.

I was looking around at everyone's face now. It was as if I were opening up—not just a can of worms, but a boxcar load of rotten meat! "It was the same three guards from the night before with the drug exchange down on the beach."

With this Brookstone shot up and began walking around shaking his head, muttering, "What the hell? This is outrageous and impossible!"

I waited, but went on, "They were your intimidators, Trimmer and his two buddies who were with him the day we came to visit you for our boards. Most likely the same guys that placed the explosive onto our van when we were talking with you inside the office."

Brookstone's glass eye appeared to be a laser beam targeting me directly. He slowly spoke, "I don't know why you may be lying. But if you are, you're going to have to deal with Trimmer directly, who ain't the nicest guy to mess with. In fact he is downright wacko. We only use him for those really, and I mean really, extreme situations."

"Sir, there is no reason for me to lie, you asked how we came to get our hands on a few gems and I'm telling you." I paused here for a moment and stated, "It had to be them. I saw them messing with our van through your window in the office and we did not stop anywhere after that, so it had to be them!"

"OK, go on."

"So we waited and when the helicopters flew off, I went over to the area where they had landed and found the opening. You know I am an investigating journalist and couldn't let something like this go."

"Then what?" Brookstone interrupted.

I asked Amber if I could get a glass of water or juice, immediately she was up and moving and I had my water.

I took a good sip and continued, "I looked around for any booby traps or hidden wires, then I pushed back the plank and shined my light down into the pit where I saw all sorts of crates, boxes and canvas sacks stacked on one another and in heaps."

At this time I thought it best to make some adjustment to my story, around what exactly took place, skirting our extraction of a few boxes. I did not lie, I just did not tell everything. Hey, I figured it was not necessary to give too much away.

"I let myself down to take a better look, and while I was looking around, checking things out I was sure I heard Theo yell something. Then I heard the chopper returning and knew I was trapped down there. It was impossible for me to get out or I would have been seen."

The girls were really listening close now. It was almost like a mystery adventure story being told. "I pushed the plank closed and managed to climb over a few bags and just made it down behind a crate on one side. This was horrible, there were rats and lots of spiders down there, they made me their runway and smorgasbord while scattering from the light."

At this juncture I began rubbing my swollen eye, but I proceeded on with the news. "Again, the same two guards were talking and then they dropped down into the pit. The one was named George, and they began to hand up more things to Trimmer above. I heard them talking about a few people, and the one guard asked George if he might grab a few more of the coins they took last time. George said sure, but shut up so Trimmer didn't know. The other guy, I forget his name, said something about they might turn them into fish food if they were found out."

By now Brookstone was intensely listening to every detail and asked, "Who was the guy who might turn you into fish food?" Brookstone asked.

I knew now that I had opened up a chamber of unknowns, and thought it best to hold back what seemed to be a key name in the game. Wally had taught us that knowledge is power and not to always be in a hurry to give all yours away. So I shrugged my shoulders and said, "I can't remember, things were a little tense for me at that time, if you can imagine. As a rat ran across my neck and I was about to sneeze, the chopper, thank God, started up and the two guards were beginning to climb out of the hole in the ground."

We could see that the girls were freaked out at the part of the entanglements with rats and spiders, Crystal had her hand over her mouth as if suppressing a squeal.

I went on with more detail, "After I made sure the chopper had gone, Theo came over and helped me out of the pit. As I climbed out, I lifted up a couple of small boxes to Theo as a piece of evidence. You know, no one would have ever believed us unless I had shown proof of such a stash. Besides, I was wondering what the heck we had found. We closed up the treasure pit and crawled over to the fence. JJ showed up and we got the heck out of there."

Brookstone stood up, looking out the windows at the city lights and the room was hushed. We knew that something big was going on here, maybe it was a big game, but the way the entire family was held in suspense I knew that gears were a-grinding. Brookstone made a few calls off in the corner while everyone sat contemplating the events. Finally we could hear Brookstone in a very serious tone, telling Jaden to get hold of Jasper and Mica and to start digging into Trimmer's extra curricular activity, and the other boys with him.

I leaned over to Amber and quietly asked her if Jasper and Mica were her other brothers and she nodded yes, adding, "This is bad, bad, bad!"

Things had changed; Brookstone did not seem to even care how much of the treasure we might have taken; there were bigger things going on. I think this was turning out to be a double take. Meaning that the Hearst Castle Security Company was taking from the treasure and using it to make deals. And then there was an inner group stealing from the HC Security stash. There might be even bigger people involved, like this Buck Skullkin character that I did not mention. The mystery just expanded. But whatever they were doing, I made it known again, we did not want any part of their goings on and I reconfirmed our position of non-involvement: a know-nothing and a leave-us-alone policy!

I was sort of sad, knowing then and there that a really great story was slipping away, never to be told. I weighed out the value of the treasure we had scored, against a story that would be around one day and gone the next. I also thought about all the people we could help with our new found wealth.

So I made my declaration, "I like those words Crystal said, 'new friends.' I think this is going to be a most interesting friendship, very different from the ones I have." And with that, I took out the third Alexandrite stone from my pocket and handed it over to Brookstone, saying, "A gift to seal our friendship!"

The phone rang, Jaden asking if the coast was clear and if they could return. Brookstone told them to get back and said let's serve dinner now. After more questions and answers back and forth, Dickson announced that dinner was being served. We were all called into the dining room, to begin the appreciation of having made new friends and lived to tell the tale. There was still tension in the air, but I shrugged it off as because of the news not being so good.

No doubt, it was a beautiful setting and a very nice feast that Dickson had prepared for this family and its two visitors. Both Theo and I were seated near to the front, up near Robbie and Brookstone, with Theo across from me, Crystal next to him and Amber on my left. Brazed salmon with golden scalloped potatoes and mushrooms came as the main dish with a variety of fresh baked breads and various servings of spiced cabbages, along with marinated everything. General questions were asked of our travels as the meal progressed. Brookstone got our full attention when he allowed a comment about Dustin's computer being hacked into a few days back. I shot him a look that did not escape his notice. Very casual like, he let it be known that our lives were now in their radar.

I could not let this pass without inquiring who might have had the opportunity to enter into Dustin's computer system. Brookstone's good eye darted and quickly glanced over at both Crystal and Amber who sat stoically, radiating their reserved smiles. As gorgeous as they were, I saw them as two smug and proud swans paddling in a deep pond of expertise, silently calling out their hacking abilities: we heard the message.

I could not help but think back on what Wally had said about being sorry for the hacker, or in this case, the hackers who had managed to invade his realm. These creatures were just too beautiful for Wally to take out his anger on. But his lessons, we would soon learn, were not of a physical nature. Between bites of delicious pastries and sips of herbal chi I thought I'd bring forth my own message. "A very wise man once told me that when a person is curious enough to open a vault and sneak around in other people's secrets, that person should be able to live with them. For once a secret is opened it cannot be returned!"

At this point our conversation took a most interesting turn. Max spoke up with his bit of wisdom, explaining that knowledge is power and there are some people who know how to use that power to achieve greater things. The idea of what was actual power and the concept of greatness might not be everyone's cup of tea. It was obvious that Theo and I were well out-numbered in points of view and out of our class. We were being made to look like kids running naked, without any protection from the wealth and power of our new made friends. I was frustrated beyond measure, for the idea of us coming over to have a nice evening with two young flowers had been replaced with our being put into a cage and told that we were at the mercy of the Hearst Castle Security Corporation. Then on top of all that, we were as if being held captive to someone else's ideals of justice, and this was not good.

As Dickson was clearing away the main dishes, Brookstone thought he would clarify our position, and with this he laid down the five stones that we had sold to his father, old man Kaamin. He then looked at us with his one clear emerald eye and spoke up. "We know where you got these stones from. How you got them and how many of them you got your hands on is still a mystery to us, but we are not too interested in that. But just letting you know that we are not going to pursue this matter, unless you persist in publishing anything. And we mean anything about our activity and about the treasure."

I let my expression of disapproval glow hot across my face and bided my time for some kind of a retort but nothing extraordinary came.

But leave it to good old Theo when he nervously asked, "You mean this is not our last meal?" and everyone broke into laughter at our expense.

Well there it was, their final ultimatum and we had no argument in our defense. For the stones did prove that we had taken a part of the treasure and it was best they did not know how much. How we had come to meet up with this family at the Phoenix Gem Show was puzzling enough, but I guessed that a gem show would be just the right place for the HC Security gang to sell some of their own stones. I had to laugh, for I, in my hot-shot move, had bought and paid dearly for some of the very treasure we had in our own possession.

Max stepped in here and added, "The treasure is going to be, and has already proven a great asset in our work. It cannot be reported to any officials. That would ruin future negotiations with unsavory organizations that are asking for funds for the exchange of captives."

Max was really covering his butt, unless he was deeper into this situation than I knew. I could understand this and nodded my head but still I did not like anyone to have something hanging over our heads as an on-going threat for later use, especially these lovely twins. If they had the ability to get into our bank accounts or investments, watch out! There was nothing I could do or say to turn the course of this situation on my own. However, as coffee was being served I felt my cell phone vibrate. I did not want to answer it and let it go until it went off again. I excused myself and asked which way was the restroom. Crystal pointed down the hall to the left and I found myself in what was a bathroom fit for kings and queens. I took out my cell and read the number and sure enough it was Wally. I redialed and within a moment, Wally, who became a refreshing voice in the wilderness, answered with, "Woe, where is yous?"

"It's a long story Wally, but we are in some very interesting company. Or you might say a hell of a lot of danger. Holding life altering discussions among new strange friends, dining with high class intimidators in Suite 77."

"Wow, wow and whoopee, sounds rather entertaining. So what else is new for you guys?"

I gave a quick run down of our circumstances and good old Wally laughed and told me not to worry. I stood there just shaking my head saying to myself, sure, don't worry. We've been found out; totally caught with our hands in the cookie jar. We were nearly blown to pieces, we are now trapped into silence and we're not sure if this covert company is going to allow us our freedom. Then on top of all that, we might have the United States Government breathing down our backs, so, "Don't worry, you say?"

However, good old Wally never failed, he came back, giving me some interesting news. In fact, he simply armed me with enough ammunition to sink a few ships, and to possibly change the entire course of these threats. His information could balance out the differences with what was equal to a cruise missile, soon on the loose. He told me to just go and enjoy my dinner and sit back and wait. I was definitely puzzled, thanked him and returned to the table completely refreshed, not knowing what the heck was going to happen.

Upon my return I saw that Theo was near white and I knew they had been pumping him for information, I only hoped he had the cool to remain a stupid surfer bum. Later on Theo told me that they were wanting to know how much of the treasure we had taken and where it was. He played dumb and said that I was the one to talk with and so they began pushing me around. Then it happened.

Brookstone's cell beeped, he looked down to see who might be calling. He excused the conversation for a moment and then began to listen to his call. We all sat quietly and I watched his face turn red like an ember ablaze, and then he went white and I thought I saw his hand shake a little. It was so obvious, the girls became concerned as their brother Bobby Brookstone went through several stages of changes.

All exchanges had stopped, then Brookstone snapped his phone closed and gestured for Crystal to come over to him. She arose and walked behind Theo and bent down to hear her brother's words. I could barely hear but enough that we heard him saying for her to go check their Hearst Castle accounts.

She left the room as old man Robbie began talking about several new stones recently found in Brazil, something about a new mineral, but I was not listening. I was wondering who Brookstone had been listening to, and had the feeling it had been Wally. Soon Crystal returned, she was whiter than her brother, finally just shaking her head in unbelief, saying, "They're empty!"

Bob Brookstone practically yelled out, "What do you mean they're empty?" It was as if we were not in the room and no longer mattered. Everyone of them began to buzz, but soon were looking at me with their stingers fully extended.

Brookstone managed to get himself under control as he told his father, "Pop, someone has hacked our accounts. All our accounts have been drained, they're empty and gone!"

"What on earth you say Bobby?"

Crystal the family computer queen mumbled, "Papa, I just checked our accounts and for some reason they show that everything was transferred out of country to an off shore bank in New Zealand."

After a few minutes of serious outrage and trying to weigh out the possibilities of what might have happened, Max turned to me saying, "Somehow Mr. Mitchner, I have the feeling you've got something to do witvh this great injustice."

Now I knew that what Wally had told me on the phone was more than serious, he had just hacked into the HC Security Corporations main accounts and transferred every penny out of country. That cruise missile had just hit its target! Now I realized the new leverage that he had given us to level the playing field. I sat quiet, acting dumb as a surf bum waiting for a massive wave, letting them reconsider our insignificance. They waited for an answer but I did not know what to say. Finally I came up with one old thought, "There be an old saying I once heard used, 'Man who stick his hand into bee hive to steal honey, many times get bit more than honey is worth,'" and I added, "In this case, also 'woman who think she too smart get bit on butt really bad!'"

I took my last sip of coffee, slid back my chair, thinking it was time for us to go, but Jaden and Brookstone shook their heads and made it clear that we were not going anywhere. I noticed Dickson take up a position in the entry way. However, I was not so intimidated at this time for the generator of power had been switched onto our side. I felt electrified at the possibilities of what to do. Dickson immediately stepped up and poured another round of hot coffee, knowing our stay had just been prolonged.

Wally had clued me in on a few things and now I asked if I might make a phone call. Brookstone nodded his approval as long as it was not the police and had something to do with this dilemma. I punched in the number to Wally and he answered laughing, "So soon you call, what is up with the situation there in Suite 77?"

I spoke aloud with everyone listening, and told him that it was time now to come up with a solution to this dilemma. I listened, took mental notes and was amazed at what I was being told. Then I hung up.

"Ok, my favorite guru has decided to make you a deal, since we are now such good friends." Everyone was quiet and listening, especially our lovely lady friends, Crystal being the most alert.

"As you know, your accounts no longer exist, but our companion in adventure is very willing to sell to you for an honest price some of the treasure or most of it we now possess." Just as Brookstone was about to explode I lifted my hand and went on, "We will agree not to interfere with your operations in any way, including no articles or books written, or inferences made. However, we have several requests from your side. First, we want to be totally left out of your reports, from your dealings; and we do not want our names to even be mentioned among your group. We would then like you to purchase back from us, at a fair market price most of the treasure we now possess."

I thought for sure all hell was going to break out, but instead, Amber began to laugh, but soon saw the fierce look on her brother's face, while her father sat there passively as if thinking all this to be humorous and entertaining.

"What then if we agree?" Brookstone asked, knowing he was in a bind and someone had hold of his future generations.

"From what we learned today, we would guess that we have about a mil and a half of stones. If you will buy those from us, we will then release all your funds back into your accounts."

"Why are you being so gracious?" Crystal interjected.

"It's this way, we do not want to be running all over the country trying to bicker and peddle gems to a hundred shows, we got other things to do. So just buy us out and your home free. You can easily resell those stones for double the mil and a half!"

Brookstone asked Dickson to bring out some of their special dealmaking brandy. After they had poured themselves a good pour and our coffee cups had been refilled, Bob sipped, "What guarantee do we have that you'll replace our funds?"

I sat my cup down and chuckled as I seriously stated, "Hey, we are friends in fate and in adventure, let us be trustworthy of one another's extraordinary friendship...right?"

Finally Theo came alive, "Yeah, didn't we just out of pure friendship give you and Jaden, and your father a good gesture of friendship?" Theo was referring to the three stones we had given to Brookstone, Robbie and Jaden.

I was surprised at Theo's sudden boldness, and then he really took me back when he tossed into the deal, "And we only ask one other tiny thing."

"What's that?" Brookstone asked thick with dubious sarcasm.

"We want to be able to come up your way and do some surfing along that long beach, maybe up at the north end where Trimmer and your guards like to surf."

I thought this to be stupid at first, but after considering its psychological possibilities, and how it more or less made us easy and innocent, I realized that Brookstone was agreeing, knowing that we would be putting ourselves into his reach; and he liked that idea. I wondered if Theo actually knew what he was saying, was he that intelligent?

Things seemed to be calming down after we made it known what we wanted out of the deal. I then offered a good will gesture, saying that we would immediately release two mil back into their account as a show of good will and our honest intent.

For the first time old man Kaamin nodded to Brookstone, as if telling him to agree and letting him know that in reality, they had nothing to lose, for they could easily resell the stones for more than they paid us. With this, Brookstone nodded and said, "Go for it, let your Wally the guru, the hairy man, enliven our account.

I punched in Wally's number, he answered, "Bank of All Mighty Corruptions," then added, "What might this humble servant do for you and what might be your needs?"

I chuckled then asked him to immediately transfer back into the HC Security account, two mil, as a good-trust gesture. He hung up laughing and shortly thereafter, a nervous Crystal brought out her laptop and with everyone looking on, they saw their account brought back up to one third of its original amount. They were impressed and Brookstone knew that he and his company had met their match with this Wally character. He figured that this guy was to be investigated to the fullest. But he realized that if he did step on our toes, there would be heck to pay and everything could be exposed. He decided to leave well enough alone; at least for now. These surf bums had somehow managed to get the big bad HC Security force's shorts caught into a full running ringer; but how?

We finally worked out the details on payment. Jaden and his father would visit Dustin's office and we would set up a loan, actually borrow the mil and a half from the HC Security Corporation and we would give them a part ownership in the new surf movie we were going to create. Of course, the girls demanded a part, and Theo could not resist but promised them a part. Surprisingly enough, both of them had lived in Maui and were acquainted with the surf and scuba diving scene there.

Thus, over fine brandy and excellent coffee, the promise was made that all funds would be restored back into their accounts as soon as the purchase of our remaining stones was paid and the surf movie loan papers were signed.

No doubt, the night drew to its end with crackling excitement. Old man Robbie Kaamin arose along with Jaden, shook our hands, letting us know that this day had to be one of the best ones he had in many days gone by, letting his words slip back into Slavic slang. He smiled and also added, "Yous granfater was most wiser man. Ands yous boys musta keeps ups the good trickies." Everyone laughed. He thanked us and nodded, but Dickson the butler shot us a dirty look and departed along with Mr. Kaamin and his son Jaden.

We arose, stretched and went onto the outside deck to view the city lights fanning out into the desert. The girls left for a moment leaving us with Brookstone and Max for a time. Our conversation was somewhat guarded but still we could feel the cement of trust forming. I was truly amazed. So much had happened in one day that I was reeling with extraordinary chunks of knowledge and I mean weighty, chunks of information. However, without knowing it, we were soon to be walked into a new garden of incredible expectations.

Chapter Twenty Five

As we stood there looking down upon the sprawling city of Phoenix, enjoying the night desert sky, another and a more personal part of this family's life was revealed. It was another far reaching—totally unexpected event, brought forth by Brookstone. I had thought that we had played all our cards and there was nothing left other than friendly exchanges; but not so, no, not at all.

As we were enjoying the soft desert breeze of the night, Brookstone cleared his voice and began talking, "Luke, I sort of like your style. You asked me a time back if we ever needed more guards, if we would consider hiring you and Theo." I nodded to this memory and Brookstone went on, "We might be needing a couple of new guys on our team. Maybe think it over." He added, "Especially since we are going to be lowering our employee count...soon!"

Then he tossed in the bomb of the night, "I know that you and your lawyer Dustin are tangled up in a ten year trial over your family inheritance. We have a lot of friends and pull in Canada. What if we could, well, possibly extricate your inheritance from that drawn-out court mess?"

This go round was nothing less than perplexing, I was truly taken aback, left speechless. How the heck did he know this? What on earth could he actually do to straighten this mess out? I also knew that these guys were heavy hitters—there was no way I wanted nefarious pressures wrongly applied on anyone for my inheritance. But this was such an incredible offer, I was flabbergasted, frozen in silent unbelief at the possibilities. The only thing I could think to say at the moment was that my lawyer, Dustin Arrow, would be in touch with him if he felt this was a good idea.

The girls had now come out onto the balcony and were listening. Crystal spoke up at this time with her thoughts," Luke, I am the one who dug up everything about your family and its loss and the fight going on over your inheritance. I know a lot about such things, I was trained as a paralegal secretary. I feel that we can turn the tide on your problems. Please consider this as an honest proposal from our family."

Then Amber added her wisdom to the conversation, "You have been caught in the legal system and from what I know, they are not going to let you go free. You'll have to get tough and fight or they will rob you blind. Better deal with this soon; maybe even set aside your surf film and get down to business to settle this mess. I think that is what your wise grandparents would have liked. They seem to have been some very savvy people; you might start with that."

This was too much, these new one-day friends were offering help that I could not ever afford and for what reason I didn't know. As a reporter I was always suspicious and looking for someone's angle. I asked, "What good would this do you, and how much would your services cost me in the long run?"

Brookstone said, "Luke, for now I cannot tell you too much but we are owed some big favors and would never be able to collect on them, so if we could use them to help you get what is rightly yours, then we will. Besides, the information you gave us this evening will probably save us some serious troubles, worth its weight in gold."

At this time, I felt the sincerity of the offer and I became a little emotional hearing about my grandparents. The pressure was on, I tried to stop tears from working their way out of my tear-well, flowing out of that brown-purple walnut shaped eye. I had to do something, so reached out and shook Brookstone's hand, feeling his missing fingers, "The name of the other man who could turn us into fish food was Buck, with a last name that sounded like Skullkin or something close to that."

Brookstone and Max both took in their breaths, standing there as stone pillars; I knew that a large bundle of dynamite had just been tossed into the fiery furnace of mysterious happenings. Some serious looks bounced back and forth between the girls, Max and Brookstone, it was like a break at a pool tournament when all the balls were bouncing in all directions. It was one of those wait and see moments—everyone waiting to see what might explode.

Brookstone, who glowed with a red angry face, nodded, conveying a serious concern to us with a grunt, and excused himself, stepping back into the suite. We could hear him on the phone giving instructions to someone and it did not sound like an order for pizza. I imagined I could hear the gears of life grinding someone into fish food. Oh boy, I thought, what did I do now?

After a time of silence out on the balcony, Brookstone returned with his normal poise. Much better composed, he nodded to Max as to say that all things were in motion. Our conversations went on in general but for sure now, there were mixed emotions floating around. Once again, I got the impression that there was a genuine good person inside that rough Brookstone container. Somehow I knew that the giving away of those three Alexandrite stones without any ties, had helped turn this night's disaster into a challenge, and now a friendship, possibly more. Whatever it was, I was glad that we had somehow come down on the good side of the Hearst Castle Security team—at least I hoped that is what had happened!

We still had a lot of questions, but both Theo and myself were mentally exhausted with all the events of the day, and of the night. Brookstone suggested that we get some rest and that we would be talking soon.

As we made our way across the living room and into the front waiting area, Brookstone decided to tell us something that was bothering him. "One more thing here Luke. We want you to know, and you probably already know this, that your inheritance is secured into a multi faceted array of industries and several corporations that will not have your best interests at heart. In fact we would like to warn you to be careful, to be on guard and take great precautions on whom you have dealings with and where you go."

I nodded my head in understanding, for Dustin had well informed me about some of the names we would have to deal with. But this warning from the HC Security group drove the point home. Money and wealth was soon to come my way and with this would come a tidal wave of power-hungry men and women. The picture of my vast inheritance was slowly merging onto the canvas of my life. I was not sure how we might deal with all the pressures but this was one reason we had begun to form a team. A team of trusted individuals who would help with the burdens of handling all my grandparents' investments and holdings.

Brookstone concluded with one last suggestion, "The Hearst Castle Security group has experience in these areas and if you feel you might need some advice or help, please feel free to contact us. Our offer to help untangling your affairs from the Canadian Court system still stands—we can help you there for sure!"

Theo and I decided to say our goodbyes. Even though the twins seemed a little disappointed, we had had enough of the Kaamin family for now, especially with the twin tricksters. In fact we had more than our share, and were most happy to get out of there with our lives still intact.

The girls escorted us down to the lobby and gave us a show of their affection with a simple goodnight kiss and pats on the back. Things had worked out rather well, and we were hoping that no further wrenches would fall or be tossed into the deal. We got to the Tripper, buzzed the locks open and climbed into our new home on wheels. When we thought to check out some of the surveillance devices that Wally had installed, we once again were shocked near fainting. Out of the back came a deep rumbling voice—Wally burst out, asking if things had gone our way.

Theo expelled gas and let out a scream of fright and I slumped over at the wheel, completely freaked by having this huge hairy man all of a sudden step out of the dark. "That will teach you guys to first check your APS to see if your Tripper had been messed with, or if anyone had entered. I set up an application that reads the surveillance devices in and out of the van, so learn to use it before you get in," the amused voice expounded the lesson.

Wally explained that he had flown back out as soon as the computer attack had been remedied. After this rude awakening we went back to the hotel, where we decided to check out and get on the road. We were just too hyped up to even think about sleep. Of course Dustin had to call in the middle of this to express his paranoia about his computer being hacked into. Wally explained how it happened, and that it was actually his fault. But no worries, all had been repaired.

We went on to explain the deal we had made.

Dustin was thrilled over the possible exchange, "Hey, that loan idea is great, you did great with that. That might save us a whole lot of trying to explain a huge chunk of money suddenly coming our way. Nice job Luke!"

I went on to explain that Brookstone had mentioned the possibility of helping us get the Canadian court jam unstuck. He was rather surprised at this news and we asked him to set up a meeting with Brookstone to extract more details. He replied that this might be a good idea, and told us to sell off as many stones along the way as possible. For he had gone through more of the boxes; we were not lacking in the rare gem area.

Our emotions were running full bore, the excitement meter was spinning nearly out of control as we drove like a bat out of hell on our way out of Arizona—and we never looked back!

The road north stretched out across the desert heading for Utah. We were filled with strong coffee and babbled on continuously, thoroughly arguing every point of our adventure. Wally had the most to tell. His exploration into the HC Security files had revealed way more than just bank accounts; we learned a lot about their activities. Brookstone was nearly killed in a café bombing in Egypt about seven years back. Several people were killed in the suicide bombing. Brookstone was severely injured while losing two companions. This was heavy stuff; we better understood why all the security, and where those scars had come from.

Then there was the reason Crystal had been able to get into Dustin's system—because Dustin had ignorantly installed a financial program that had a backdoor. She found her way in and took a good look around, spying on our activities. Now she pretty well knew our business, which was not much as of yet. For a time she was able to block our accounts, but Wally had reversed this attack and took it back to the Hearst Castle Security accounts, where he had transferred every penny to a secret account offshore. Fortunately, Theo and myself had outside accounts, but Dustin's accounts had been hacked. Wally admitted that the Crystal or Amber chick did have some skills as a hacker, but completely lacked the real skills of a professional. I told Wally that he might want to spend some special time and give them some personal tutoring. We all laughed at this, knowing that Wally would have his large hands full dealing with those Kaamin gems!

Wally went on telling us that this was no ordinary family; they knew high ranking people all over the world. They had connections reaching up to the White House and were well known in behind-the-scenes military groups. He suggested that we could spend time getting to know them, and join their efforts from a distance, whenever events allowed. Better to have them as friends than be on their bad side; they ain't people to mess with.

I thought back at my arrogance of the night, wondering if Brookstone would have been so kind to us if the girls and their father hadn't been there. Wally told us about one of the other brothers, Morgan, who had once gone underground as a guard into a federal prison in order to infiltrate one of the most notorious gangs. All I could think was that my little freelance journalistic work was a picnic compared to living inside a stinking rotten prison.

Then there was Max. During an earlier call, Dustin had explained that yes, Max was a Fed and again we had come near to revealing his cover. He had been working underground, inside the Kaamin family for several years now. They were his key into many ongoing investigations in the world of trade and exchanges. But Wally laughed, saying that it was unlikely that the Kaamin family did not know that Max was a Fed. In fact, he indicated that Max was most likely a double or maybe even a triple agent, if there could be such a thing.

Wally had found the Hearst Castle security team to be what we might consider legitimately honest, with a few missing chapters in their story. My opinion had somewhat altered towards Max, but I guessed that for now, we would have to leave well enough alone.

Dawn found us standing on the Glenn Canyon Dam looking out at the great Lake Powell. We could feel the vibration of the generators under our feet and saw from one side the pleasant calm lake. On the other side of the road was a deep canyon rumbling with torrents of water gushing out of the dam; it was a good picture of what we had been through in the last few weeks. We had truly found adventure and serious intrigue. We had come from a pleasant business trip, then suddenly been forced through a spinning turbine, and spewed into a deep canyon of intrigue and possible wealth. It seemed that every twisting curve in this canyon brought some new danger, all in the name of treasure. We were crossing a great bridge, passing from one state to another, looking for what we hoped would be a calm horizon and a better time for us and our friends.

Somehow through this difficult situation, the providence of good fortune had come our way. Theo could lay the ground-work for his planned film. We could assist Wally in getting his incredible programs up and running as he so wanted. Dustin and I would now be able to hire the proper lawyers to begin working through the loose ends of my inheritance. Plus, now we had the offer from the Kaamin family to expedite the entire court and law suit mess. There seemed to be complications since my grandparents were from Canada and their holdings and various charities were scattered all over the world. Their will, along with their trusts, was entangled in several courts, but with this new friendship, possibly we could proceed in straightening it all out.

The work of upholding the various charities and outreach programs that my grandparents had set up would now fall into my hands. For now, the worst part of the entire court thing was that the charities that my grandparents had dedicated funds to could not receive any monies from the established trusts. This was one of the most upsetting aspects of man's greed. These charities would be a lifetime of careful and serious concern, and I had all intention of fulfilling my grandparent's lifetime work after their passing three years earlier in the fated plane crash.

Then there was Theo's older brother Jay, who had called and informed us of the value of the treasure we had left with him, which alone was considerable. He also had followed up on the San Bella ship wreck and wanted to put a dive together to try to locate it. Possibly it was not too far off shore from where we had found the skeletons. Theo was already making arrangements over our new connections to his friends in Hawaii, scheduling technicians for the upcoming winter wave season. That was exciting in itself. I also had received several article requests from two different magazines, and it looked like our schedule was filled up even though we had not even crossed into Utah. We were just wanting a quiet peaceful trip home, but I had my doubts!

I had to laugh when Theo said, "Just think, all this from a malfunctioning fuel pump just at the right time!"

"Oh no, you better toss in an earthquake and a skull and a smugglers cove too," I made mention.

CHAPTER TWENTY SEVEN

THORTIN GETS BURNED

The morning was wearing on as we stood there, looking down into the deep Glenn Canyon, listening to the roar of the outflow of the dam and feeling the power of the spinning turbines deep inside the massive cement and steel structure. Then the satellite phone rang and everything suddenly changed again.

Thortin's voice came through but almost so far away I couldn't hear him. Immediately I got the feeling it was going to be bad news. He began as though he were in the final inning in the last game of the world series and his team was one point behind; he was desperate to get this man out. Thortin sounded tired and shortly the reason came clear. He delivered the news as a highly paid pitcher would throw his fastest speed ball. His newspaper office had been set on fire. It was a total loss, nothing left—zilch, just lots of ash and enough coals to barbeque a herd of elephants!

He went on while we listened in shock. There had been a few strange calls warning him not to publish anything more on the finding of the San Bella bell or any more hinting at what might be a lost shipwreck on the coast. Thortin refused to heed the warning, thinking it was a crank call, laughing that there were treasure hunters out there who didn't want any more treasure hunters in the area. He went ahead and published one more story in the series. The next night the office was torched. Thortin concluded with a good number of colorful but rather dark phrases. He knew now that this story was dangerous and certainly could have more to it than all of us realized!

We hurried back to the Tripper, now sitting in Utah, and called him back, asking a hundred questions. After hanging up, we went into conference mode. Our planned trip was altered. We headed towards the northwest, to Salt Lake City for a gem show, selling a good number of smaller gems. Then over to Vegas, where we sold a batch more, and then up to Reno where we sold another five stones.

For now, our plans had been rearranged. We informed Thortin to locate another building and to estimate the cost of new equipment to start up again. We told him that we would be there in a few days, and to get things started. He was more than taken aback and hesitated because of the costs involved. He did not know about our new ability to help, we just told him not to worry, we wanted cost estimates as soon as possible. It was as if you could hear him saying, "You surf bums, where you gonna get the bucks to front this print operation?"

It was the third day since the bad news came through and we were just headed out of Sacramento towards San Francisco when Thortin got back to us. Fortunately they had all their files and data stored on a secure cloud server, but they would need new computers, new printing presses, copiers, and a new stock of inks, papers and assorted business paraphernalia. He was describing several hundred thousands dollars worth of equipment alone. There was some insurance to come, but due to the suspicious origin of the fire, it would be months before any insurance money would come their way. The costs were manageable on our part, so we told Thortin to get started and begin ordering everything he needed to get up and running. There was a nice office warehouse down the street, even a better setting than what they had before. We told him to go for it. He was hesitant, but we told him that this would be a loan from the surf film fund that we had recently built up, and it would be against his future incoming insurance. Not to worry, just get started!

What was so fantastic about this entire situation was that we were now in a position to actually help. I don't care what anyone might say, money is power and if you got it, there are few things that can prevent you from getting things done.

Chapter Twenty Eight

New Print Shop Up And Running

When we arrived in San Luis Obispo the following morning, we took a nice room in town a short way from the new office. We found Thortin supervising ten different projects at once; workers moved in and around stacks of crates and boxes with delivery vans coming and going. People were all over the place, painting and building walls; it looked like a bee hive had been knocked over. Thortin was on the ball, getting things organized. He was happy to see us and invited us to stay at his place, but we told him we had settled in at the Mission Inn down the road for the night.

Dustin had already made arrangements with Brookstone to meet. But after hearing the news of the fire at the Tribune Newspaper he had decided to come up our way and hold the meeting there. We asked Thortin where we might help; he just shook his head saying that the entire town had been there since yesterday helping them move in and get things set up. Much of the larger equipment had been ordered and would be delivered in a few days but all the smaller things were being set up. Dustin had informed Thortin to send the billing to his office and they would be handled through his business accounts.

Thortin wanted to know how all this was going to work, but we assured him that monies from out of the surf film would work for us and for him until his insurance paid off. In a round-about way we told him that it was best he just concentrate on getting the paper back up and running; everything would take its course. In all honesty, we felt that we carried some guilt in this situation; it was our crazy Hearst Castle lost treasure story that had brought Thortin and his news-paper into these woes.

We were given a tour around the new location. We suggested that the upstairs areas could be turned into a couple of office rentals and at least two apartments. Thortin was hesitant at this advice; but again, we encouraged him to move forward and get it done, for we would be interested in renting one apartment and an office for future stays and business.

Thortin was surprised that we might want to carry on some business on this part of the coast. He led us into what would be his office and closed the door. We sat down in this new bare-walled room and began asking questions about the fire. Half way through this sit down talk, Dustin arrived and he had JJ with him. We said our hellos and told JJ how nice he was looking before sending him out to get pizzas for all the helpers out in the shop.

Of course, the first thing he asked was, "No problem friends, but no dough without the dough, if you know what I mean…" Theo interrupted with "Please do not call us 'jelly beans'!"

Dustin handed over his debit card and told him, "Pizzas only now and go, go."

JJ was playing cool, checking out the group, but Dustin shot him a stern look to get going. When he finally left we continued probing, trying to connect the dots, if there were any to be connected.

"I'm sure you have been questioned by the police and the insurance. Is there any news on how or who might have started the fires?" Wally asked.

"No, but it looks like someone used some type of starter in

the print room to get things going. The fire was pretty well on its way by the time the fire department arrived, not much was saved other than a number of files from the front office."

My phone went off; I didn't recognize the number, but I stood back out of the group to answer. I listened and gave my approval. Theo looked over at me after I had shut off, wondering who it was, "It was Brookstone, he wants to come see us and visit with me for a talk."

Thortin continued and we listened. There was some doubt about the strange threatening phone call that Thortin had received, but there was no proof on who might have been behind it. I knew it wasn't the Hearst Castle Security Company. Who might want to stop the San Bella treasure hunt from being advertised was the question of the week.

Dustin had arranged the meeting between Brookstone and me, the information that Brookstone was about to share was rather sensitive, best not to be shared with others until I had made my decisions, whatever they were to be.

Brookstone arrived with both Crystal and Amber and found us sitting around Thortin's new conference table. Everyone was introduced and after the preliminary exchanges, Brookstone asked if the scheduled meeting could take place. Thortin knew that Dustin had arranged for me to meet with Brookstone, so he invited Theo, Wally and the girls to go to lunch with him. I insisted that Dustin stay with me and Brookstone, I needed another brain there to deal with what I thought was coming.

As Wally and Crystal exited the office I laughed. Oh boy, this was going to be good, I thought. Wally and Crystal? He was going to tangle with that sweet bomb of a woman who had hacked his programs. I called out, "Hey Wally, maybe you might begin your special get-even tutoring with pretty Crystal over lunch. Hope it works out OK, but hey, don't attack, or should I say hack, her programs too much!"

Crystal shot me a dirty look knowing that Wally was the master who had bested her attempts to dominate us. But I just gave her my twenty dollar smile and got back a fifty dollar smirk.

After the room had emptied, the door closed, Brookstone began by jumping right into the matter of the fires.
"To begin with, we're pretty sure that the fire was set by our
ex-commando pilot Charly Trimmer, or the Cat, and his
boys." I started to say something but Brookstone waved me
quiet and said, "Let me finish and I'll tell you why. If you
want to explain to Thortin later, you can."

"With the publication of the bell of San Bella story, Trimmer
and his behind-the-scenes boss named Buck Skullkin knew
that someone had found the treasure. They did not have
the means to get out all the treasure, so they wanted to shut
down any chances of furthering the treasure-hunt idea, or
you might say quenching the fires of treasure hunting. They
targeted the newspaper office to stop any further exposure."

"People could have been hurt in the fire," Dustin stated.

"These guys are true psychopaths, and life or the lack of it is
no concern to them."

Brookstone nodded to me that my experiences with this
Trimmer and his buddies were most accurate, even though
this was hard for him to admit, and was expressed hesitantly.

I guessed that this admission was not easy, because it had a
direct reflection on their reputation and overall operations.
It opened a hole that a herd of elephants could run through,
and I had started the stampede.

Dustin said, "Now I don't want to cast sand into your fine
running machine, but why on earth would you allow such

despicable characters around, even have them working for you at the Hearst Castle Security headquarters?"

Brookstone sat back, pyramided his finger tips and began his explanation. "Nearly a year back, we were extracting four rather important people from a jungle camp in Nairobi, when the chopper was taken down. We lost both our pilots, two good men they were, and one of the escapees. We found ourselves having to re-negotiate our extraction, and Trimmer and his two companions were the only experienced chopper pilots for 500 miles.

We hired them to bring our captives out and they did a great job. Turns out that Trimmer is one hell of a chopper pilot. His two friends are excellent mechanics, and they came as a package. We were not that happy with their attitudes, but we were able to use them to get in and out of some of the worst places. How long we were going to use them was being debated."

He let this information sink in for a moment, then went on. "Seems like we did them more of a favor, than they did for us. A massive manhunt was going on for the three of them. They had escaped a military prison a month earlier and were desperate to get out of the country. In our own desperation we were put in contact with them. At the time, we did not have much choice and went with them, using their expertise. I have to admit that Trimmer is one heck of a good pilot. He did prove his value to our efforts, at least for the meantime."

Brookstone skipped over much of the details that I would have liked to hear, but he wanted to get on with his ultimate reason for this meeting. "Soon the Trimmer boys won't be any more problem, once we have found them and dealt with them, and well—are sent away, and I mean far away."

This struck me sharp; knowing that these people did not mess around with sub-operational intruders or misguided gang members. From what we had learned, they weren't pussy-footing kiss-ass American do-gooders, a rehab club out of Washington DC! I did not ask further, I did not want to know if we were going to be connected to people disappearing or becoming fish food. I had to ask, "You mean you don't know where they are?"

Brookstone in all his coolness went on, "For now, this little glitch is on its way to being repaired." He casually waved his arm, as if saying "NO big deal."

I interjected, "But won't they go after the rest of the treasure?"

"Don't think so. We could not take any more chances, either with the FBI or the Trimmer gang, so we went in with major equipment and extracted the entire treasure out of the gully. In fact we're going through the trench with a fine tooth comb as we speak. The treasure will be kept in a safe place: no longer left to be damaged or found by other curious beach combers."

I was saddened by this. Maybe, just maybe, I wanted to go back and dig deeper into the hidden artifacts. That was no longer possible. I still had a thousand questions, but I knew we were there for another reason.

"Before we get into the details of this meeting, what was going on with Trimmer and his buddies? And, Oh yes, who was the Ruthie woman that we saw taken off the raft that night?" I wanted to know.

Brookstone hurried along, "Just leave it up to human nature, and greed will find a way to get its claws into things it shouldn't touch. Trimmer was ripping off bits and pieces of the treasure, as you saw. They had an old fence dealer in Frisco named Buck Skullkin, a very unsavory character. He was not only using Trimmer and his crew to steal the art-works, but he arranged to bring in illegals and dope at the same time. They would pay for the dope with different pieces of the art and some of the jewels. The woman was one of two women who were kidnapped in Mexico, about six months back, maybe you remember reading about it."

"I don't remember myself," I admitted. I thought back six months and remembered that I was probably up in Canada being escorted from one court to another in pursuit of the inheritance that had been willed to me.

"She was an executive with Jet Blue Airlines but they have not found the other woman yet. This Skullkin character, along with the back stabbing Trimmer gang, had blueprinted our operation, and even used parts of the treasure to trade off in exchange for captives.

They would make contact with various drug gangs and set up rendezvous where the abducted victims would be exchanged and traded for cash and treasure. The cove has been a long known haven for these types of nefarious operations. It was a near perfect operation, until two surf bums came along and managed to undo the whole thing."

I inquired, "How long was this going on? And what is the big deal about old Hearst art treasures?"

"Actually, that hole you saw in the pit, about eight foot square? that was about six chopper flights out. So we are thinking that it had been going on for about six months. But they still managed to get away with a good bit of wealth."

"Listen Luke, you might be thinking that this lost Hearst treasure is a bunch of bull, but let me explain just a few of the situations we have to deal with.

HC Security has had to deal with some of the worst of human scum. We have to negotiate with a few groups that have more wealth than the United States spends on its 100 secret wars. Many of those we confront do not want more money, they got enough to last them and their tribes for 1000 years. What they want are things that no one else has. This is where we came into existence and began to actually use our art treasures and masterpieces to trade for lives.

Ten million dollars is nothing to some of these shell families which own palaces and play-homes worth more money than some nation's annual budgets. They want rare art and things that no one else owns. Thus, we offered these things. And to tell you the truth, we became quite successful in having many hostages released. Some for nothing more than a one-of a-kind-painted Fabergé egg from the Czarist dynasty.

We so happened upon a collection of Fabergé jewelry which soon became some of our highest demanded pieces. Sorry to say that we only had a limited number of this jewelry, but we're hoping that there will be more found in the remainder of the collections." He paused as my attention was riveted on this new disclosure about their inner operations. "We have been at grand parties where a gold-encrusted statue of a naked lady was revealed, and we had ten weary souls released that very night. Some of these families have killed one another in the attempt to steal rare icons. The whole matter is insane. But we say—let them go insane as long as we can get innocent hostages released."

Brookstone shifted gears after this last statement and changed subjects. "You know Luke, at our first meeting I did not make the connection. But after the girls did their research and came up with your relationship to the Mitchner's, to them being your grandparents, I had to marvel at how coincidence often makes for strange experiences. I want to tell you that we knew your grandparents, and they were more than fine folks."

Not again. This had to be more than flabbergasting—another revelation beyond what I thought I knew. When would it end? It seemed as though every time we made a move or took a step forward, we were trumped by greater news or insights. I was taken aback, and I squirmed in my chair until I had to get up and move around the office. I was numb in my thoughts over this latest chunk of information, it was too much.

Brookstone kept his good eye on me and went on, "As you know now, we have various operations throughout the world and many important ones scattered throughout the worst parts of Africa, specifically East Africa right now. Your grandparents in their benevolent calling helped establish several medical clinics, one or two small hospitals and several orphanages.

When your grandparents, Stewart and Gladys, made their annual visits to these distant outposts, it was our teams who were assigned to guard them. Some of these areas are of the worst kind, few white men walk in and return. But because of the work your folks were doing, we found it advantageous to make sure they were kept safe. There were times when your grandparents protested our shadowing them, but after a few attempted kidnappings, they came to appreciate our being on the scene."

The use of their personal names by Brookstone hit me deeply. I had not heard anyone use their names for such a long time that this was almost a spiritual experience for me. A few moments passed before I inquired, "Why would you be so interested in protecting a couple of old people who were visiting charitable operations they sponsored?"

"It is this way," Brookstone continued. "Many of our extractions are from both the East and West African countries; especially since the Somali piracy hijackings off the northeast coast reached epidemic proportions. Your grandparents' village hospitals in the Ivory Coast areas and in Nigeria became vital locations for negotiations. Some of the captives were injured, and the only medical help could be found in those tiny clinics.

Our teams of negotiators would make the contacts, and once a deal was struck, the captives would receive the best medical care possible while all the arrangements were being worked out. We would ship in the cash, the jewels, the gold coins and the art work inside the medical crates, and if all went well, we would bring in a chopper and extract the captives. It was the only way to handle the entire operation without suspicion."

"Amazing. I knew my grandparents had a lot of things going on, but never did I realize that they were ever in danger, or had hands-on experience in this kind of scene."

"Now since your grandparents are gone, killed in that air crash, things have become more difficult for us; our hands are somewhat tied. The medical facilities along with the outpost hospitals are not receiving the help they once got."

This was hard for me to understand. But Dustin had told me that since the lawyers set their eyes on my grandparent's fortune, the Canadian court system had tied everything in knots. The trusts were locked up, the funds set aside for these operations were up for grabs. This is not what my grandparents wanted; they had been setting up trusts to run things long after they were gone. But I did not know much about their philanthropic operations.

Things were a mess and it was almost overwhelming; there were a hundred liens and law suits against their estate. Apparently, their efforts to complete and set everything up on a permanent basis had been cut short with their deaths.

Brookstone saw my anxiety, mixed with curiosity about his knowing more than I knew about my own grandparents' lives.

He continued, "Your grandparents pretty well kept those medical facilities and philanthropic operations up and running. We found them to be excellent doors, in and out of some very bad places. Now that your grand parents' monies have been caught in the jaws of the international court systems, those distant charitable operations are drying up. We would like to know your intent, if you were to get the inheritance that was provided for you by your grandparents."

"In what manner do you ask?" I said with reservations and of course, with suspicion.

"I'll be right up front with you. If you have the heart to continue on with their work and keep their dreams alive by providing continuous hope to the hospitals and medical facilities, we will take steps to make sure that your inheritance is freed up, and you get everything that is rightfully yours.

If you have no intention of carrying on with your grandparents' wishes, then it will do us no good to use up our personal resources on your problems. That will be left up to you and your own funds and connections. But I think you and Dustin both know that without some help, those hungry lawyers could easily execute enough influence to cut your inheritance down to a trickle, and still drag it out for another few years."

Dustin spoke up, "You make it sound so easy. What is your ultimate reason for this offered assistance?"

"What we are asking you is—if we help you free up the Mitchner inheritance and it comes to you, as your godparents wanted it—we are asking that you would continue to support those operations that they established. I often spoke with Stewart and knew his intentions. Their dreams were to use their wealth to help others.

I think they knew that you also had this same kind of heart and will, and that is why they left most everything in your hands. You are young, and you have a sharp mind, and you loved them enough to fulfill their lifetime work.

This would involve keeping the small organizations they established, using their investments wisely, and making sure that funding for good went on in their names. Without a doubt, we have a stake in all this. We won't pretend we don't. But those little medical facilities do a lot of good for a lot of people, even outside our needs. When we are gone from there, they will continue to do good. In the meantime, our own people can be helped through these facilities. That is why we want them kept open and funded."

"If they are so important, why don't you fund them your-selves?" I remarked back.

"We might be able to do this for a short time, but we do not have such financial resources. The government is not stupid, they would soon realize our hand in these countries and that would be a no-no. But your grandparents have a long established relationship with these people and places. Their reputations are respected, and we don't want to take a chance on damaging this trust."

My mind went to opportunity, then to benevolence, in following the trail of charity that my grandparents had made. I could still continue on with my journalistic ideals. In fact the idea of traveling, helping, and getting into places such as the ones mentioned by Brookstone would be a perfect opportunity to accomplish another step beyond what my grandparents had created. News and information about atrocities or political situations could be exposed and help of all sorts might be sent. This could work out on a scale never before dreamed of by my little article writing mind.

"In a way, we would be working together," Brookstone interrupted my ponderings. "I think if I remember correctly, back at our headquarters I heard you say that you might be looking for a job if we had any openings. Now Luke, letting you know, with the removal of Trimmer and his crew and the breaking up of the San Francisco ring, that Buck Skullkin has disappeared. There is a need for someone of your caliber, and to tell you the truth, we would enjoy having you and Theo on our team rather than just anybody."

"I ain't no chopper pilot, or a jungle crawling commando," I retorted.

Brookstone smiled saying, "Well, not yet you ain't, but you never know!"

I was thinking maybe Trimmer and his buddies had become fish food; but Brookstone did not expound on this. They were just gone and I felt that was enough for now along those lines.

Brookstone let all this sink in while sipping his coffee. Then he cleared his throat, "To tell you the truth, you and your journalistic reputation would work well. You would fit into just about any situation. You could also become a courier, maybe even one of our negotiators."

"So now we have a good sized hole in our operations and we are looking for some good men," Brookstone added as a further thought.

I had to laugh, "You mean that we have suddenly graduated from surf bums up to good men and ambassadors?"

Brookstone had to laugh himself, "Please now, we want you to remain two surf bums, or should I say one good photographer and one upcoming journalist. But I think you have proved yourselves to be valuable prospects— far more than just surf bums, but actually very capable individuals."

"Ha, good men worth millions I'm guessing."

"Sure, that never hurts, but you're free to do whatever you want with your wealth; you will have more than you'll know how to spend. You could fully feed twenty charitable operations just with the interest on your banking operations alone.

We do think, and warn you though, that you strive to remain anonymous as you can. Don't flaunt your wealth and become a high-roller buzzing around the world as a target. Hell, we might have to come do some serious negotiations for your skinny butts in time."

We all laughed at this. "If I agree to this, how long before things could get settled up with the inheritance in the courts?"

"Maybe six to ten months or there-about."

This was almost impossible to believe. Dustin and a few other of our hired lawyers had been working for nearly three years already, getting almost nowhere but deeper in debt. I had to ask, "Will there be any violence attached to your persuasions?"

"No, of course not. All our behind the scene influences will be on a very personal, one to one level. No arm twisting in a physical form, but there might be some financial persuasions made along the way." He saw my eyes fill with question marks and immediately added, "Don't worry, we have more than enough funds to handle this end of things, your funds will not be used in this manner. So, no trace back to you."

I looked over at Dustin who was taking down notes, to measure his reaction. So far, everything had been directed towards me because I was going to be the center of this settlement. The final decisions would be up to me. But I would not make such an important decision without Dustin's approval and he knew this.

I was thinking of the islands and the movie we wanted to make. This few months could give us the time we needed to head to the islands to make the first part of our surf flick. I asked, "How much involvement would I have to be in for?"

"Actually, Dustin would be your acting power of attorney; this would keep you out of the light and off the scene. In fact we would recommend that you stay away and off the stage. Court discussions can get rather heated, and the newspapers will be there to report every detail. After all, we're talking about a good sized fortune that reaches into many companies, and several countries."

With all the changes in court rulings it was hard to keep track of the worth and the behind-the-scene value of my grandparents' investments and trusts. We were not even sure of the extent of the investments, the properties, and the many smaller industries entangled in their lifelong holdings. So I thought to inquire, "I know this might sound stupid, but since my grandparents' deaths and all this court finagling, I sort of lost track of things concerning their estates.

What do you think it might be worth?"

"You do know that several of their companies were sold off, but the funds were not transferred and finalized until after the plane crash. Their lawyer discovered there was some hesitancy to pay off after their reported deaths, and that is still being worked out. This will add a nice number to your estate, not exactly determined yet, due to the Canadian tax laws." Brookstone looked down at his hand held computer, punched in some numbers and looked up at us, shaking his head.

He finally said, "So far, we are not sure of all the different company values. But with stocks, investments, mines, properties and out-of-country holdings, you're looking at something between four-hundred to five-hundred million and more. That's a good part of it so far, then you have interest and annual income off the stocks and bonds."

Brookstone waited to let this sink in. Then he tossed out a real, true incentive, one that we all knew had weight to it. "If the lawyers and courts have their way, they'll drag this out another five years, and you can pretty well kiss away most everything and die from a nervous breakdown."

The room went silent, my head spun with unbelief. I got up and had to walk around. Going to the window, I just stared out at the passing traffic and the leaves blowing in the wind. I could hear Dustin asking Brookstone questions, while the world went on around us without a thought to my life or this fortune waiting for me. All this was way too much for me to handle at once. Finally I turned back and quietly said, "Let me think on all this for a day or so, and I would like to talk with Dustin and my team."

"Of course, this is a huge decision, which will not only

change your life, but it will also affect everyone that you come into contact with. So you talk it over, then let us know as soon as possible."

With this, Brookstone leaned forward, and made one last statement, "Just imagine how many people you would be able to help with your inheritance. It's a fantastic opportunity, not only to do good, but to enhance your journalistic endeavors. Ah hell, you can buy your very own newspaper if you want."

He reached over and opening my hand, he dropped in eight beautiful emerald stones, as a sign of friendship from his entire family, letting me know that their friendship was equal to ours.

Nodding, he shook our hands, and turned to leave, but stopped. With that piercing green eye as if looking into my soul, he said, "I think your grandparents must have done a really good job with you Luke. Even without an inheritance, you can always be thankful of having had such people in your life."

Once again he asked us to keep every bit of these events secret. It could easily invite more problems and bring more complications to our lives.

I was left standing there, considering this offer. No doubt, it had to be the greatest decision ever to come to me, involving hundreds of people, millions of dollars, and a complete life style change. If I could keep myself in the background and have others run the show, I might be able to keep my freelance freedom and my easy-going life style. Maybe!

I found myself looking out the window laughing. Dustin asked me what I was laughing at. "Oh nothing really. Our so-called treasure just became a river pebble in a box of gold nuggets."

"Hey, the game is not over, don't discount anything yet," Dustin warned me.

Everything seemed to be falling in place with the loose ends getting tied off. But the earthquakes were not over, Theo came barging in the door holding his cell phone to his ear. His jabbering was intense; excitedly he gestured for me to take the phone. I got a little perturbed at his intrusion but he ignored my dirty looks and shoved his phone over. He told me that I better take this call.

Reluctantly I put the phone to my ear, and heard Theo's brother Jay's voice rambling on about something to do with my apartment.

"Hey, slow down. Start over. What are you trying to tell me, Jay?" I finally got his attention.

He began in a calmer voice telling me that my apartment, that he had been staying in, had been broken into and trashed. Someone broke in while he was gone to his boat. Apparently they were looking for, and he was guessing here, but he said, "Most likely the treasure."

I asked him how bad was the damage and was anything taken. He was not sure, but my desktop computer had been opened and it looks like they took my hard-drive.

He went on to say, "I must have just left for my boat when these guys, or whoever, showed up and broke in. I had taken my own laptop with me to do some work while on the Serendipity. Good thing, I have most of my research on those things you left with me on my laptop." He paused for a moment, then asked, "Do you think I might be in trouble or in any danger? It looks like these guys were pretty intense and serious with your place."

"Did anyone get a look at them?" I asked.

He went on saying that my neighbors were taking out the trash that morning and had seen a van parked in the alley. Two rough looking characters had gone through the back alley gate earlier that morning. I continued asking, questioning Jay, trying to establish the extent of damage and what they might have taken. I was curious about some of my personal things in the apartment. From what I could get, whoever it was must have been looking for the treasure.

This relieved me to some degree, for I had not left anything around or any clues about the treasure in my place. The only thing that I had on my desktop were my journals, traveling notes and my articles but all that was on an on-line backup system. When it came to the Hearst Castle stash, I kept all correspondence to a minimum on my laptop, especially after the near disaster we had with the HC Security team, and Dustin's emails to me about the San Bella.

After Jay calmed down somewhat, he got around to asking me, "What should I do now?"

I pondered for a while, realizing that this entire adventure was spreading out like a mucky tar-ball encompassing, possibly endangering others. Finally I told him to go stay aboard his boat, but be double careful that he was not followed out there. I told him that I would probably call someone to come out and do a double-take on the damage to see what might have been done. I tried to reassure him that he was in no danger if he stayed out of the way, but to lay low and make sure the items we left with him were kept safe and off the internet for now.

So much was happening that I was not sure what to do, but told him he could sail over to Catalina with a few friends quietly, but stay in touch without revealing where he was. Theo and I were on our way home and we might join him there.

Brookstone was listening to the call and after I told Jay we would be there soon, Brookstone was nodding his head as if knowing, already one step ahead of us. He had made a call while I was talking.

"So that is where they are," Brookstone announced as he arose.

"Who?" Dustin asked.

"It's obvious. That has to be the loose cannon. Trimmer, better known as the Cat, and his crew trying to find out how much you guys know."

Dustin doesn't cuss often but I heard him say, "What the hell kind of a name is Cat or Trimmer?"

"Many call him Cat, his initials for Charly Anthony Trimmer. It's an alias he changed to after he escaped from a South American prison. Thought it would be cool to lift up his status among the mercenary groups."

"But how would they know where I live?" I spoke up.

"Simple my friend, we knew just about everything about you before you ever came up to retrieve your boards and laptop. And it would not have been any big deal for Trimmer to copy your files and find out your address. Even the size of your shoes."

I shot Brookstone a serious look, but I knew this was all part of the game that had been going on since our van's break-down. For one split second I swore to myself, if any part of my life ever needed repair, nothing more or less than a fuel pump, it was going to be taken care of right then. No more leaving things up to happenstance!

That would be a mighty work to accomplish. For my entire life, no less my journalistic career, was created through and by fortuitous lotteries, but without winnings. It ran like the golden thread through every aspect of my life. Just like this

Hearst episode, which started with such a small happening that blossomed to a manifestation with worldwide consequences—events reaching from Africa, across Europe, and entangling one of the wealthiest families known around the world, swallowing me into what has become a massive sink hole.

Brookstone broke my distant stare by asking me if it would be alright with us, if he and a few of his team members came down to our area to continue their search. He mentioned that Trimmer and his crew might still be watching for us and that we better take extra precautions to make sure we didn't meet them in the middle of the night. "These were no fools to mess with. The Cat is cunning."

Dustin was looking at me, nodding his approval. I spoke up saying, "Sure. We need all the help we can get. Maybe we can put this whole thing to rest with some help."

We said our personal goodbyes and told Brookstone and the girls to stay in touch and said our hurried goodbyes to Thortin and wished him the best in his new building. We hit the road and were on our way home when Theo got another call.

I only heard him growl, "Oh crap," and knew another foaming wave had sucked us under.

Sure enough, it was Sally from the surf shop. She and her sister Cinder had gone in that morning, and the shop had been broken into. It looked like everything had been gone through, but no boards or diving equipment had been taken; someone must have been looking for something else. Theo said that we would be there in a few hours. Lock up the best they could and get out of there. And no, do not call the police!

There it was again. The sticky net had been cast out another time, nearly catching others. Thankfully, the girls were not at the shop, or hadn't walked in during the break-in.

"Looks like the Cat again, looking for clues to what we have, trying to find out what we know about him and his buddies," Theo spoke out in disgust.

JJ somehow managed to get his question into our discussion. "Hey, this should be cool. Don't you have hidden cameras taking pictures at your shop?"

"Right. Wow, why didn't I remember that?" Theo said. He grabbed his laptop and fired it up. "In fact, I spent all that time setting it all up. Now, watch this!" he added.

As the computer booted up, JJ added, "Sounds like you sold your last ride to the surf gods and forgot to get paid. That is why you old farts need me around, someone's gotta show you the wave and keep you out of the foam."

Theo shot JJ a dirty look but without a retort, he was locked into silent agreement.

Within a minute, Theo had connected to a wireless router on one of his sites and began reviewing last night's camera recordings.

"Crapoid, look at that," JJ was looking over Theo's shoulder and watching everything that went on in Theo's Surf and Water Shop from last night.

Sure enough, two guys jimmied the side door and shut down the alarm systems. However, even though they found and busted the main viewing camera to pieces, they did not know there were several others, along with listening devices. There they were, Trimmer and his buddy George. They seemed impressed with the rows of fantastic boards but had to move on. Trimmer told George to begin his search in the back storage areas while he searched the computer. Apparently, Trimmer knew his stuff, for he booted up, clicked around and searched the files but found nothing concerning the treasure.

JJ asked in his favorite sarcastic tone, the one we came to despise, while using the opportunity to stick a sharp lesson to Theo, "Hey professor, where are your passwords and computer codes that you're supposed to be using?"

"Ah, I don't bother with that, I don't keep much on my shop computer, other than sales records and contacts," Theo retorted in an irritated voice, knowing he had been nailed.

"Wanko, your sonic board has more brains than you do? You're three strokes short of catching foam. But OK, yeah, sure thing," JJ laughed.

Then at the last minutes of their search, Trimmer finally opened the till. There was nothing but a few bills for change and some quarters. But he lifted the drawer and smiled as he said, "Now look at this George." He held up a five sided Spanish gold coin and studied it for a few moments, then said, "I knew those shits had got into the ditch!"

"That's the same kind of coin that we found in one of the boxes, isn't it?" George was asking as he reached into his pocket and pulled out a matching coin. Trimmer grabbed it and compared it with the one from the drawer. "Exactly the same. I knew it."

Then Trimmer looked up at George and asked in a suspicious tone, where did you get this one George?"

Ah, well, when me and Drake were down in the pit, there was one box that was broken open and a few coins were pressed down into the dirt. We didn't want them to go getting lost, so me and Drake took a few."

Trimmer nodded, as if saying that he would deal with this later and put the two coins in his pocket. George wanted to protest, but thought it best to shut up for the present.

I turned to Theo, "What the heck did you leave that there for? I thought we were going to put our things into a safety deposit box, just to prevent this type of thing." I shot out my question.

"I was going to take that over to my folks' antique store yesterday, but we ended up coming here instead."

Now JJ's curiosity was aroused, "Thundering crash in shallow waters. Hey guys, thought all that stuff was nothing but circus props. Aah? Seems like Mr. Theodore Vontempskii got his jock filled with sharp rocks that time."

"It was, we thought, for we did find a few coins buried in the sand on the beach, and we were not sure what they were," I covered up to prevent him from further inquiry. But JJ's suspicions were aroused, knowing that two heavy hitters had broken into the shop and the apartment. It must have been for something worthwhile. Not for an unknown worthless piece of copper.

I suggested to JJ to be silent for now, and asked frustrated Theo to call Brookstone and let him know what was going on. Theo called and told Brookstone that it was Trimmer and George who broke into the surf shop, we had them on film. He said he would see us at the shop in a few hours and hung up.

Then Theo called his brother Jay back and warned him to stay low and on the look out. He described Trimmer and this guy George. Jay admitted that these guys sounded scary, and they fit the description that Luke's neighbors had given of the two visitors to Luke's castle apartment in the sky. He would take extra care to stay low while making ready his schooner for a quick trip to Catalina.

With fervent protests from our young traveling friend, we dropped off JJ and went to my apartment. Sure enough, what a mess! But although things were tossed, no terrible damage had been done. We guessed that they didn't want to make too much noise by breaking things up. They were looking for specific items, and nothing on my shelves fit the bill.

We were straightening things out when Brookstone called from Theo's shop. We headed over there to meet Brookstone and his brother Jaden where we downloaded the film and recordings from the surveillance cameras. Theo brewed up some of his famous killer coffee and we all sat there sipping hot java while reviewing the movies of break-in thugs.

Brookstone was impressed with Theo's surveillance system and made mention that they might want to borrow his expertise one of these days.

Brookstone made it known that this Trimmer would be back. They knew that we had gotten hold of part of the treasure and they were desperate because they'd been cut off from the Hearst Castle Security resources. I also told Brookstone that we had photographed everything inside Trimmer's wallet, including all the numbers from his little booklet.

Brookstone's arms flew up in the air as he exclaimed, "Oh sheeet, no wonder he is looking for you guys. You have no idea what you have in your possession. I would also like to have a copy of all of it." He exhibited his frustration with us by walking back and forth, then went on blasting us. "Why didn't you tell us earlier? You got yourself into some deep do-do with those names." I always forbid my men to carry or make written record of any names or places, but Trimmer had his own agenda. This is why he's more than dangerous and must be removed."

I flashed back to Brookstone's irritation back at the HC Security headquarters about the notes written by Trimmer, when he said, "Too much information!"

Now we were frightened. For the level of adventure had crossed the safe boundary, bringing us into the danger zone. Theo and I were not happy campers. Brookstone thought it over awhile and decided that the only way out of this was to lay a trap for them, and well, catch the rats. We asked how this might be. Brookstone rubbed his face a little and shrugged his shoulders and finally said that we were going to have to be the bait in the trap. There was no other way.

Theo cried out, "No way! That is not a good plan."

"Do you have anything better?" Brookstone shot back a bit perturbed.

"Sure, we can call the police and let them handle it."

"Ha, sure. Have those guys make a deal for the treasure while you young gents are turned into jail bait? Taking their places while they head out to Brazil?"

I saw the dilemma we were in, "OK, so what kind of a trap do you plan?"

"Easy, you guys hang out at your castle in the sky and they'll most likely come around and find you. We'll be there watching and step in to handle them from that point on."

"Step in, huh? Hells-bells, you gonna let those guys turn us into chicken chunks before you show? What if they get nasty with us?" Theo got riled with Brookstone.

"Nah, don't sweat the little stuff. They might. But again, we won't let them get that far. Maybe to chickens, but never to chunks," Brookstone, as if sealing his words, pounded his right fist into his left palm with a few good snaps. "Besides, they want the portion of the treasure you guys took, right?"

"Hey, we is that little stuff we're sweating. What do you mean by 'that far'? I don't like you pounding your fist, that is not a good sign," Theo held up his hands in front of him as if in defense.

"Oh great. Sounds real good. What if they got guns, knives and all those good things?" I joined in with Theo.

"Just be cool. I assure yourself they do. But they won't want to use them, too much noise," Brookstone nonchalantly stated.

Theo gulped while grabbing his neck, "Hey knives don't make a bunch of noise. Just one swish across my neck and the only one to hear me would be the great person inside of me that's never had the chance to really live!"

Jaden, who had been standing in the background just observing, finally laughed at the overstatement of what he thought to be our over-concerns. But Brookstone said, "Again you got to trust us, we'll bring in a few more of our guys and take care of this once and for all."

So the plot was hatched and we were set up as the broken eggs in the omelet to-be. We did not want to get anyone else involved, so Theo shut down his shop; hung a sign out that said he was gone surfing for a few days and would be back. We headed out to my apartment, considering the plan, the so-called plot with the HC Enforcers, which I was now calling them.

In rain or shine, and in this case, threats of murder, our practice was to ride our bikes while on the peninsula or on Balboa Island. Parking for the new Tripper was not easy to come by. And unless we had to travel outside our immediate area, we preferred to ride our bikes in and out of all the little back streets. Before leaving the Surf and Water Shop, Brookstone told Theo that his camera systems were done nicely but his locks fell far short of discouraging the least of invaders, as the break-in revealed. In Brookstone's professional concern, as long as Trimmer and his boys were still out there, most likely looking for us, he made us put tiny button trackers into our belts, telling us to pay attention to everything going on around us. This did create some concerns with us, but apparently not enough. His worries would manifest soon, way too soon!

Brookstone and Jaden would meet us at my place but they had to go first to the John Wayne Airport to pick up a few more of his security team members. He was bringing them in to help hunt Trimmer's gang down. He told us to go pack a few things for a stay on Jay's boat until they had dealt with the threats. This sounded good to us, so Theo locked up and we headed out. We were definitely alert, letting our eyes scan every person twice and searched out each shadow for possible threats. On our arrival to my castle in the sky, after securing our bikes into the downstairs area, we made it up the three flights of stairs, feeling rather safe.

Upon entering, our worst fears came to be. I was more concerned about the condition of my place and not really paying much attention, just thinking that at least we had pretty well cleaned up the castle in the sky earlier. As we entered and were passing through the kitchen, we were both over shadowed while I felt something cold and dull pressed against my neck. I knew it was a gun! The world exploded and my wounded body was flung across the room until I hit the floor. A blast of glaring light shot into my head, and pain like I never knew flashed through my entire body. Both Theo and I found out later that we had been Tasered with high powered stun guns.

We finally came to and found ourselves tied and bound onto two kitchen chairs. I had been beat up before, by a gang of drunken Malibu surf freaks, and kicked around on some of my journalistic assignments, but this near dead feeling affixed to every one of my muscles felt like liquid lead oozing through my veins. It had to be the worst blue ribbon Pulitzer Prize hang-over feeling ever reached! My mind began to clear and once my eyes uncrossed and began to focus, I saw sure enough, it was the Trimmer man with his two companions, George and Drake. I recognized them from the cove night scene, and the helicopter visit to the treasure trench. They meant business.

Trimmer began by splashing cold water in my face and slapping me around, Theo was not quite awake yet, they wanted to know everything we knew and how much of the treasure we actually took. But his greatest concern was what I had done while having his wallet in my possession. Apparently those numbers and codes, if they fell into the wrong hands, could bring down serious retribution on him.

I played drowsy and began the role of an ignoramus, as if still brain dead from the shock and I could not remember. Trimmer was in no mood for my foolery and held the stun gun up to my forehead and growled with words that sounded like a garbage disposer grinding up glass. "Maybe another good blast might restart your already mummified brain, let's see—humm?"

"No, no. OK. Somehow I am starting to remember a little now," I mumbled, not wanting to have my brain scrambled with fifty thousand watts of electricity. I guess I still had the hope of Brookstone's words, "We'll be there!"

It was obvious, that if the HC Enforcement Team did not show up soon, both Theo and I knew were bound to become fish food. It was only logical, these guys could not let us go and identify them, they wanted no witnesses. Theo was still dazed from the shock of the taser and most of the questioning and knocking around was aimed at me. They knew that we had spilled the beans to Brookstone because the treasure trench had been completely cleaned out. Somehow they had found out that we had sold off some of the stones to the Kaamin family in Phoenix. They hinted that they had someone working on the inside and it was no use trying to keep our bit of the treasure quiet. They even knew of the thirty thousand dollars we had received. That was one of the things they were searching for. I immediately knew that the inside person must have been the Phoenix butler Dickson, or James, up in Suite 77. I knew that guy was not who he said he was; it had to be him.

Apparently they had found out that Brookstone was onto them. Their behind the scene theft and drug operations with this Buck guy from Frisco and their behind the door game was up. They wanted information and whatever part of the treasure we had taken. There was only one thing that we had going for us and that was they didn't know that Brookstone and Jaden had gone to the airport to pick up a few more of the HC Security team and hopefully meet us back at my place.

Mr. Charles Anthony Trimmer, was pissed to say the least. He was not only angry at their having been discovered but they were now on the run. They were desperate, and it looked like they needed every penny to make their escape. He was demanding that I hand over the money from the sale of the stones and take them to where the rest of the treasure was stored.

Our new traveling coach the Tripper was parked at the storage yard where the vault held the rest of the larger treasure items. Each of its three safes were stocked with all the cash, stones and coins that we had set aside from our sales and accounting. The Tripper van was a perfect hiding place. We could just go there and drive away any time and take a treasure trove with us. Theo, Dustin and I along with Wally knew this, but there was no way I would give this information over. I had to come up with something and stall for time, but what?

I tried denying that we had any more of the treasure. But Trimmer held up the five sided gold Spanish coin that he had found in Theo's till, to my face and yelled, "Stop your lying, this is proof that you got your hands on some of those boxes down in the trench."

Wiping off his spit from my face with my elbow I barked back, "No, the only thing we took from the trench was the San Bella bell. If we knew there was a treasure stored somewhere nearby, believe me, we would have been on it like flies on dead meat!"

Theo spoke up at this time and mumbled that this coin was his brother's, from a diving trip down in Mexico and he was going to list it for sale on eBay. George stepped up and smashed his fist into Theo's face. He flew across the room and went down, still tied to the chair. George stood over him and told him to stop lying and unless we came up with the rest of the coins it was soon over for us. He went on to outline the various stages of dead meat!

I saw a blue bruise form on Theo's cheek while a trickle of blood began from Theo's lower lip. I yelled, "Hey, that is bullshit. If you want my cooperation, then lay off. I'll get you the cash, but we better move along, the bank might be closing soon."

I knew that I had to stall for time. We did have a few stones and some monies in a deposit box and maybe that would give us some time. For Brookstone was sure to show up soon; I hoped it would be in time. Trimmer took the hook and ran with it, I was just hoping that the line would hold.

I told Trimmer that I had deposited the cash and the few stones we had into a safety deposit box at my bank. He seemed to gain back some composure with this information, removed the stun gun from between my eyes and said, "Good, we'll start there," and cut me loose from my bonds.

As I was rubbing life back into my arms the phone began to ring. Everyone stood still for a moment until Trimmer told me to answer it but put it on speaker.

I hit the speaker button on my cell and answered, "Hello, this is Luke Mitchner."

"Oh Luke, glad I caught you. This is Thortin."

I tried to remain casual and asked, "Yeah Thortin, how's it going for you up there?"

"Things are getting interesting, and more so than ever," he

started out.

I was stalling for time, dragging my talk out. It was obvious that Trimmer was fit to be tied as he stuck the stun gun into my side to tell me to get going. I said into the phone, "What do you mean on that one?"

"Well, looks like a couple of the HC Security guys may have caught the firebug who burned me out."

"Really, tell me about it. You're right, that does sound interesting," I answered excitedly while looking directly at Trimmer.

Thortin went on to explain that two of the volunteers that were working inside the new print building were recognized by Brookstone's volunteers. It ended up that they were actually spying for the Trimmer guy.

With this I saw Trimmer turn red and go stiff, uttering "Sheet." He was losing it, as if getting ready to club me, but I held up my hand real quick, asking Thortin what that meant.

"It means that with a little friendly persuasion from the HC Security team, these guys confessed that they were hired by Trimmer to burn us out, and they were getting ready to do it all over again."

"Wow, is that so?" I exclaimed.

"Yeah, there's a statewide all points bulletin out for that Trimmer character and his companions."

Trimmer reached over and took the phone and punched it off, then smashed it against the wall! I was about ready to announce my protest when he stuck the stun gun into my back. Grumbling with his glass crunching voice, "Let's go."

Without further disagreement, I calmly inquired, "Where

to?"

"You idiot, to your bank to get the monies, that's where!"

Trimmer turned to George and Drake, who stood back watching our interrogation, and told them to stay here. Hold this other surf nut, pointing down at Theo. Then he said "I'll be back soon."

"Charly, why can't we all go?" George asked with doubt in his voice.

""Because it would look too suspicious with all of us piled into our van. Besides it's easier this way, we got a hostage, in case this punk gets funny with the money," Trimmer laughed a little at his stupid rhyme.

Theo looked up at me, knowing that the money in the bank would never satisfy these guys. I could see his concern for his own life if things did not change for us soon. I gave him a quick shrug of my shoulders as if telling him to be patient my friend; knowing my gesture might take his mind off of death—trying to figure out what it meant.

Trimmer shoved me out the door and warned me not to try anything. He pushed what I felt to be a gun in my side as we made our way down the stairs. I was really scared, not so much for myself but for Theo. I felt guilty in getting him involved in this mess, a mess that might cost us our lives. For some dumb reason I was hoping that Theo's parents would never find out about this scene.

We got into their small mini van, Trimmer made me drive and we headed out to my bank. This is where my mind went into high gear. I really had to come up with something, but what, I did not know. I started asking him questions, "So you're Charles Anthony Trimmer, the famous Cat, wherever did you get that name? Were your parents some kind of animal lovers, maybe song writers?"

"Shut up and drive!"

My eyes searched out every obstacle on the road which normally would never have trapped me. I got behind every old lady, and even a school bus, to take up time. But nervous Trimmer jammed his gun into my ribs and told me to get my butt in gear, we didn't have all day. It never fails—I wanted a traffic jam somewhere along the way but no way—a perfect green light run all the way. I have an old saying that I use now and then, it goes something like this, "Fake it for now, and figure it out later!" Oh boy, was I going to have to fake it for now.

I headed south on the coast highway and drove over the New Port Bay bridge and finally pulled into the Coastal Bay Bank. We parked in a side lot and again, Trimmer warned me not to get funny because good old Theo would be the one to suffer the consequences. He stressed that George and Drake were both crazies, expert lovers of pain and slow death. Brookstone had promised a trap, sure. But this was a trap alright, and we were locked into its jaws.

I crossed the traffic and turned into the bank's lot off to one side. I got out as slow as I could. Then we walked to the front door. I was scanning the area for my rescuers, but no such luck. I looked around as we entered the air conditioned bank, and turned off to the left towards a woman who sat at her desk working near the vault room where the safety deposit boxes were kept. As I walked up to the woman, she turned from her computer with smiling recognition, looking up to greet me, "Well hello there Mr. Mitchner, glad to see you today, how may we help you?" She smiled while checking both of us out.

I recognized her as Molly, the same lady who had originally assigned the deposit box to me. "Just here to get something out of my box, is there still time to get in?"

"Sure thing. No problem, let me get my matching key." She opened her key drawer and went through her files, then arose to open the vault door. My mind was racing full steam now, and I had a tiny idea cooking, one that I had moved up to the front burner; but everything depended on rules. We followed her into the vault room. She went over to my box #87 and put her key in and turned. Holding out her hand, she asked for my matching key. Every box had to be opened with two keys, one from the bank and another one from the depositor. The idea had reached full boiling point now, so I used the steam to start whistling. I began looking into my wallet. Not there. Then I was frantically digging through my pockets one by one and patting them. I looked up at Trimmer and suddenly slapped my forehead. "Oh crap, in all our rush, I forgot the stupid key!"

Trimmer's anger flared while his tattoos began to dance on his arms, but he managed to hold his cool, "Is it really necessary to have two keys?"

Oh was I praying that some extra good will would not be allowed for my stupidity. It could be just my luck that Molly would make exception for me, the good old sweet talker. I was not normally much of a rule keeper, but this time, I was a full convert to rule keeping—please!

But we could see immediately that rules were rules, and she had no intention of breaking them. This lovely and most honorable clerk, Molly Conover, suddenly found great favor with me. I would show my gratitude if I lived through this. With kind authority she nodded, "Oh yes, Mr. Mitchner, this is necessary. Otherwise anyone that works at the bank can open up someone's box and take a look. Now you wouldn't like that would you?"

I knew this all along but I pretended total frustration as I asked Trimmer if we could go back to the apartment to get the key. My mind went dead for a minute, for I could see the red hot idea Trimmer had, right then and there holding up the gun to make innocent Molly open the box. He must have realized that this would do no good because she didn't have the second key. My mind restarted itself.

I apologized to wise and rule-keeping Molly and said we would be back shortly. We walked outside and for sure my armed escort was furious with me, pushing me along, calling me every despicable name, telling me that he knew my game and it was nothing but lame.

I thought I was done for, but received a reprieve at the van. He in anger asked me where my key was. I told him there were several keys in a kitchen drawer and maybe have George bring all of them. I didn't know which one was the right key. He immediately called George, the red faced brute, and told him to get the keys out of the kitchen drawer and to bring the other surf punk to the bank. Make it quick.

There fell a monkey wrench into Trimmers's plan when wise old George asked, "How the hell do you expect me to get over there? You want me to hire a cab or what?"

"You're as dumb as spit. Go have Drake steal a car, there's tons of them on the street right there. Get moving." He hung up.

We sat down in the van to wait. I asked, "What does that mean? 'As dumb as spit.'"

"Shut your brain. You're gonna find out real soon."

No doubt, I was scared for Theo and worried for my own life. It was apparent that the HC Security gang was no where to be found.

However, at this time, we did not know it, but Brookstone had been tracing the tracker units and was puzzled over my leaving the apartment for the coast highway. They had split up the team and at that very moment we were being watched by Brookstone and Jaden. The other part of the team was on its way to the apartment. Soon things were going to start happening in our favor, but of course, I did not know this, nor which side of favor we would fall on. I just sat there sweating.

As usual, in these precarious moments, my mind has the tendency to analyze events and circumstances. I flashed back on the earthquake at the beginning of this experience and went through the different aspects of the Hearst Castle's lost treasure. It was one of the better adventures in my life, but would it be the last one? Did that quake really mean a shake up in my life? So far, it was not a shake up, but a full fledged shakedown into the ground!

Well, I had meant some rather incredible people in the last month or so but 'so what?' Then I began pondering on my inheritance and thought that I might bargain our way out of this mess by offering a really nice reward to the Cat man and his gang if they would just let us go. I was possibly about to offer this meaty bone to this real bad dog when my thoughts were broken.

While we waited, someone returned to the car next to us and backed out. Shortly thereafter, a custom van with darkened windows pulled in and sat there. The passenger got out and walked around the back of the van and across the parking lot headed to the bank. We could not see who was inside because of the smoked windows. Music was playing inside the van and we were waiting. It was rather warm and I asked Trimmer if we could roll down the windows for some ocean breeze. He agreed and we sat back while he held his phone, ready to receive a return call from George, or maybe send a death call for Theo.

Soon Trimmers's phone rang. It was George who seemed a little nervous but said he would be there in a few minutes. I was wondering what the heck was going on but, just as George had promised, he pulled in right behind us and got out of a nice car, looked around like a scared rabbit and hesitantly walked up to us. The Trimmer was just getting out of the passenger side when George said, "It's up for us Trimmer."

"What are you talking about George?"

"I mean that Brookstone's men are here right now. They got an explosive strapped to me. If I make a wrong move, you and me are going to be bits and pieces of meat scattered around the parking lot."

Trimmers head shot around looking for Brookstone or a way out. He was puzzled, not yet seeing the threat. He stretched out his arm that held the Taser gun to stun me another time, but the van door next to us opened. It was beautiful Brookstone. Yes, I say wonderful Brookstone, the man of many talents, calmly stepped out, with a nasty looking taser gun, long and dark, he pressed it to Trimmer's neck. Real cool like, Brookstone quietly said, "Mr.Catman, if you don't drop your gun, you're going to find yourself with a cooked brain by this mother of all tasers."

Someone slid open the van door and pushed George, Drake and Trimmer into the waiting hands of several other men.

They were roughly searched then handcuffed to the arms of the back seat. All done within a minute or so. I had backed out of Trimmers's reach and was rubbing my neck, looking around to see how many citizens were watching, but no one was even looking at this unusual collection of world wide mercenaries—or whatever you wanted to call them.

Then Theo came limping over to me with one huge smile on his face. Other than a new black eye, a swollen jaw and a swollen lip he looked pretty good. In fact, I was actually happy to see him so happy! "OK, mister cool, looks like the matter is now being settled, let's get out of here."

Brookstone came over to my side of the car, "OK, members in adventure, go home, change your shorts and you guys return this rental. We'll be in touch."

We never heard or saw Trimmer, George or Drake again. Whatever happened to them, we do not know and do not want to find out. But we suspect that they are dwelling in an east African tribal compound as official miners, or worse, they are now fish food in the Pacific, off the San Simeon coast line.

Later, after we had resettled our nerves and regained our senses we met at Dustin's office. We told Brookstone about the inside man in their team. He did not want to say much about this, but as usual, I pressed him for the real deal. I thought it expedient to inquire on the butler-doorman Dickson or James Kilgore, so we would not have to worry about any hidden matters. I related my feelings about his being the inside man for Trimmer or that Buck Skullkin character.

Brookstone shook his head in a negative, as if not wanting to recall this individual, but I persisted. "Oh well, you might as well know. The South African authorities discovered who Dickson really was and we made a deal with him before they moved in on his life. We persuaded him that it would be better to return to the States and help us in our search for more captives where he might have a better chance at some justice, rather than rotting in an African jail. So we brought him back and gave him a bit of freedom in exchange for his many years of contacts."

Brookstone's glass eye looked straight ahead, as his good eye scanned the room and finally fixed itself on me, and went on. He nodded and admitted to us that Dickson was really the long wanted mastermind of the Symbionese Liberation Army (SLA) who had been lured back to the states by the Hearst Castle Security Company by offering him a safe haven. The family had known who he was and were trying to determine his connections, before he was handed over for prosecution. They had come to learn much through his stay with them. One important point in cracking the case was our personal dealings in the cove with Trimmer. The connection was made with the selling of information to Buck Skullkin, the man who Trimmer was working with.

Brookstone was tired but wanted to tie all the loose ends up, "We were going to give him a good deal until he turned on us and joined with Trimmer and the Buck Skullkin mob, in their dirty deals behind our backs. So my young friends, we allowed Max to recapture him for the FBI. Max increased his rankings and we gained some points along the way and that is the end of our dealings with the SLA gang."

What amazed me was that look on Dickson's face as I remembered when I walked into Suite 77 and called him James. That was his real name and he must have been shaken up by this; how did I know?

We now had another loose end tied up. There were lots more but the most threatening of the bunch, were seemingly taken care of. We thought that we might get on with our lives.

The next three weeks were as though a huge hundred thousand watt generator had been turned down in our lives, from full speed to idling. This high powered adventure, or whatever it might be called, had originally sparked itself into a blazing serendipitous adventure from one little trip down the California coast heading home from the annual International Surf And Water Sports Show.

The more electrifying aspects to these entangled events had slowed down, with the drama of interactive circumstances smoothing themselves out like a spent wave on a flat sandy beach. Since my momentous decision to proceed with the help of the HC Security Company's help, another unseen set of incredible waves were on their way.

Our newly created team had adapted the name MAVIN Associates—Mitchner-Arrow-Vontemski International. After all, a team had to have a name to identify itself and this name managed to add a bit of purpose to our merging ideas. It was as though our minds had been lifted up onto another level; we became aware of something greater going on around us, rather than just good surf and sunny days. We could relate to ourselves as something more than a gang of bumbling beach barnacles. Interesting, how unexpected circumstances can bring about such change, gathering together a group of strange ingredients to mix them into one very flavorful recipe.

No doubt, the fine gears of banking and international court intrigue were turning. We were told to step back and stay out

of the reach of anyone who made inquiry about the untangling of my inheritance from out of the machinery of the Canadian court system. Now our team had a whole new set of decisions to make.

Looking back at our experiences on the beach and the drama of being caught up in a boiling caldron of danger and international intrigue and then the adoption into one of the most incredible families was somewhat frightening, but at the same time exhilarating. I did not want to think about what might lay ahead in the arena of responsibility, but we often sat around trying to comprehend how we were going to deal with the financial storm ahead. I personally was amazed how this strange team had been brought together; it had to be divine intervention! I had a good feeling that we could accomplish good things. For there was no way I was considering leaving the team out of the possible wealth and the responsibility of our hopes. There would be a lot to deal with and I needed people around me that I could trust. We were all going to work together to avoid the seasons of those Perfect Storms, no matter what form they might arrive in! It had not yet been settled but a handsome wage would be paid to our team members. They would be given access to resources that would be there to help them accomplish the MAVIN's charitableness along with the challenges we would come to know.

The birth of the team had taken place unexpectedly. We had an experienced lawyer named Dustin Arrow, we had a computer programmer who was the geek of all geeks, named Wally Justin. And there was Theodore Vontempski, genius inventor and man of many talents as well as owner of a well established Surf and Water Shop. Then there was myself, somewhat of an investigative journalist and adventurer. Add

in Jay, Theo's brother, another quiet genius sailor and antique master who fit in well. Then there was JJ, but we still had not brought him into the team as a full member. He needed further growth and maturity. We were considering Max Colton but he had too many faces and we were not sure about his loyalty. Then of course, we had the entire Kaamin family, starting with Brookstone himself. Without a doubt, we had the makings of a very interesting team of qualified and well rounded men and women of experience to begin moving forward in adventure and intrigue.

On one of our more important brainstorming sessions, after weighing out all the options, we were stymied to figure out ways to begin introducing our new found wealth into the light. Dustin had talked with several new lawyers that the HC Security Corp had put to work on my inheritance case, and it looked like it would be at least six months to a year before the way had been cleared—but it was now on its way. Dustin suggested that Theo and I head out for the islands and get busy making our surf movie as soon as possible. It would be dangerous for us to sit around spending money. This might bring trouble our way, attracting attention to ourselves with large purchases. It would not be wise to begin introducing large amounts of monies into view of Uncle Sam. The movie could become a conduit for all of us to show return and even if it was a flop, we could begin inserting our own funds into its showings and returns, and we could write the losses off our taxes.

We realized that the HC Security Team was right in trying to keep us under the government's radar. No need to suddenly buy big, go extravagant and become a flash bang item. We stepped up with further ideas on how we might work with our new found wealth. We did not want to set the scene for the media to take notice, so we set our goals towards the big wave movie.

We possibly had ten months before our life would be changed by greater circumstances so we began laying out the plans for the big wave season out in the Pacific. Theo had taken that end of things up and had us scheduled on a small personal cruise ship to the islands. We could ship over the Tripper van packed with all the necessary equipment and camera systems to produce a high quality surf and water sport movie. We were going to have to ship over all our gear and camera systems anyhow, so why not put them into a ready to drive away container? We could also use this week on the Pacific to think things through and outline the next few months of traveling. Thus, then and there our new film making company—the World Wave Watchers—WWW—was born.

Theo handed over his surf and water shop to his brother Jay, who was going to continue tracing down and establishing the value of some of the unusual art pieces. JJ, the surf kid, was put back under our care during this working vacation. Wally would fly over later, but Dustin, along with Brookstone and Max Colton, were headed north to Canada for the next few months of court and lawyer battles before joining us in the islands. Colton was traveling with Dustin to make sure he was safe. These proceedings involved millions; and where there were such tempting sums, there always existed evil to demand its share. Everything seemed to be ready for the next adventure.

One of the best things that came from all this was that I had my own by-line in the San Louis Obispo Tribune. Thortin had decided that the face of the newspaper was going to change and my articles would have a safe and sound place to be published. This alone was one of the fulfillments of my dreams. All the frustrations of the past months had been washed away with the introduction of the Kaamin family and their possible assistance. Then there were those two incredible Kaamin gems, Crystal and Amber. Wow, I must admit we were humbled by their skills in business, in law and in international issues, not counting their poise and beauty. But within all this, they had a real down to earth quality to them and Theo had arranged for their presence on site, and a place in the film. After all, they were now official investors in our movie company, what could we say?

What all this meant to our futures was most unpredictable. But from that time on, everything in my life would become most unpredictable!

The deal between HC Security and myself was officially struck into an agreeable contract. Their operation went into high gear and both Dustin and Brookstone were gone for a time. Theo and I had our new Tripper shipped to Hawaii and we began setting up our film operation. We first headquartered our film team in a nice beach home just south of Lahaina Maui on a beach called the Shark Pit! At first many were reluctant to get involved with movie makers, thinking we were just two dreamy surf bums trying to make it big. But as time went on, some of our connections were cemented into a working relationship. This might have been due to my published surf articles and Theo's established Water and Surf Shop in Newport. His experimental sonic board was slowly catching on with some of the Hawaiian surf shops, many big surf kahunas came sniffing around, considering the possibility of furthering their name and fame as sonic powered magicians.

The best part of this film was that Brookstone had asked us

to take the two lovelies along. They were deserving of a get away and would be able to help organize every detail, which was how they had been trained. Theo and I more or less looked upon them as spies sent to watch over us, Oh-boy, but what spies!

It became evident that the two Kaamin girls were way more than surf and scuba queens. One day on the beach several local brutes tried to extract and waylay some of our equipment until we paid their personal beach fees. This is where we learned for sure that our sweet spies, as we called them, were not ordinary beach chicks.

As the two big locals began pushing us around, and demanded payment for the use of the beach to film on, sweet innocent Amber, stepped up and simply put her arm around big man Ho, as if to cling to him. Her right hand took hold of his neck nerve and squeezed it. We watched in amazement as he struggled, but within a moment she released him and he fell like a huge log, flat on his face. His big bad buddy Yo came alive with fury but sweet Crystal simply made a casual twist and out shot her pointed toe, catching him right on the upper leg near his hip. He crumpled onto his side and lay there screaming obscenities. People came around, but by then, the girls had stepped back, and we were thought to be the culprits. Soon, a few of the oafs' other beach friends came around and helped them to their van. Theo and I just stood there dumb struck, wondering what the heck had we gotten ourselves into now, and was there a way out of this?

Looking at these two wonder birds, standing there all innocent, Theo, with his fists on his hips, was in form, "Blistering belly-buttons, float me baby to the giant wave in the sky, I'm three strokes short of catching the big one! Holy molly what in this world do we have here?"

The End

Crystal slyly announced, all smiles, "Just get your fi
and let us know when we're going to be in it." She
to suggest that we do everything possible to make
success, meaning of course, to have some really ni
girls in it, meaning her and Amber, maybe a love
had to laugh at this one.

"No problem dear ladies, but first we are signing

classes in your 'Kick The Shit Arts," Theo manag
announce. And soon after, we were enrolled in s
personal lessons of self defense.

My left eye had not healed itself and I was worr
might carry a strange purple mark on my lid fo
my life. The girls did not seem to mind this, af
their family were either scarred or had parts m
deal about a little purple eye. Hey, I began to
the family now.

Then the days of long walks, quiet nights and
the right waves kept us in constant contact w
gemologists. To tell you the truth, not many
come near their beauty, their poise and, oh t
ligence. What a package we had brought wi
I myself took more than a liking to Amber,
spending more time walking on the beach
had to remind him we were here to film an
the next filming place. However, our frien
Kaamin family would slowly weld itself in
We would soon realize that it does make a
have the right friends. Especially in highe
Canadian Courts!

THE LUKE MITCHNER SERIES

Michael M. Tickenoff

www.storynetadventures.com

Made in the USA
Coppell, TX
18 February 2022